THE SECRET OF THE STONES

A SEAN WYATT ADVENTURE

ERNEST DEMPSEY

JOIN THE ADVENTURE

Visit ernestdempsey.net to get a free copy of the not-sold-in-stores short story, RED GOLD.

You'll also get access to exclusive content not available anywhere else.

FOR MY FRIEND ZENA GIBSON.

"The greatest zeal of man is not for love or money, but for immortality"

-Anonymous

PROLOGUE

NORTHWEST GEORGIA, 1838

A young native appeared from a patch of early morning fog, sprinting through the undergrowth of the forest. He recklessly ducked and weaved his way through the trees and brush. Twigs snapped and leaves crunched under his moccasins with every quick step. He was glad that he'd kept some of his old traditional clothing around. The soft breeches and cream-colored tunic were light and made movement considerably easier.

Despite his excellent conditioning, John Burse was out of breath and stopped to risk a moment of rest against a tall poplar. He squinted his deep-brown eyes as he searched the surroundings for a route that might help him escape. He sucked in the cool spring air in huge gasps; the scent of dry leaves and pine needles filled his nostrils.

Then, his fears were realized as he heard the sounds of the dogs drawing closer and voices mingling with the howls of the animals. Two hundred feet behind him, a group of a dozen or so men with three hunting dogs came into view through the hazy mist.

John had known the dangers of what he'd been asked to do during the secret meeting the night before. The tribal council had trusted him with a mission of utmost importance. Being caught not only meant certain death, but could also, ultimately, lead to the downfall of his Cherokee people.

With a new resolve, he tightened his tan leather satchel and took off again, glancing back occasionally as he made his way through the maze of tree trunks. The group was still far behind him but well within shooting distance. Just as that thought occurred, he heard a familiar popping sound followed by a musket ball smashing into a nearby tree; the shot narrowly missed him by a few feet. The close call made his pace quicken.

His slender legs burned from the exertion, and his lungs continued to gasp for more and more air. Hunting had kept him in good shape. Often, he and his father would chase down deer for miles after shooting them. Deer could manage to live a long time even with a critical wound from a gun or bow. But today he was the hunted, and the burden John carried made his journey that much more difficult.

Exhaustion was beginning to take its toll as he crested a small ridge; suddenly, he tumbled over the top and down into a small gulley, where he rolled to a stop at the edge of a large creek.

He'd been here many times. The expanse was about forty feet across and at the deepest point appeared to be only about six feet deep. He could see the soldiers and their dogs in the distance closing on him fast. The little river foamed and churned as it flowed around a small bend just downstream. The young Indian knew the area well, probably better than even the most seasoned of soldiers. With little hesitation, he decided what he had to do and jumped into the icy, rushing waters.

The hunting party stopped at the same spot where their quarry had entered the river. A tracker busily inspected the ground near the edge. Footprints stopped there with no sign of them leading anywhere else. The dogs were restless, confused as to what happened to the trail they had been following. To the animal mind, it was as if the Indian had simply disappeared.

"Clever feller," a leather-skinned officer muttered before spitting out a slug of tobacco juice. He had a few marks of rank on his dark-blue United States Army uniform and was obviously the man in charge. His matching cavalry hat had a few dirt streaks on it, but the distinct golden tassel still stood out proudly. The week-old stubble on his face was a patchwork of gray and light brown. He scratched his neck while considering the next move.

"He's gone into the water, boys," he said to his men in a matter of fact manner. "Thompson, take three others and the dogs, and cross the creek. Check back two hundred feet upstream along the edge to see if there is any sign he came out. I'll take the rest of the men downstream. If he's in the water, he's movin' slow."

Ten minutes later, the main group from the hunting party came to a waterfall. It was a seventy-foot drop to the bottom, where a shallow-looking pool churned with the falling liquid. A small hill on the left dropped sharply over the edge. There was no way the Indian went that direction. The sheer cliffs meant he had to go to the right. That way led down to the bottom gradually by means of a faint path. A cold spray shot up both sides of the falls all the way up to where the men were standing.

"Sir, if he went over, I doubt he survived," a young soldier chimed in, half hoping their running was done for the day.

The keen leader didn't buy it. This Indian had been far too smart to come so far and then just fall over a cliff. "He didn't go over, Private. Men, get down there and search the area. Someone get into that pool and check every inch of the bottom. Check the ground surrounding it too. If he came out of there, I want to know where. We can't let him get away."

The soldiers took off immediately, heading down by way of the path to the right of the falls. Thompson's men and the dogs had just finished their check of the other side of the creek and were standing across from the old officer.

"Find anything, Lieutenant?"

"No, sir. Not a thing, Colonel."

"How far did you check upstream?" The lead officer looked toward the direction from where the water was coming.

"Three hundred feet, sir, just to be safe." Thompson's voice was firm.

The Colonel frowned then turned his head and spit the other direction. His eyes narrowed, scanning the forest undergrowth. "Good man, Lieutenant. Get back over here, and head down there with the others. He must have gone that direction. Not sure if he jumped, but if he did, we should find him shortly."

"Yes, sir."

The remaining men and the dogs scampered back through the icy water and made their way down the little path. The old officer peered around the surrounding woods but could find no sign of the Indian. Deliberately, he turned and stalked down the trail to join his soldiers at the bottom.

Crouching in the dark, the Indian waited anxiously. The soldiers chasing him had surely not seen where he had gone. He must have just barely slipped from sight before they arrived at the river. He had moved carefully as he made his way from the water at the lip of the cliffs to the left of the falls. It had been a risky maneuver to lower himself down to an almost unnoticeable rock ledge that led behind the mist to a small cave.

From his hiding place, he could barely hear the orders of the officer and the confusion of the men below. It was difficult to understand what was being said over the rush of falling water, but there was obvious frustration among the group. Leaning back against the rocks, he took the chance to catch his breath. His only option was to wait and make his way out of the rocks when they were gone. Slowly, he stretched out his legs on the cold, moist stone and tried to relax, a difficult task given the circumstances. He hoped they didn't notice the hidden ledge on the cliff. Unless one already knew it was there, the narrow path was almost invisible.

An hour or so had passed, and the soldiers had found nothing. The officer in charge had been barking out orders for the last five minutes and was clearly unhappy about the Indian's odd disappearance. From behind the mist and falling water, he could make out that the blurry shapes of the soldiers were taking off farther downstream.

Apparently, they thought he had jumped over the falls and continued on in the river. Again, he laid his head back on the satchel and let himself fall into an exhausted sleep, confident that the immediate threat was gone.

The young brave suddenly snapped awake. He must have been asleep for many hours. Twilight had settled into the forest, and soon it would be dark. He figured night was probably a safer time to travel. Dogs could sense him, but men would have a much shorter field of vision. Before dozing off, he had considered what to do with his precious cargo. His mission was to keep it safe from the hands of the army. The United States government was to never learn of its whereabouts or contents. Today, he had nearly failed. If he were to leave his hiding place and try to make it west, he could be caught and lose everything that generations of his people had fought to protect.

Then he considered the place where he was sitting. Only members of the tribe knew about this little nook behind the waterfall. Indeed, who would even consider climbing out on the slippery ledge? Sitting quietly, he considered the options and risks.

Closing his eyes, he prayed a quiet prayer to the Great Spirit. There was really only one choice. His orders had been to take the satchel west and do whatever it took to keep it from the United States Army. Now, he was disobeying the council, unsure if it was right to do so.

He carefully laid the leather bag in the deepest recesses of the cave and untied the straps. His people had known what the United States government wanted. For over a decade, the Cherokee had worked to earn the trust of the government. They'd adopted their way of life, even worn clothes like the white man. But the Cherokee chiefs had always known that, eventually, greed would take over the hearts of the white men. They wanted gold and would do anything to get it. John stared at the beautiful, yellow metal. It seemed somewhat dull in the darkness.

With great care, he removed two gold bars and placed them in a small stack against the wall. It was difficult to see in the hollow rock, but, just to be safe, he scattered a few loose stones over the bricks to conceal them.

Climbing from his refuge, he looked back inside to make certain the stash was not visible to the casual eye. Acceptable for now, he thought. Hopefully, his people would only be gone for a year or two and then could return to their ancient lands—only then could he retrieve the gold. For the moment, though, it would be safe.

He tightly gripped the, now, much lighter satchel. The burden of the gold bars had been cumbersome, but what still lay within his leather pouch was far more weighty.

With that thought, he carefully shuffled out onto the cliff ledge and made his way back up to the top of the waterfall, backtracking toward his village. If he hurried, he might just make it back in time to blend in with the last migration caravan.

Several miles away, the search party had set up camp for the night. Sitting alone in his tent with a candle burning, the old officer was busy rereading a correspondence. The letter had been written on parchment and bore the seal of The president of the United States. A younger officer, probably no older than nineteen, stepped into the tent and cleared his throat, awaiting recognition. His uniform looked remarkably clean considering the circumstances.

"Permission to speak with you, sir?" The young man seemed a bit uneasy about interrupting his commander and stood rigid, awaiting confirmation of his request.

The colonel finished up what he was reading as if no one was even there then folded up the letter and put his reading glasses down on a small box next to his cot.

"At ease, Charles," the officer finally replied. He directed the soldier to a small stool in the corner of the tent. "What is it, Son?"

"Well, sir, we have been tracking this Indian for three days. I'm not complaining, sir. Don't get me wrong. I will follow orders no matter what. I'm just curious: What is so special about this one Indian? There must be dozens that escape the relocation caravans every day, all over the South. Why bother with chasing down this one?"

The old man smiled and looked down at the letter he had been reading, clenching it a little tighter. He was not annoyed by the question. In fact, he would have probably been asking the same thing thirty years ago if the positions were reversed. It did seem odd. And Charles's point was valid. He decided to tell the lieutenant just enough to ease his mind without spilling the beans altogether.

"Charles, this is no ordinary Indian. And our group is no ordinary military platoon. You have been chosen to be part of an elite government operation. This entire unit of soldiers was not assigned by random chance. We took the best of the best from the United States Army and were careful to make sure not a single one of you had any family because of the dangerous nature of our missions. You're an orphan, aren't you, Charles?"

"Yes, sir." Confusion filled his face.

"Every single man in this group has a similar background and did unusually well during their military training. Each one of you shoots better, runs faster, and has been found to be far more intelligent than the rest of your peers."

Charles was still listening. With the kind words from the hard man, pride certainly showed in his youthful grin, but he was still uncertain where the explanation was going.

"This unit has been put together by the highest office in the land. It was ordered directly by the president himself. We are to protect the national security of the United States at all costs. That boy holds something that is considered a threat to the safety of our government and this country's future."

The colonel let the words sink in with the young man.

"I cannot give you all the details, Charles. It has been deemed 'for my eyes only.' However, I will tell you one thing since I believe it necessary to keep up your morale and to ensure we handle this situation quickly."

The young man leaned forward, his anticipation rising.

"The Indians have been fighting us for a long time now. Their little wars against the United States have been desperately futile. We have greater numbers and much better weapons. They seem to get sick easily and are primitive in many ways when it comes to battle tactics. Up until now, their uprisings have been trampled, for the most part. And now the Cherokee and what's left of the Creek Nation are being moved west.

"Nearly all our campaigns against them have been successful because their efforts are scattered and largely independent. However, if the Indians could find a way to unite all the tribes, they might just have enough to cause problems for us. That is one of the reasons we are separatin' the tribes. We must not let them consort with one another. A united Indian nation could drag out fighting for a decade. To make matters worse, there is something in existence that could unite all of the tribes. And with this thing, they could possibly lure a union with the Spanish, British, or even the French."

"And this Indian we are chasing is carrying something that could do all of that?" The young officer was still unsure.

A nod of the head was his only reply.

"What is it?"

The older man paused. He had probably already told the kid too much as it was. But one more little bit of information would only help intensify their search.

"Gold," he said simply.

It was difficult for the young man to comprehend for a moment. He leaned back, obviously disappointed with the answer.

"That's it?"

"It is."

"Please forgive me, sir, but I seriously doubt that one Indian can carry enough gold to unite all the tribes as well as bring in reinforcements from England, Spain, or France."

"It isn't the gold he has with him, Charles, though he surely has a sample. No, what he has is the knowledge of where the rest of it is. That is what we are after."

"A map?" The young man's interest was piqued again.

"Exactly."

1

ATLANTA

Frank Borringer stared hard at the ancient script. It just didn't make sense. If what his associate had told him was true about where this item had come from, the implications would be enormous. He leaned back in his chair, removing the reading glasses from his face. With the other hand, he wiped his eyes and pinched his nose. Inside his brown tweed blazer, his body perspired from the mental exertion. His fingers struggled against the constriction of the light-blue bow tie around his neck.

He wondered how long he'd been in there. It was easy to lose track of time when your brain was in overdrive from extensive research on a particularly interesting project.

The library was dark save for a few lamps spilling tiny pools of light here and there. He usually visited after hours, though he doubted this near-anachronism of a place was in demand these days. With the advent of the Internet, it was possible to do nearly all of one's research from home. Still, Frank enjoyed the feel of a library: surrounded by books, works from thousands of years, and all in a material, concrete presence. With a computer, sure, the information was there, but there was no feeling.

He'd let himself get distracted by the thoughts and shook his head in frustration. Frank had been a professor of world and ancient history at Kennesaw State University for fifteen years now. During that time, he had been blessed with the opportunity to travel to many different countries as a special guest of numerous IAA excavations.

The IAA, or International Archaeology Agency, traveled the globe in search of ancient artifacts, most of which modern historians didn't believe existed. Fortunately for him, the IAA headquarters was near his home in Atlanta. The proximity, and his expertise on so many ancient cultures and languages, often guaranteed him as the first choice for many of the agency's research expeditions.

Over the last decade he had been to the Far East, Europe several times, Central and South America, and the most fascinating of all to him, the Middle East. In recent years, he had turned his attention from foreign countries to his own. Growing up in Northwest Georgia, he had a special interest in the history of the country now called the United States. Frank began concentrating most of his efforts on the history of the Native Americans, where they came from, how they got there, and what they left behind.

Sitting there at a work table in the Kennesaw State library, he stared at something that both puzzled him and aroused the childlike wonder inside of him.

Forcing himself back to task, he propped the spectacles back onto his nose and started reading again. "The chambers shall light your way."

Borringer sat alone at the table, staring at a small, circular stone etched with a script from a time long forgotten, and a place far from the Southern United States. The engraved disc arrived a week ago. Frank had promised the friend who'd sent it that he would analyze the piece as soon as there was a moment to spare. Until yesterday, he had yet to open the box in which it had been delivered. Frustrated with himself now for not looking at this miraculous piece sooner, a chill went up his spine at the implications of both its existence and message as he turned it over carefully, inspecting the smooth surface with the greatest of attention.

Mesmerized, he could hardly believe what he was reading. Impossible. Could the four chambers really exist? He'd thought them to be a legend from ancient tribes, something they talked about, much like the stories of a fountain of youth or El Dorado. But just like with those famous legends, the Golden Chambers had so far never been found. Yet here was a piece of evidence that suggested they were out there, somewhere.

Thinking back, he remembered the first time that he had heard of the four mystical rooms. One of his good friends had told him a story about Native gold in Northern Georgia.

There were several stories, actually. As kids, he had even witnessed some things that made him believe there might be a huge repository of the precious metal somewhere nearby. But nothing was ever found— simply rumors, stories. Notions of an ancient Native treasure had been abandoned long ago.

The stone was shaped like an inch-thick coin, about the diameter of the average human palm. On one side of it was an odd picture of what appeared to be two birds. The opposite face contained some kind of writing in a very odd script. At first glance, the inscriptions had been confusing. There were marks that looked like hieroglyphs, but there were others that appeared to be ancient Hebrew. Still more of the engraved characters appeared to be cuneiform.

It had been an astounding epiphany when he realized that what he was looking at were four ancient languages combined into a singular code. Once he had come to that conclusion, the translation of the phrases had been much easier. But how had these ancient languages come to be on something so obviously Native American? These writings should only be found in ancient parts of the Middle East, and certainly not together on one piece.

Perhaps even more unsettling was the riddle the words spelled out.

He pored over the two sheets of paper on which he'd written the translations. One was a letter to his friend who'd sent the artifact. The other was to a colleague from the IAA.

Glancing down at his watch, Frank realized how late it was

getting. He placed a call from his cell phone to his wife at home so she wouldn't be worried and started packing up his things. After storing sheets of paper, pens, and other items into his laptop case, he returned to his computer. Better to print the stuff off, make some copies, and come back to it tomorrow. The thrill of discovery made him want to stay and work further, but he knew there would already be hell to pay at home for his tardiness.

He slid the laptop into its bag with his other research materials and casually walked over to the librarians' desk. The library had closed about an hour ago, but being a professor had its privileges. All of the staff workers were very kind about letting him lock up for the night. Stepping around the corner of the front counter, he pulled out the papers onto which he had just finished the translations of the stone disc. After making copies and a brief notation, he put one set into envelopes and addressed them. Slipping the letters into a special basket for outgoing mail, he then walked hastily around the front desk and out the door to the sidewalk.

A brisk autumn breeze greeted him as he strode down the promenade toward his car. There was a renewed feeling in his mind as he deeply breathed in the crisp air. Maybe it was the weather or the fact that he felt like this new discovery was going to be something that was talked about for generations? Perhaps it was both. Frank smiled and turned the corner around the library building that led to the parking lot.

The university was situated on the north side of Atlanta in an area outside the sprawling ring of the I-285 bypass. Kennesaw was largely a suburban community. Safety while walking around at night had never even been a concern. For some reason, though, tonight he found himself glancing around, uncertain as to what would make him paranoid. Frank had never had any problems working with the IAA, though he had heard stories about some of their agents, one in particular.

Shrugging off the brief moment of worry, he walked over to his car and put the key in the door. Why should he worry about anything? No one knew what he was working on except his friend.

Besides, he had only been researching this new find for the last couple of days.

Frank smiled, thinking about some small amount of accolades. Maybe, after more information came to light, he would receive an award for his assistance in the unraveling of the ancient mystery. Opening the back door of his car, he plopped the laptop case into the backseat. After slamming it shut, he moved to the front door and started to pull the handle when suddenly he heard a footstep behind him followed by a sharp pain in his lower back.

His initial thought was to turn and face his attacker, but there was no feeling or control in his legs, and his body crumpled to the ground a moment later. He tried to move his arms back to feel the wound, but he couldn't control them either. They just lay limply at his side. Panic set in with the realization that he was paralyzed.

Borringer saw a pair of black shoes stepping over him and the back door of his sedan being opened as he stared, helplessly, from the pavement. He struggled to move his head just enough to see the assailant, but all he could make out was a silhouette in the back of his car, searching through his laptop case.

After what seemed like an eternity, the shoes and black pants stood over him. Then the attacker's face came into view. A blond man, probably in his late twenties or early thirties, looked down at him angrily.

"Where is it, old man?" A cold German voice demanded.

The world was spinning now, and Frank's vision had begun to blur. Haze crept into the corners of his eyes, overshadowing the numbness of his body.

The voice grew louder. "Tell me where the stone is, Professor."

"You will never find what you seek," Borringer gasped, desperately fighting unconsciousness.

Grabbing the professor's shirt, the blond man lifted him off the ground a few inches, sending new waves of pain through Frank's body.

"I need the stone." The attacker shook him violently, clenching his teeth. "Tell me where it is."

"If you couldn't find it before now," he gasped, "you were never meant to have it."

The firm grip on the shirt released, and Frank's limp body fell to the ground. Borringer's head smacked against the pavement, jarring any coherent thoughts he may have still had.

The menacing voice sounded distant. "I *will* find the stone. And when I do, nothing will stand in our way."

Frank barely heard the last words before surrendering to the darkness.

2

ATLANTA

Tommy Schultz sipped a white coffee while sitting in the breakfast nook of his kitchen. He'd learned of the drink while visiting Spain one summer. It was similar to a latte, except that it was made with regular coffee instead of espresso. It had more milk than a café con leche, so the flavor was less bitter. There was a paused look of satisfaction on his face as he savored the warm, toasty flavor. He had a lot to do today, but no matter how busy his morning might look, there was always time for good coffee. That was something he felt the Europeans had right. They always made time for coffee or tea, especially in the afternoons. Most Americans viewed it more as an energy drink, something to be gulped and discarded. Terrible waste.

These and other frivolous thoughts played through Schultz's head as he finished up the last bit of java in his cup. He looked at the empty vessel with a small amount of disappointment, wishing there were a little more.

Tommy stood and sauntered into the kitchen, straightening his red-and-white striped necktie as he moved. The tie didn't have to be perfect since the rest of his outfit was fairly casual: tan chinos with a textured white button-up and a pair of brown Skechers.

Standing by the little bistro table, he gazed for a moment at the figure in the mirror. He didn't think he looked old. After all, he was only thirty-three. But inside he felt much too tired for someone his age.

There were only a few lines underneath his dark-brown eyes, probably from the years of being on digs in sunny, hot places. The sun always made him squint. It was rare that he found a gray hair in the tussle of chocolate coloring on his head. Tommy smiled at his vanity and grabbed his keys off the table.

Tommy Schultz had founded the International Archaeological Agency a few years before. His parents had been fairly wealthy, and when they died suddenly, Tommy had inherited everything. His career in archaeology had barely begun when the accident happened. For a short time, he'd moped around, trying to find his life's direction. Then the idea for the agency had come to him one night while sitting alone at a bar. A news story about treasure hunters played on the television. He began to wonder what it might be like if he started an agency that recovered ancient artifacts and returned them to the rightful governments. At that moment, he began planning the IAA.

He took a deep breath and suppressed the tear that was trying to sneak out of his right eye. It had been more than a decade since Tommy's parents had died in the accident, but from time to time, memories crept into his mind.

Reaching over a chair, he grabbed his computer case from the table and headed for the door that led into the garage. Out of the corner of his eye, he noticed through the dining room window that there was a car sitting in his driveway. Curious, he stopped and walked toward the glass to see what the vehicle was doing there. It wasn't one that he recognized.

The auto was a gigantic Hummer, larger than most he'd seen. He wondered how anyone could drive such a large truck and still afford the gas prices. Odd, though. No one was inside it.

He frowned in confusion and walked back toward the front door of the house, half expecting to find the driver of the vehicle about to ring the doorbell. Suddenly, an arm wrapped around his neck from behind and squeezed tight.

From the shadows of the hallway, a tall blond man appeared wearing an English-style trench coat. "Hello, Mr. Schultz." The voice sounded German.

"What the..." Tommy started to respond, but the arm around his neck pulled tighter, cutting off the air he needed to breathe and speak.

"It will all be explained to you later. For now, you must come with us."

The tall man nodded, and again the arm squeezed harder. Lights and scenery started blending together in a blur. He felt a small prick of pain in his arm as a syringe injected something into his bloodstream. A cool feeling eased up his arm; it was only a few seconds before Tommy was unconscious.

Due to the odd morning hours that he went in to work, no one noticed the three men carrying Tommy's limp body out to the truck and stuffing it in the back of the SUV.

3

MIDTOWN ATLANTA

"So, how does it affect your personal relationships to be gone so often? Must be difficult to make anything last with friends or romantic interests. Or maybe you prefer it that way."

She looked at her victim in the khaki pants and olive green button-up jacket with a genuinely curious glance, even though the tone of her comment had been lathered in sarcasm. Her head was cocked to the side, a playful shimmer in her hazel eyes. The sounds of coffee grinders and cappuccino machines humming loudly in the background afforded no awkward silence.

Sean Wyatt sat, somewhat uncomfortably, across from Allyson Webster, journalist for the *Atlanta Sentinel*. He scratched his messy blond hair for a moment while considering her line of questioning. The noises and the people bustling about enjoying their morning java did nothing to ease his mind. She'd requested to meet with Wyatt to ask a few questions about the International Archaeological Agency, the driving force behind the construction of the Georgia Historical Center. In fact, most of the artifacts on display were pieces recovered by IAA agents, one of whom in particular had been involved on more of the recovery missions than most.

Sean was that agent, and Allyson wanted to speak to him

regarding some of the inner workings of the IAA. After ordering two lattes, the two had sat down in a couple of large cushioned chairs in the corner of the coffee shop, preferring their interview remain at least a little private.

Sean had been hesitant about answering questions regarding his job. He didn't feel like it was something glamorous the public wanted or needed to know about. There had been a few dramatic incidents, but nothing he felt the need to reveal to the readers of the *Sentinel*.

For a moment, he looked out the wall-sized window, lost in thought. Downtown Buckhead was busy with pedestrians and commuters hurriedly heading to work or other appoint-ments. Across Peachtree Street, a woman in a cream-colored dress stood staring at a storefront window, oblivious to the morning pandemonium.

He sipped his drink, drawing out the seconds before answering. "Well, if you really want to know, I prefer it that way," he replied with a wry smile.

"Really?" Her eyes squinted in suspicion.

"Yeah."

"And why is that?"

"Because in my line of work, attachment is not a good thing. I'm hardly ever home. And when I am, it isn't usually for very long; maybe a few weeks at a time. But I most definitely like it that way."

"So you're a loner?" she asked with a lifted eyebrow.

A slight snort came out of his nose to accompany the grin. "I guess I am." He set the cup onto a small end table that was positioned between the two sofa chairs.

She returned the smirk with one of her own. "Fair enough. So, how about you tell me the details of your escapades down in Peru? What exactly went on down there? I've heard some pretty interesting bits and pieces from that little adventure."

Again, he took on a half-embarrassed appearance. "I'm sure most of what you might have heard was somewhat exaggerated. It was a pretty uneventful trip."

Something in his gray eyes told her that he wasn't telling the truth. "Really? Because I seem to remember hearing something about an altercation with some South American drug cartel."

He was a terrible bluffer, and he knew it. His uncomfortable wriggling probably didn't help. "Ms. Webster, I'm not sure what you heard, but I don't think any of that really matters. We went in, got the artifact we were looking for, then donated it to the Peruvian government. Of course, we did accept a small reward for locating and delivering the piece."

"Of course," she added, her face stoic and cynical. "But why don't you just tell me about what really happened down there?"

He leaned in closer toward her. The scent of her curly hair smelled like apples mingled with a slightly sweet perfume; vanilla perhaps. With the way her head was tilted, the rich brown curls cascaded off of her shoulder. There must have been a school for professional women to attend just to make their hair do that. Sean tried to ignore his heightened sense of attraction by taking another gulp of latte.

"I'm sorry. I don't know what you think you heard about the expedition in Peru, but, I assure you, it wasn't really that exciting, except from a historical discovery perspective."

"Are you trying to tell me that there wasn't a run-in with any drug smugglers down there and that you weren't taken captive by their leader only to narrowly escape and get away with some statue that you had been looking for?" She took a long breath of air.

Sean continued squirming in his chair. "Again, Ms. Webster, I'd rather not comment on the specifics of some of our expeditions. The one to Peru had a few snags along the way, but everyone came out fine. The Peruvians were able to retrieve an enormous part of their history due to the IAA's assistance. They were very grateful, I might add."

She could see there was no getting him to talk, even though he was clearly leaving something out.

Changing the subject, she asked, "Is it true that you were in some kind of special government operations unit after you went to college?"

Again, his face turned red, and he could not seem to get situated in his seat. She was good. "I'm afraid that I can't tell you that, Ms. Webster."

The way that he said her name made her blush, just slightly. "And why is that? Because you'd have to kill me?"

"Something like that."

"So what *can* you tell me?"

"I can tell you that the IAA has recovered lost artifacts for over twenty different governments. We span the globe, looking for what others do not. I guess you could say that we dig where no one else does."

"Why the gun then?" She motioned with a nod toward his khaki jacket that had fallen open just enough to reveal the .40-caliber Ruger he always carried.

He pulled the jacket around, covering the piece. "That's mine. We don't have standard agency-issued weapons, if that's what you're thinking. Got a permit for it, if it bothers you."

"What bothers me, Mr. Wyatt, is that there are stories going around about all kinds of stuff that your organization has been involved with, but you won't throw me a bone." She huffed and her face flushed red. His dodgy answers were exasperating.

"What can I say? I don't like to kiss and tell."

Allyson let out a frustrated sigh. This interview had been pointless. She stuffed her notepad into her laptop bag and grabbed her coffee as she stood.

"Thank you for your time, Mr. Wyatt. But this has been a waste of mine. Sorry for the inconvenience."

"Not at all," he stood with her. "I was going to come here for coffee anyway. At least let me walk you out."

"That won't be necessary."

"I insist." He extended his hand politely.

Not agreeing but not disagreeing either, she simply headed for the door. Sean fell right into line behind her then quickly extended his arm to open the door for her. She shot him an angry glance, not about to thank him for the seemingly long-lost courtesy.

Defiant, she strode quickly to her black four-door Honda Civic and beeped the alarm off as she approached the driver's side door.

Again, Sean reached out to open the door for her, but this time, she beat him to it. "Thanks again, Mr. Wyatt. Have a nice..."

Her face changed suddenly as she noticed two men in black suits walking toward them from across the pavement. About halfway there, they simultaneously reached into their jackets, removing black pistols.

Sean saw her eyes grow large at whatever she was seeing on the other side of the lot. His reaction was instantaneous; years of government training and field missions kicked in. With a surprising amount of force, he shoved Allyson into the front seat of the car.

"Stay down!" He barked the order quickly.

In another fluid motion, he whirled behind the open car door and pulled it all the way forward, shielding himself from the two gunmen. In another second, he'd ripped his own weapon from inside his jacket. Silent pops pounded the door in front of him as bullets blasted the plastic and leather interior.

They had sound suppressors. His own weapon, unfortunately, would not be so discreet. Risking a peek around the edge of the door, he saw that the two brutish men were still stalking toward the car. They were only about twenty feet away now.

Only one way to play this one, Sean thought. Dropping to the ground below the bottom edge of the door, he extended his weapon and squeezed off four shots at the feet and shins of the approaching attackers.

One man's foot exploded in a mass of Italian black leather and blood. The other man's right shin splintered instantly from the impact of the bullet. Both assailants dropped to their knees with the unbearable pain surging up through their legs. One dropped his gun to the ground while the other held it to his side; both were grasping at their new wounds. That was all Wyatt needed.

Spinning around the outside of the door, he stood and fired off two more shots. The suit with the shin injury fell over backward, a blackish-red hole about the size of a nickel etched into his head. The other clutched at his neck, furiously trying to contain the sudden fountain of blood leaving his body. That struggle only lasted a dozen or so seconds before he fell forward.

Sean looked around anxiously. There was no one else in the parking lot, but his shots must have been heard inside the shop. People on the sidewalks were screaming and running away from the scene in a panic.

He stepped back over to the open door and found Allyson curled up inside, terrified.

"We have to leave."

"What?" She asked, shock on her face.

"Now, Allyson."

He reached down and grabbed her arm, yanking her from the car. Again, the amount of strength he showed for a man his size was surprising.

Allyson stared blankly at the two bodies lying on the asphalt.

"Are they...?" she began.

"Yeah," he answered before she could finish her sentence.

He reholstered his gun. The yellow parking lights flashed on a nearby carbon gray 1969 Camaro.

"We'll take my car."

She was too stunned and scared to disagree at this point.

Questions swirled in both their heads amid the confusion. What was going on? Why were those two men trying to kill them?

Sean opened the passenger door for her and, as gently as possible, forced her into the seat. He skipped around the back of the car quickly, taking one last look around the parking lot.

He turned the key, and the engine revved to life. Trying not to draw too much attention, he stepped on the gas and steered the car out of the back exit.

4

NEVADA

Through a giant arched window, the last rays of afternoon sun shone onto the dark walnut floor. A man with gray hair and a wrinkled, weathered face gazed out at the mountainous scene. He was known by a few loyal followers as The Prophet, a leader during a time of spiritual and religious weakness. They didn't need to know that the title was self imposed. All that mattered was that they believed in what he was doing. His mind was occupied, busy with a task few knew about. An old phone on a large oak desk rang the way phones did twenty years ago. Aroused from his thoughts, the old figure sitting in the shadows of his study reached over to answer.

"Have you begun?" His voice was direct and commanding.

"Yes. Everything is in place as you wished, sir." The voice on the other end of the line was foreign.

"And you are certain that Schultz will lead you to the answers we seek?"

"One hundred percent sure."

"And Wyatt?"

"He will not be a problem."

"Is he dead?"

"No. But he does not have access to the information."

"Why is he still alive?" Irritation laced the old man's words.

"Do not worry, sir. The homing beacon on Wyatt's vehicle is working. I will know every move he makes. He is predictable if nothing else."

"I am not worried. I simply know exactly what this Sean Wyatt is capable of. You are the expert in these matters, so I expect you to know exactly what I am talking about. We are proceeding with the plan that you presented, but if at any moment I feel like things are getting out of control, I will not hesitate to pull you." The threat created silence on the other end for a moment before the shadowed figured continued. "Keep me informed of any further developments. And Jens..."

"Yes, sir?"

"Dispose of the woman. She can serve no purpose for us."

"Of course, sir."

The dark figure in the high leatherback chair gently laid the receiver back onto the phone base and returned to gazing through the large study window.

Soon, he thought, *the whole world would change.*

5

ATLANTA

It had been a busy day already for Detective Trent Morris. He had been working since 7 a.m., and now, right in the middle of the morning, he gets a call for a double homicide at a coffee shop in Buckhead. And from the sound of it, it wasn't going to be a routine call.

When he arrived on the scene, one of the CSI guys already there informed him that they were unable to find any identification on the two victims. Both were males, roughly the same muscular build, dark-brown hair, and wearing very similar suits with long black coats. Each one was wearing sunglasses as well.

If he didn't know better, Morris would have sworn the guys were Secret Service. Unaware of any possible presidential visit to North Atlanta today, that was an easy thought to swear off.

Morris was an imposing presence and commanded a great deal of respect with his coworkers. He had grown up in Atlanta with six brothers and sisters just southeast of the city. Being the oldest had taught him a great deal about responsibility. He walked with purpose through the police tape, lifting his badge that dangled on a lanyard from his neck as he passed the officer working the perimeter. Nodding a thank you to the cop lifting the tape for him, Trent breathed in the mild city air. An array of odors mingled in his nose: restaurants, trees, car exhaust, and cigarette smoke from a couple of the other detectives already on the scene.

"What do we got here, Will?" He spoke as he neared a familiar face kneeling over one of the bodies.

His partner, Will Hastings, had been transferred to the department a few weeks ago. The twentysomething white kid had been a breath of fresh air to the investigation unit, and he and Trent had developed an instant chemistry. The younger cop had a go-getter attitude much like Morris had when he joined the police force. But something about the kid seemed seasoned, not too eager like so many rookies he'd seen.

Will turned at the sound of his name and stood up, pulling off the latex gloves he'd been using. "Hey, buddy." He glanced down at the mess. "At least we got the call in the morning. Usually this kind of thing happens at the end of a shift."

"Just thinking that myself, Brother. So what's the story here?" Trent strode over to the body Will had just been inspecting and looked down. "This where they were done?"

"Looks that way. Shots were from up close. From the looks of it, they came from over there near that black car. This one's fatal wound was to the head," he motioned to one victim. "This guy here," he pointed to the second, "was shot in the throat. Probably only took him a minute to die." One victim lay sprawled on his back, arms splayed in different directions. The other was positioned facedown on the asphalt, in a pool of blood from the exit hole in the back of his skull.

"One fell forward, and the other guy just collapsed back." Trent continued his partner's line of thought.

"We know who these guys are yet?"

"We're trying to ID them right now, but they didn't have anything on them."

"Robbed?" Trent was trying to piece this together as quick as possible. Hunger gnawed at him. As if hearing his stomach grumbling, a young beat cop walked up with a fresh cup of coffee from inside the shop. "Coffee, sir?"

"You read my mind, Kyle. Thanks."

The young officer seemed pleased with the gratitude and walked back over to the perimeter to relieve the cop Trent had seen when he first arrived.

Will responded to the previous question. "I don't think it was a robbery. These guys both had Glock 9 mm's. Powder residue on their hands indicates they took some shots, too, and there are bullet casings all over the ground matching their weapons."

"What kind of gun did them?"

"Ballistics hasn't said yet, but I'd say it was probably a .40 of some kind. Sort of looks like a hit gone wrong."

"Great," Trent thought. That was the last thing the town needed on top of the rising level of gang violence. Through the years, Atlanta had seen its fair share of corruption, but for the most part, organized crime had not been able to take root. With so many international corporations transplanting to the growing city, there had not been room for the much more localized operations of the Mob.

"So, are we talking Mafia type? I mean, shouldn't assassinations be someone we've heard of?"

"Doubt it. Got a witness over there. Said he saw the whole thing. Claims it was a man and a woman. The department's artist is over there right now getting their description. He speaks with some kind of accent. Sounds like German to me, but I can't really tell."

Trent looked over at the witness sitting on one of the patio chairs and looking about as unnerved as a person could look. The guy had probably never seen a murder before, much less two. He was blond, late twenties/early thirties, probably around six-two, two hundred pounds. His jaw was distinct much like the rest of his bone structure. Wearing a police-issue blanket around his shoulders, he looked visibly upset as he described the suspects to the artist.

"Any sign of the weapons?" Morris took a sip of his coffee, pleasantly surprised that it was just how he liked it. He raised his cup in appreciation as he looked over at Kyle, who returned the gesture with a simple nod and a wave of the hand.

"Haven't found them yet. We got a team going through the nooks and crannies in the surrounding blocks but nothing so far. Witness said that the two suspects hopped in a car and tore out the back entrance."

"A male and a female? Did the witness get a good look at the car?" Trent dared to hope.

"I'll go you one better. 1969 Camaro, silver with black trim, and the witness even got the plates memorized. So, odds are, we aren't going to need those sketches anyway."

Trent could not believe what he was hearing. This might actually be over within an hour. "Have I told you lately that I love you?"

"No. But you can buy me a beer later instead." Will returned the smile.

"Done. So who do the plates belong to?"

"Car is registered to a Sean Wyatt. Lives out near Dunwoody on the north side of town. No word on the occupation yet, but we got three units headed that way right now to check it out."

"Good. Let's get up there and see what this is all about."

The two detectives turned and walked away from the victims, who were now being bagged in nondescript coroner body bags. Trent nodded again to Kyle as they slipped under the police line and opened the doors to the car.

He looked through the windshield at the witness apparently finishing up with the sketch artist; the young man looked as though he were about to puke. "Poor kid," he remarked. "Bet he'll never get that vision out of his head."

"Yep," Will agreed. "Some people just aren't built to handle that sort of thing."

6

ATLANTA

Sean reached up and clicked the remote to the front gate of his home a few seconds before they pulled in. From the street, it was difficult to see what lay beyond the huge brick wall and the spruce trees behind it, which was kind of the point of the wall. He swung the car into the driveway as the gate opened completely. Once the car passed through, it began closing again.

Allyson gazed, open-mouthed, at the property. She'd not said anything since leaving the coffee shop. He assumed her entire life had been spent far away from things like the shooting in the parking lot.

Vast collections of trees, shrubs, and flowers decorated the whole estate. Giant magnolias dotted the large yard with their dark, waxy leaves. Azaleas surrounded the unmanned gatehouse, along with a few of those long grassy plants common to golf courses and suburban neighborhoods. Poplars, Bradford pears, and even some coniferous spruce trees stood in rows in the enormous yard. More hardwoods lined the driveway on both sides.

"Are those maples?" Allyson broke the silence with the sound of awe at the beautiful landscaping.

"Good eye," Sean responded, glad to see she wasn't comatose. "I planted alternating varieties so when the fall colors peaked there would be a more contrasting display of color. There are silver, chalk, sugar, and my personal favorites, the crimson king maples. The colors have started to change, but it will be another week or two before they really look amazing."

"They're beautiful." Allyson continued to look around as the car sped up the driveway.

"I'm kind of a plant lover. Worked my way through college doing landscaping for a local family."

"I think it's wonderful," she said with a squinting glance. Even though she was talking, her voice was still distant. Her mind was probably still replaying the incident over and over.

"You've killed men before, haven't you?"

He had anticipated this question and had been pondering what to tell and what not to tell. After all, she was a reporter.

"Yes. I've killed before. But only out of necessity—situations where it was either me or the other guy."

"Do you think about it a lot? I mean, ending another human's life is pretty heavy."

"To tell you the truth, I don't think about it too much. I just look at it like it was something that had to be done. It's always been survival. Nothing more. When I worked for the government, it was just part of the job."

She didn't pursue the government topic, though she was curious.

A beautiful tan-colored house stood at the top of the driveway. The two-story Mediterranean villa with a Spanish-tile roof was not large by any stretch. It could not have been more than two thousand square feet. She had expected a grand mansion to accompany such a palatial garden scene. Instead, the home before her was certainly nice, but it was humble in a way.

"Bought it six years ago," Sean started again. "Since I live alone, I didn't need a big house, but I loved the property here. I spend a lot of my free time out here working."

"Gardening?"

"I enjoy the work. There's something liberating about manual labor." His reply was honest.

He pulled the machine around the back of the house to a large four-door garage that was behind and below the house. Invisible from the approach up the driveway, the car house stretched out perpendicular from the basement and seemed to be nearly half as large as the dwelling. When one of the four wooden garage doors opened, Allyson could see there was another car in the spot where they were about to park. Then she realized that the garage had doors on both sides. Convenient for a person with a lot of cars to park. In Sean's case, a few cars and many motorcycles.

Sean parked the car, and they stepped out into a small collection of old and new bikes. Allyson's gaze went past the Nissan Maxima in front of her to at least two dozen motorcycles of varying types. There were cruisers and sport bikes from different eras: Harley Davidson, Indian, Buell, and all of the Japanese makers were represented. A few British café-style racers sat quietly together as well.

"Those two are my favorite." Sean read the fascination on her face and acknowledged the machines with a nod. "The Norton and the Triumph. I love the raw style those bikes have. No fairings. No tricked-out special parts. Just the bike and the road. The way it should be."

"Do you ride them or just collect them?"

"I'm a rider first. A collector second." He smiled. "Those guys that just collect them blow my mind. Never made a lot of sense to me." The garage door started closing behind them; the Maxima beeped and then revved to life.

"Sorry that I can't take you for a ride on one right now, but I think it's best if we don't stick around here."

"Why? Won't we be safe here?"

"I doubt it." His reply was blunt. "My guess is the cops will be here soon. And then there is the concern about the person following us."

Instant paranoia struck Allyson's face as she turned around, trying to see out of the garage windows.

"Don't freak out," he said calmly. "I doubt we have a tail. But I am pretty sure we have a homing device on my Camaro. That's one of two reasons we're changing cars."

"What's the other reason?

"At the coffee shop, I noticed a guy in a Lexus in the parking lot just sitting there. His windows were tinted, so I didn't get a good look at him. At first, I thought he was just waiting to meet someone. But he was still sitting there when we left. It was almost like he was trying to look casual, even had a newspaper with him. Just struck me as odd, given the bullets flying around and all."

"So you think he saw the plates?"

"I think he had already looked at them. I keep a spare set of fake tags here in the shop, registered to a very old friend. They're on the Nissan, so I'm hoping that will buy us some time. The police will come here and find my car, search my house, etc."

"Just a typical day for Sean Wyatt, huh?" Her sarcasm was cute.

"The cops mean well, or at least I think they do. Nothing will be taken from my house. I just hope things are left as they found them."

"You get searched often?"

He ignored the question. "Don't worry. We're going to figure this out, and trust me, you'll be back in the office in no time. But I just killed two guys back there, and if that guy in the car has anything to do with it, I don't think we are on the right side of the law at the moment. Call it a hunch."

His words didn't ease her mind much.

He walked quickly over to the running car. "We should probably be going. I'll be glad to give you a tour of the whole place some other time."

She was amazed that he could still flirt at a time like this. She followed him and opened the front passenger door simultaneously with him.

"Promise?" Her voice was playful as she slid into the front of the car. Apparently, she had put the double homicide behind her for the moment.

He smiled at her, careful not to show the concern in his mind. He wasn't sure he trusted her. She shows up, and then all of the sudden he's getting shot at. And was her fear legitimate or an act? He couldn't tell at the moment, but it was a little odd how one moment she had been terrified and the next she was ready to hop in the car and go. A normal person might have tried to escape.

Suddenly, she screamed at the top of her lungs.

In the reflection of the tinted black windows, he saw a quick movement.

Sean's reaction was immediate and fluid. He dropped to his knee to avoid the swinging elbow that was intended for the back of his neck. His fist launched at the attacker's groin, and a confirming groan of pain assured him he'd found the vulnerable area.

Hunched over, the attacker, dressed in a black sweater, staggered toward his prey, who had sidestepped quickly over to a row of garden tools.

The man's recovery was too slow. Sean's hands moved quickly, scooping up a shovel and bringing the head of it crashing against the face of the intruder. The stunned assailant crumpled into an unconscious heap on the floor of the garage.

Sean dropped the shovel and jumped in the car. Allyson's mouth was agape as she stared at the scene.

"We have to go." His voice had become very direct.

"Are you just going to leave him there?"

"Yeah."

The black Maxima sped down a different, much shorter driveway on the backside of the property. It led into a dark, tiny forest of pines and oaks. Another gate within the tree cover was already open for them, and Sean guided the car out and onto a quiet suburban street.

7

ATLANTA

Trent Morris was less than happy. The warrant had come through quickly since Will had phoned in for it before Trent had even arrived at the coffee shop. Units got to the scene at the suspect's house soon after. It had taken only minutes to get access to the property, and yet all they found was an empty house and a garage full of motorcycles. Of course, the car they were looking for was there, also empty, the hood still faintly warm. They must have just missed them.

Investigators were busy checking out the car, removing panels and checking the undercarriage while inside the house, another group was performing a similar search of the residence. He already knew they wouldn't find anything there. He believed the suspects hadn't even gone inside the house. They had come here, got out of the car, probably to get into another, and left just as quickly as they had arrived.

Will stepped into the garage from the door that led into the house. He looked equally annoyed at the situation. "Find anything?"

A frustrated glance was the only answer he needed. "They must have left a few minutes before we got here. Came in, changed cars, and left."

Will filled in the other details. "Everything in the house is in order. I don't think they even went inside."

"I was thinking that too." He looked around at the scene. "What kind of car are we looking for now?"

"No idea."

A latex-gloved officer was busily examining the trunk while another was facedown in the front seat, checking under the dash of the Camaro.

"What do you mean, no idea? If they switched cars, the other car has to be registered to Wyatt. This is his house, isn't it?" Something didn't seem right. What Morris had thought would be a simple operation was starting to look like anything but.

"Yeah," Will answered. "That would make sense. But the only car Wyatt has on record is this Camaro. All of the bikes checked out," he said with a slight hand gesture toward the collection of motorcycles. "All of them are here and accounted for?"

"As far as we know." His tone was determined. "They left in a car, but we don't have any idea what kind of car—the color, the tags, nothing." Morris scanned the room, perhaps hoping there would be some sort of clue. "Let's get back to the station. I want to know more about this guy."

The two detectives started to walk out the garage door to their car when suddenly, the young officer whose face was down under the dash popped up. "Detective Morris?" His voice was mixed curiosity and excitement. "I found something."

Will and Trent stopped and turned back. "What you got?" Morris walked back over to the car where the cop was now kneeling in the driver's seat holding something in a white-gloved hand.

"Looks like a homing device, sir."

"That's not one of ours," Trent said, inspecting the device. It was tiny, about the size of a nickel, and looked much like a small battery one might find in a watch.

Will had come over to look at the find as well. "I don't think it's the feds' either."

"No. And why would someone have put it there?" If Morris was confused before, he was completely baffled now. An archaeologist from the IAA along with a journalist from a local newspaper murder two nameless guys in a parking lot, run back to the house, get into a car that doesn't exist, and leave behind a car with a homing beacon on it. The whole thing was weird.

Gears were turning in his mind. Finally, Trent broke the silence as the discovering officer and Will looked at him as if waiting for directions. "You guys finish up here. I am going to head back to the office."

"What are you going to do?" Will asked.

"Find out exactly who this Sean Wyatt is."

8

NEVADA

The old man was sitting quietly in the courtyard of his lavish estate. A servant brought a pot of fresh coffee to him along with a slice of tiramisu. He thanked the young man, who returned through the large oak double doors whence he came. After pouring the brown liquid into a gray tea cup and mixing in a dash of sugar and cream, he leaned back and savored the aroma.

It had been several hours since he had heard from Jens Ulrich, and that was disconcerting. Since the beginning of this operation, his operative had been in contact with him every day to provide progress updates. Perhaps he had chosen the wrong man for the job.

A light breeze moved across the courtyard. Two butterflies fluttered from a small bush and settled down on another. The sound of a bee buzzing around a flower nearby signaled the full onset of spring.

Setting the small cup down on the bistro table, he took a look at his Bulgari watch, annoyed. He wondered what was taking Ulrich so long.

Right on cue, the cell phone in his jacket pocket rang to life. Sitting up a little straighter, though no one was looking at him, he answered the phone. "I do not like being kept waiting."

"Sorry for the inconvenience sir. I have been..." he paused, "busy."

"It's quite all right...it's just that..." he wasn't sure if the younger man on the other end of the line could tell his boss was not nearly as composed as other employers he'd had in the past. "It's just that this is something that we need done quickly and quietly, and it makes me a little nervous when you don't check in."

"With all due respect, sir, I am paid very well for what I do. There are a great number of people all over the world that would gladly pay for my services, and they would have the common decency to expect that job get done without my having to check in every day." His tone had become somewhat irritated. "You hired me to take care of this, and I will. Do I make myself clear?"

The bluntness of the younger man's voice struck him as both cold and somewhat threatening. Indeed, he was of a reputation as one to not be angered. Still, some respect must be paid. "Why is Wyatt still alive?"

There was a pause on the other line. "How do you know he is?"

"Because I have not heard otherwise. The police are looking for him though. Are you trying to use that to your advantage?"

Maybe this old guy wasn't so dumb after all. "I have changed plans, sir. He could prove useful to us after all."

"I'm glad you consulted me about this," the old man fought his anger then thinking for a moment, he said, "No, this is why I hired you. You think on your feet, and I know from your reputation that you have always been successful. Better that I not know what you are going to do with Wyatt. Just let me know when you have the map."

"Thank you, sir. That is all I ask. The map will be in your possession soon, I assure you."

The line went dead, and the old man slid the phone back into his pocket. He paused momentarily, looking up at the mountain that shadowed the mansion, deep in thought. "It better be," he said finally and took a bite of his dessert.

Back in Atlanta, Ulrich set his phone down in the center console of the black Lexus IS 250. Its motor hummed quietly as he maneuvered through the back streets of Buckhead.

He turned to the man that had tried to ambush Wyatt at his

house. The hired gun still clenched his jaw from the heavy blow of the shovel.

"It wasn't my fault. I had no idea Wyatt would react so fast." He could feel his boss's eyes glaring at him, and his reply to the gaze sounded like an elementary schoolchild after being caught throwing food in the cafeteria.

"I warned you to be cautious, but you didn't listen."

"I said I was sorry. It won't happen again."

Glancing over, the driver replied coldly, "Well, that's true." Before the man even realized what was happening, there was a puff of smoke accompanied by the cough of a silencer. At first, the hole in the man's head just looked like a black dot. Moments later, dark-red liquid began oozing from the wound as the head toppled over against the window, lifeless. Vacant eyes stared at the ceiling. Ulrich pulled the car over next to a church on Vine Street. He moved quickly to slip the body out of the car and onto the pavement. Only a minute passed before he was cruising down the street again. Glancing over at a small splotch of blood on the passenger's seat, his only thought was that he was glad he'd got the leather package. It would be easier to clean than fabric.

Ulrich wiped off the stain with a handkerchief; satisfied it was gone, he simply tossed the cloth out the window and continued down the street, headed to where the beeping dot on the LCD screen indicated the direction of his quarry.

9

ATLANTA

Detective Morris sat staring at his computer with a look of indignation. He had been there for hours poring over paperwork and searching international databases for anything about Sean Wyatt. Nothing he had found indicated anything unusual. The man had been everywhere on missions for the IAA, but he was apparently a ghost the few years before he worked there.

Born and raised just a few hours north near Chattanooga, Tennessee, Sean had attended a small private high school. His parents still lived in the area, experiencing the joys of retirement on the many beautiful golf courses the region had to offer. This luxury was certainly helped in no small part by contributions from Sean's six-figure IAA salary.

After high school, Wyatt had earned a bachelor's degree in psychology from the University of Tennessee in Knoxville, a master's degree in archaeology four years later. Usually, a master's program only took two to three years, but students had up to six to complete their coursework. During that time, Wyatt's file claimed that he had been employed by a local businessman as his personal gardener/landscaper. Again, nothing out of the ordinary. No wife. No kids. Not even a girlfriend. A loner. That explained the motorcycles at least.

Trent leaned back in his black standard-issue fake leather chair and scratched his head. The blue-and-white striped tie he'd been wearing earlier had long since been discarded on top of mounds of paper. Leaning forward again, he took a deep breath and gazed at the file on Tommy Schultz.

Schultz had met Wyatt in high school. Their love of sports and history and a similar sense of humor caused them to be nearly inseparable, with the exception of when teachers had to actually separate them into different parts of the classrooms.

As it turned out, Schultz's parents had quite a large sum of money they had kept secret. From the lifestyle they lived, no one would have guessed that they had possessed such wealth. The Schultz family home was moderately sized, and neither of Tommy's parents drove fancy cars. Luxuries were few and far between to the outside observer. Yet when his parents died unexpectedly, he inherited a sum just over $18 million. With some keen financial guidance and shrewd investment maneuvers, that money had grown into just over $40 million in a little over a decade.

Thomas Schultz set up several charitable organizations, the primary nonprofit being the International Archaeological Agency. With seemingly unlimited funding, the IAA, established in 2001, had recovered an inestimable amount of artifacts in its first seven years of existence. The discovery of the Sahara Temple was one of the most fascinating. In a seemingly endless array of sand dunes, the IAA was able to uncover what was believed to be an ancient Egyptian colony for priestly training. In South America, an ancient Incan city was discovered in a part of rain forest thought to be completely vacant of any prior civilizations.

Perhaps their greatest achievement, though, came from last year's amazing find. A ship, dating back to the early twelfth century, was located off the coast of Alabama. This was something that rocked the history world. Of course, most historians claimed it had been misdated or perhaps was simply the result of one European country being unable to keep up with evolving technology in sea faring. However, after intense study and analysis, it was confirmed that the ancient ship was indeed over eight hundred years old.

That was always the case. Whenever some kind of evidence came around that might shake up what everyone was taught in the history books, a throng of people was waiting to hide it, discredit it, or simply bash it into the ground. Heaven forbid the world had been taught an incorrect history up until this point. To some, it seemed ignorance was indeed bliss.

The more that Detective Morris read into the IAA, the more fascinated he became. This was not a group that searched the world for known archaeological locations or artifacts. It seemed that they specialized in finding things that were both lost to the eye *and* to history.

None of this was making sense. These two guys weren't murderers. And Trent was fairly sure that Allyson wasn't either. She was a reputable reporter: young, with a devoted following of readers yet not so well-known that she could just up and leave her current job. From the looks of her file, it didn't add up.

He plopped the stack of paper down onto his desk and stood up, stretching his arms out and twisting his back a little. There was no one else in the building except a couple of beat cops talking in the breakroom. Morris didn't envy those guys. He had done that job a long time ago. There were some parts of Atlanta he was glad to avoid on the routes they had to cover. As a detective, he had the luxury of showing up after the crime was committed and a safe perimeter had been established. Too many times, he had been shot at, once successfully. Fortunately, the bullet only grazed his side, but a few inches to the right and...

Shaking the thought, he walked toward the breakroom to get a cup of what passed at the station for coffee. The officers who had been talking casually gave a polite, "Evening, Detective."

To which Trent replied, "How's the joe, boys?"

One of them snickered. "How's it always taste? Like crap."

"Yeah, well, one of these days I am going to spring for some good stuff." He poured a cup of the steamy black sludge into a paper cup. After placing the hot coffee pot back in its place, he stepped over to the fridge. As he opened the door, the other officer who hadn't spoken said, "We're out of creamer too, sir."

Crap. A forlorn look down at the hot liquid in his cup signaled he was actually considering dumping it down the drain. "I heard you guys talkin' about a murder when I walked in? The KSU thing?" He changed the subject from the topic of bad coffee, hoping the medicine might go down a little better. Taking a sip, he realized it hadn't helped. "Any word on that?"

"The professor that got killed? Nothing new yet, sir." This time, the taller one spoke up.

"Murder weapon been found yet?" Trent took another pull from the coffee and grimaced as he swallowed.

"No sign of it. Heard it was a large blade though." The short cop reached over and confirmed a stereotype by grabbing a chocolate glazed doughnut from a box on the counter.

This was nothing new to Morris. "What was this guy a professor of?" he asked casually, trying to free his mind from the case that had been numbing him for the last eight hours.

"Ancient languages and cultures. He taught unconventional history courses there. Did a lot of work with the IAA. Apparently he was an expert in..."

Trent immediately interrupted, the light bulb going on in his head. "Did you say he worked with the IAA?"

"Yeah, I think so. That's what the bio said."

"Who's on the case?"

"Thompson, I think. Why?" the tall cop said as he, too, grabbed a doughnut.

"Just curious." Trent tossed the nearly full cup into the trash and walked quickly out the door. "Thanks, fellas."

"No problem." The two beat cops went back to finishing their sugary pastries.

10

ATLANTA

S ean had driven around the outskirts of the city for a few hours, uncertain of what to do. He'd chanced a stop in a drive-through burger joint to get a little food for Allyson and himself. Being out of sorts wasn't something he was accustomed to.

Interrupting his thoughts, the cell phone ringtone sang from his left front pocket. Two attacks within forty-five minutes had caused both him and his passenger more than just mere concern. When the phone rang, it was just one more in a growing line of surprises.

Fishing the device out of his pocket, he looked at the number. It was an Atlanta area code, but the number was unfamiliar. Normally, he tried to avoid answering calls from unknown numbers, but after what had just transpired, he decided to give it a try.

"Wyatt here." His answer was simple and direct.

"Sean Wyatt?" The voice on the other end sought confirmation.

"Yeah. Who is this?"

"Mr. Wyatt, this is Detective Trent Morris from Atlanta PD. We'd like you to come in to answer a few questions."

This wasn't good. "Questions about what?"

"Mr. Wyatt," the cop on the line began again, "we have reason to believe that you were involved in a double homicide this afternoon in

Buckhead." The man paused. "Of course, if you don't come voluntarily, we can always bring you in."

"Sorry, Detective. No can do. The two guys from the coffee shop shot at us first."

"Seems like you handled the situation more than adequately." Morris changed gears. "Look, we just need to find out more about what happened. Odds are, a man like yourself with your resources won't even be held for more than thirty minutes. Do you have any idea who those men were that you killed?"

"No."

There was a pause on the line then, "What do you know about Tommy Schultz's disappearance?"

A look of immediate concern crossed Sean's face. "What are you talking about?"

"About twenty-four hours ago, your friend Schultz went missing. We were hoping you could enlighten us. Normally," he added, "someone who is missing for such a short time would not have raised any alarm. However, Schultz was due to give a press conference yesterday concerning one of his new finds. He never showed."

Tommy had told Sean about the discovery and that he was going to announce it at the Georgia Historical Center during a special press conference.

Now this cop was telling him that his friend was missing?

"I assume you went to Tommy's house," Sean posed.

"Of course; we have people still there as we speak. There was no evidence of forced entry. And there was no sign of a confrontation. So, whoever took Schultz either knew him or was invited in. Both of those signs point to you, Mr. Wyatt."

Sean realized that the good policeman was trying to keep him on the line so that they could trace his location. He figured they had about thirty more seconds before pinpointing him. "I was unaware of Tommy disappearing. But I can assure you, I will find him." Then he went back to the incidents from earlier.

"The two dead guys from the parking lot came out of nowhere. I have no idea why they attacked us or what they wanted. They just started shooting. About twenty minutes later, I knocked out another one at my house, though I doubt he's still there."

"At your house?"

"Yeah, don't think I killed him though." Sean hurried, "Look, Trent, I don't mean to be rude, but I have to go."

"Sean, wait!" Morris was desperate. "What do you know about the Borringer murder?"

Wyatt pressed the end button. Borringer murder? Had he heard correctly? Sean had been out of town for a few weeks and hadn't heard anything about it. He'd worked with Frank Borringer a few times on a couple of projects. The man was a foremost expert on ancient dead languages. The professor was one of only a few people in the world who could interpret Sumerian and ancient Hebrew text and was an asset to the university in Kennesaw.

Now he was dead?

The rush of new information was unsettling. His best friend had been kidnapped. Frank was apparently dead. And now there were two separate attempts on his own life.

He had no idea what was going on, but he intended to find out. Turning the car down a side street, he changed directions.

Sean's look of concern transmitted to Allyson.

"What is it?" she asked. Her head and fingers trembled like a drug addict on day two of going clean.

"That was someone from the Atlanta Police Department. They want us—me—to come in to answer some questions about the two guys I shot today."

"Good. Maybe they can help us."

"I don't think so. Pretty sure I'm a suspect, not a victim."

"But it was self-defense. I was there. I can be a witness for you." She had a pleading look on her face.

Sean felt bad that she was all of a sudden pulled into this, whatever it was. Odds were, she'd been implicated as well.

"The cop said that Tommy Schultz has disappeared, and a professor that we have worked with a few times has turned up murdered. They think that I had something to do with it. At least, that's what they're saying."

"Your friend from IAA? What can we do?" Her green eyes looked so innocent.

"We have to find Tommy."

"How are we going to do that?"

"Whatever it was that Tommy was working on, he must have been using Dr. Borringer for some part of it. That's the only connection I can make."

"Do you know what he was doing?"

"Only that it was part of his ongoing search for an ancient Native American treasure called the Golden Chambers. He told me about it a few times, but I never really took much interest. Seemed like another El Dorado story to me."

"So, where are we going?" The shock of the day's events seemed to melt away into a firm resolve.

This girl was tougher than she looked.

"Dr. Borringer's house. If Tommy had been working with Frank on something, maybe his wife will know about it."

The gray sedan veered onto another street and crossed the interstate toward West Atlanta.

11

BLUE RIDGE MOUNTAINS

Tommy struggled to free himself from the wooden chair, bound by tightly wound twine. He was in a study, which overlooked what seemed to be a fairly substantial estate. A large yard surrounding the building ended abruptly at a thick, rolling forest. The room where he was constrained must have been at least four stories up. If it was a home, it was certainly large by any standard.

Twisting his head around, he took a better inventory of the room around him. The dark walnut floor led to an open, arched doorway. It was difficult to see beyond the corner, but he assumed it led into a hall. On either side of him were shelves of books that went all the way up to where the ceiling angled into a kind of conical-shaped glass sunroof. To access the highly shelved books, a library ladder was in place. A large square window sat before him, framed by cream-colored drapes. The window loomed enormously, allowing for an amazing view of the property and beyond.

Scooting the chair of bondage around, he found himself behind a large desk that matched the dark, rich cocoa of the floor. Whoever he was, this villain certainly had good taste. On top of the desk, an LCD widescreen displayed a screensaver of pictures from some random

European towns. Directly next to him, a much more comfortable looking high-backed leather desk chair mocked his less-than-desirable seating arrangement. Two smaller guest chairs sat opposite on the other side of the desk, giving the appearance that the study was more of an office in some ways.

Wrenching his body around again to get a better perspective of where he was, Tommy inched closer toward the window.

"I trust you like the view, Thomas." The foreign accent came unexpectedly from the direction of the open doorway.

"I would like it a lot more if I wasn't tied down to this uncomfortable chair." Even in a dire situation, Tommy hadn't lost his sense of humor. "I would have much preferred you tie me up to that bad boy right there," he continued, motioning with his head to the much more comfortable leather option.

"My apologies," the blond bowed slightly. "It is a regrettable scenario, having to hold you captive like this. Unfortunately, it is necessary."

"And why is that?"

"You have spent the better part of the last decade looking for something. Though several times you have found clues, nothing has pointed so directly to the answers you seek as what you discovered a few weeks ago."

"I have no idea what you are talking about." Tommy figured the guy knew about the stone disc. He was glad it was not in his possession.

Blondie had been standing politely, hands folded behind his back, wearing a very Euro-trendy suit. His vibrant tie looked like it was about three decades behind the current fashion, which, oddly enough, must have made it the current fashion.

"There is no need to play coy with me," he began. "We are aware of the stone disc. I also know that you were in contact with Dr. Borringer at the university in Kennesaw. You sent him something you could not decipher."

So far, this guy seemed to be right on the money. "Frank and I are colleagues. I use him as a point of reference all the time with my work. But I'm not sure what stone disc you are talking about," he lied.

"Still in denial." The stranger shook his head, making a clicking sound with his mouth, and took a few steps toward the desk. Leaning over and placing both hands palms down on the top, he stared directly into Tommy's eyes. "Thomas, it would be better for you if you would just tell us where the stone is. As soon as we have it, I will let you go. We will also need the translations Dr. Borringer gave you."

Tommy sincerely had no clue if Frank had even started working on those documents, much less finished translating them. He started to relay that information then decided to keep that to himself. "It would be better for you if you wouldn't wear such brightly colored ties."

The blond captor was thrown off slightly by the comment, glancing down at the fabric. Then, standing, he resumed his icy façade. "You think you are funny?"

"I'm better in a bar."

"Well, Thomas, I wonder if you think this is funny." Reaching over to the corner of the desk, he grabbed a remote control and switched on a 20-inch flat panel LCD TV that was mounted to the wall at a corner of the cone-shaped ceiling.

The screen flicked onto a feed from a closed circuit security camera. Tommy's heart nearly stopped. They were looking at an image of Sean's parents' home. "You son of a ..."

"Now, now," the blond said before he could finish, "the Wyatts will be fine. All you need to do is help me find what I want."

Tommy struggled against the twine. Unfortunately, whoever did the tying must have been one heck of a Boy Scout. He could barely move. "You better not touch them."

"Oh, we won't touch them, Thomas. They will simply be victims of an unfortunate accident. Many innocent people have died over the centuries during times of conflict. Millions have given up their lives during religious wars. Our mission is a new crusade. It has been blessed by God." He cocked his head as if talking to an elementary schoolchild. "If sacrifices are necessary, who are we to deny them?"

The tone in which he was speaking told of a great religious conviction inside the shell of a madman. That was a very dangerous thing, and the smile on his face was even more disturbing.

"I've heard this speech before," Tommy spat out. "The world has seen dozens of lunatics like you. Usually, they end up taking the easy way out when justice catches up with them."

The young blond man paused in midstride. A sinister smile crept across his face. "You would compare me to the Hitlers and Napoleons of history?" Leaning close, his voice lowered to a near whisper. "If those men possessed what it is we seek, the world may well have been a different place." He stood straight again before continuing. "All the more proof that they were not meant to have it."

"The Wyatts are good people and have nothing to do with this," Tommy said, thinking a change of subject might help the situation.

"Nothing to do with what, Thomas?"

Catching himself, Tommy realized he may have just hooked himself without knowing. Or maybe he'd just bought himself and the Wyatts some time.

"Fine," he said with hesitation. "I'll do whatever you want. Just leave them out of this." Desperation was in his voice.

"What happens to them is determined by our success." He stepped closer, around the desk, and leaned in so that Tommy could smell the pungent and probably overpriced cologne the man was wearing. A cruel grin crossed his face. "Now, tell me everything."

"What do I call you?"

Standing erect, as if considering what harm could come from his prisoner knowing his name, he then responded, "I have had many names, but you may call me Jens Ulrich."

12

ATLANTA

The campus at Kennesaw State University sits about twenty minutes northwest of Downtown Atlanta, just outside of the I-285 perimeter. Some of the more socially concerned citizens of the city look down on those who lived outside of the encompassing highway. *Silly,* Morris thought, *that people would think in such terms.* It was the modern day version of living on the wrong side of the tracks, though, in many ways, this particular wrong side of the tracks seemed much more enviable. Even with the encroaching urban sprawl, the area to the northwest of Atlanta had remained a nice place. Just one exit down from the university, a shopping center had grown from what was once just a mall to a town unto itself.

Even more impressive was the university. Quite young, as colleges go, Kennesaw State had only been established in 1963. However, in just forty years, the campus had grown to become the third largest school in the state, boasting an enrollment of over sixteen thousand students. The newest addition was the remarkable student village that had been constructed over the last three years. A school that only a decade ago had no student housing now possessed one of the nicest dorms in the country. It made him wish he were a freshman in college again. The brick and stucco combinations were topped by neo-Dutch roofing. The promenades and brick walkways that led from one housing hall to another were designed like those of a European town, complete with fountains in the middle of small plazas, Euro-style cafes, and a village convenience store.

The school was renowned as one of the top baseball programs in the country. KSU had also won NCAA Division II National Titles in women's soccer and men's basketball, all remarkable achievements and all in such a short time.

Trent eyed his surroundings as he walked along the concrete toward the library. He lived fairly close to the university, depending on the time of day. If it was from 7 a.m. until 10 a.m. or 3 in the afternoon until 8 at night, it would take him more than an hour or so to get from one point to the other. Otherwise, it would only take him fifteen minutes.

He hated the traffic. The city had done all it could to create as many lanes as possible to keep the traffic problem to a minimum, but to no avail. Atlanta had recently been deemed the city with the worst traffic in America.

He rounded the corner of one of the older buildings on campus and entered the parking lot of the library. Directly in front of the structure, a flag flew at half mast. He'd noticed a few others on campus paying the same tribute. The crime scene had been scrubbed, replaced by flowers and candles in the spot where the killing had taken place. The library was back in business, though at this time of day was not bustling with the rush of students desperate to finish papers and projects. Of course, with the arrival of the Internet, libraries had become less of a valuable commodity. Those who needed to research a topic nowadays simply had to search on Google or Yahoo. Seemingly endless amounts of knowledge pouring down from the ages were available at the click of a button. The antiquated libraries full of musty old books had been replaced by laptops at a Barnes & Noble or any number of coffee shops that offered free Wi-Fi.

Thinking about things like that made Trent feel like he was

getting older. He was only thirty-eight, but a time when the Internet and email didn't exist or when people didn't have cell phones seemed like ancient history.

All of these things ran through his mind and made him smile, just slightly, as he swung open the door to the main entrance. The library itself was not very large. It was one of the first buildings constructed during the initial building phase in the 1960s—when the college had been established. Apparently, expansion had only occurred as necessary. He made his way over to the librarian desk to where a short, redhaired woman was busily stamping books. She looked to be in her midforties. As he stepped up to the counter, her attention went from the books to the tall black man in a trench coat at her desk.

"Can I help you?" she asked with a smile, setting aside what she was doing.

He returned a polite smile of his own. "Yes, ma'am," he pulled his wallet from inside the jacket to show his identification. "My name is Detective Trent Morris. I was wondering if someone here could answer a few questions for me."

The redhead looked at him, a quizzical look on her face. "Well, I'm the one you would need to speak with. I am the head librarian here," she paused, "but I thought the police had already finished up their investigation."

"They have." And since he wasn't assigned to this case, he needed to cover his tracks a little. "I was just stopping by to do a little follow-up. You know, make sure that everything has gone back to normal as much as possible. It's kind of a new customer service thing we're doing at the department. Gives a better image of the police and all that."

Apparently, she bought it and smiled. "Well, I appreciate you checking on us. Things are starting to get going again, but it will be a long time before things are back to normal." Her eyes seemed to focus on a random spot on the carpet ten feet away. "Dr. Borringer was a well-liked man here. Lots of people knew him. It truly is a great loss for the university family and the community."

"You didn't happen to see him the night he died, did you?"

She looked down at the desk, a tear forming in the corner of her eye. "Yes. I saw him just before I closed up."

"I'm sorry to put you through this again. Please forgive..."

"It's okay," she cut him off, "really. Dr. Borringer had a key I had given him. It was a common thing for him to stay here later with whatever project he was working on, so I just let him lock up when he was done. Other than the person that killed him, I think I was the last person to see Frank before he died."

Trent gave her a moment to have that thought. Then he pressed on. "Do you happen to know what he was working on that night?"

She wiped her eyes with a tissue from a nearby box and gave a slight sniffle. "I don't really know. Dr. Borringer was in here all the time. It's anybody's guess what he may have been doing."

Somewhere upstairs, a vacuum was running. The clock on the wall read 7:08. On the way to the library, he had called Will to find out if he knew anything about the murder. From what he'd heard, they had no suspects and no leads, only Wyatt.

Looking down at her nametag, he revived the conversation, "Darcy, is it?"

"Yes."

"I appreciate you taking the time to talk to me. I just wanted to stop by and make sure things were getting along as best as could be expected." He handed her his business card. "Please let me know if there is anything I can do for you or if you come across anything unusual you think we should know about."

The smile returned to her face. "Thanks. I will."

"Pleasure to meet you." He finished and walked out through the metal detectors and out the glass front doors. It was a shot in the dark, hoping to connect anything with this murder. Still, something nagged at him as he walked down the concrete ramp leading back to the parking lot.

"Detective!" The voice came from the entrance of the library. A young woman in a denim skirt and white blouse stood holding the door open. "Wait a sec!" The brunette trotted over to him as he turned around; he was unsure of what this girl wanted. "My name is Emily Meyers. I helped Dr. Borringer every once in a while on some of his projects."

Trent looked at her. "Did you talk to any of the other police that came around here?"

"No, sir," she put her head down. "I was scared to talk to them. I didn't really have any information that I thought would help them." A guilty look came over her face. "That is, until I heard you talking to Ms. Darcy a minute ago."

"Do you know what Dr. Borringer was working on?" Trent quizzed her.

"I can't be sure. I was just an assistant for him. But I had been working with him the day before he died. He had me doing a lot of hieratic comparisons—sorry, those concern ancient writing systems, mostly in ancient Egypt. Very confusing stuff. Dr. B never showed me where he got some of these writings, but I know this: whatever he was working on contained a lot of ancient Egyptian, Sumerian, and Old Hebrew."

"So you weren't working here for him the night that he died?"

A sad look shadowed her face. "No. Dr. B had told me he was nearly finished and wouldn't need me that night. I met up with some friends at a coffee shop for a little study session then went home."

Morris was a little annoyed. "You felt like you didn't need to tell the police any of this?"

She raised her eyes from the ground. "I wasn't here when the cops arrived the first time. But I was working here in the library when that tall blond cop came around."

"Tall blond cop?" Trent knew all his fellow detectives, and none of them fit this description.

"Yeah, I overheard him asking a lot of the same questions you were asking. I think he said his name was Jurgenson or something like that. He talked kind of funny, real deliberate. I couldn't tell for certain, but I thought I heard a foreign accent a few times."

Jurgenson? He'd never heard of that name before and, there were certainly not any cops that he knew of with accents, other than Southern, working for the department.

"What exactly did this blond cop ask about?"

"He kept bugging the head librarian about where Dr. Borringer did most of his research, which computer he was using, any mail that he might have sent out that day. Stuff like that."

"What did she tell him?"

"Not too sure, but it didn't sound like she really knew too much about what the professor was working on. Jurgenson didn't seem very happy about her lack of information. He stormed out of the library, slamming a stack of books to the floor as he left." The girl looked down in thought. "I don't guess he found anything he was looking for."

"Do you know what he was looking for?" Something about the girl's demeanor led him to think she knew more than she was letting on.

She looked up from the sidewalk. "No, not really."

"What do you know?"

"Only that I think Dr. B was doing this project as a favor to someone over at the IAA. Pretty sure it wasn't for himself."

Bingo. "You don't happen to remember the name of the person at the IAA he was helping, do you?"

She looked around a moment, trying to recall the name. "Seems like it was Thomas...something."

"Schultz?" He finished the sentence for her.

"Yeah, that's it," she said with recognition in her voice.

So there *was* a connection. "Thank you, Ms. Meyers. You have been very helpful."

"You're welcome." She started to turn around and walk back into the library while he spun in the opposite direction.

"Detective?" she called out again.

"Yes," he turned around, stopping in his tracks.

"I'm not going to get into any trouble for not talking to that Officer Jurgenson, am I?"

"I'll take care of it," he replied, walking backward away from the girl and then turned the corner at a jog.

This story wasn't making sense, but now he had a connection. Sense could come later. Who was this Jurgenson? Sounded like there was another player involved in this fiasco. For the moment, though, his only thought was to check out the IAA headquarters and see if he could find anything else about Schultz and more importantly, Wyatt.

13

ATLANTA

Sean Wyatt's carbon-colored Maxima eased into a parking spot in front of the Borringers' house. He and Allyson got out and looked around; the neighborhood was completely lifeless save for the stereotypical random dog barking in the distance. Even for a Thursday, it was unusually inactive. Sean supposed the outrageous late-night board games would have to wait for the weekend for the suburbanites. It was not a life he'd been interested in pursuing.

Most of his friends from college had made such a life change. The endless parties and sleepless lifestyle had been traded in for mini-vans with soccer balls on the back window and family nights watching wholesome television. For people who had, at one point, been persuaded to take a spur-of-the-moment trip to the beach, six hours away, spontaneity now represented itself in an all-expenses-paid venture to the local fast food playground. On nights of true exhilaration, the couple might be allowed a quick visit to the local video store to rent a movie, though with the advent of Netflix, that *inconvenience* had been remedied, removing the necessity to pack up the car with the kids and go out.

Sean saw some of those people on the rare occasion when they could find a babysitter. They would always pester him with the same questions: "When are you going to settle down? Don't you want kids? Isn't it time for you to be getting married?"

His responses had always been to the point and not the least bit sensitive. Though he was not a mean person or in any way cruel, marriage and family was a topic that simply annoyed Sean. He was always quick to point out that if he wanted to go to a movie, he simply looked up the show times online and went. If he wanted to go out for dinner, he just got in his car and drove to whichever restaurant he chose. Freedom, he always explained, was far better than changing diapers or watching those annoying kids' TV shows.

There was always the same counterargument, too. "Don't you want to carry on your name?" they would say. To which he would always assure them that there were plenty of Wyatts in the world to take care of that problem.

He wasn't a loner, just an island of sorts. Maybe he just hadn't met the right girl. Among the primary annoyers was his father, constantly nagging about the injustice Sean was doing to his parents by not giving them any grandchildren. This, though bothersome, always made him laugh a little bit. His father's accusation was that he was too selfish, to which Sean wholeheartedly admitted. Ironically, his dad would always say, "Don't you want any kids so that when you are older you will have someone to take care of you?"

Sean didn't feel the need to point out the ironic absurdity in that argument. The conversations always ended with his father not understanding and Sean being content to let the older man remain frustrated. The need to procreate was something the younger Wyatt did not possess or simply ignored.

Now, he stood in the middle of what surely must have been the capital of the nuclear family. It was like an updated version of something out of a 1950s TV show. Allyson interrupted his thoughts. "This the place?" she asked and pointed to a two-story ranch-style home that stuck out like a sore thumb in the midst of cookie cutter urban development.

"Yeah." He left the car and strode purposefully up the walkway toward the front door. Allyson followed less confidently behind.

Lights were still on in what he assumed to be the living room and in a few other windows upstairs. As he approached the porch, he could see a television on inside. "Looks like she's awake," Allyson observed.

"She probably won't sleep well for a while," he empathized.

As the two stepped up to the door, a cat appeared in the glass partition of the doorframe. The animal looked at the visitors as if he were a butler receiving guests. Sean rang the doorbell, and a few moments later, the door cracked open slightly. A woman, probably in her midfifties, judging by the streaks of gray in her thick brown hair, peeked around the corner just below a latched chain.

"Yes?" Her voice strained like it was an effort to speak, much less be cordial.

"Mrs. Borringer, my name is Sean Wyatt, and I was an associate of your husband's. Would it be all right if my colleague and I came in for a minute?"

"You were a friend of Frank's?" Her question came from a suspicious face.

"No, ma'am," he answered. "I wouldn't lie to you and say I was. I met him a few times and referred to him for a few questions on occasion. I work for the IAA."

"I know who you work for, Mr. Wyatt. My husband had a great deal of respect for you. I'd hoped you would come by eventually. Please, do come in." Her slight English accent had become more prevalent since her mood seemed to have lifted slightly.

She unlatched the chain on the door and opened it wide for the two of them to enter. "Please excuse the mess; quite a lot of things to do the last week or so since the incident."

Mrs. Borringer stood to the side to let the two visitors in. She was casually dressed, wearing a pair of khaki pants and an Atlanta Braves sweater. The woman must have been a neat freak. There were a few boxes lying about, a small stack of letters on the table, and a small array of baking pans filled with various foods, presumably brought over by well-wishers and mourners. Hardly in disorder, though.

"Please, come in." She closed the door and locked it behind

them, ushering the newcomers to a sitting room near a fireplace. "By all means, have a seat." The lady motioned to a very soft-looking couch. The décor was best described as inconsistent. While the outside of the house portrayed a more neoclassical-North-western look, the interior appeared more of a kind of mosque/syna-gogue than a home. There were very few pieces of furniture save for a dark walnut table that matched the hardwood in the living room and hallways. The walls were decorated with different reli-gious emblems and pictures from differing theologies. It seemed that each wall was dedicated to a different ancient culture or religion.

"This is a very interesting home you have here, Mrs. Borringer." Allyson broke the proverbial ice with her ambiguous compliment.

"Thank you, dear." The woman's smile was sincere. "Frank respected all religions and cultures and appreciated each one's contributions to the world." She drifted off in thought then returned. "He believed that we all came from one place in history and that what had once been a singular view became twisted and changed over the years. But remaining in every religion, every cultural belief system, a part of the truth still existed." She stood and asked if the two visitors would like coffee. "I can't have any, though, too late in the day for me. That stuff would keep me up 'til the morning. But I can make a pot if you'd like." She waited expectantly.

Her generous smile was irresistible. "That would be great, if it's not too much trouble," Sean answered.

The lady smiled down at him. "No trouble at all, Sean." She spoke like she had known him for years.

While she was in the kitchen, he decided to continue the conver-sation. "Did you know what it was that your husband was working on the last few weeks just before he died?"

Sounds of pots being filled with water and dishes being moved around preceded the answer. "I don't know what he was working on." There was a pause before she continued. "The police came by twice and asked me the same thing both times."

"I'm sorry Mrs. Borringer. I didn't mean to..."

"Oh, it's okay, dear. I know you didn't." There was a minute of silence before she reappeared.

Allyson smiled at her as she came through the doorway of the kitchen, a small plate of cookies in her right hand.

Mrs. Borringer returned the smile. "Yes," she began, "I doubt those incompetents at the police department will ever find the villains that did this to poor Frank. He never crossed anybody, never hurt anybody." Her face grew resolute. "My husband was a good man in a world of horrible people. And I fear that we may never know who took him away." Rather than breaking down, an odd sort of anger had taken over her demeanor.

Sean was interested in the police department's role in this whole turn of events. Allyson had taken a cookie and was nibbling on it, listening intently. "You said the police came by a couple of times?" he stated the question when it felt like the lady could answer.

She snapped out of her daze with a start. "Yes. Yes," emphasizing an oddity about the answer. "It seemed strange to me that the investigators that came to visit me were, on each occasion, different people."

It was Sean's turn to perk up. "What did they look like, Mrs. Borringer, the two detectives?"

A slightly confused look appeared on her face. "The first officer was very polite. He was probably just under six feet tall, had dark hair, white guy." Then, her thoughts wrapped around the details. "Now, the second fellow was taller, probably six-three or so. He had a trench coat on, but I could tell he must have been pretty strong. His attitude was impatient, though, not very friendly. I much preferred the other policeman." Her words sounded like a child speaking about a preference of pastries.

Allyson and Sean had finished their snacks. "This second man, did he produce any identification?" Sean had become more curious.

The older woman gave a look of confirmation. "Yes. Said his name was Detective Jurgenson." She stood and walked back into the kitchen to retrieve the coffee. "Cream or sugar?" she called to them from the open doorway.

"Both," the two of them responded at the same time.

"When he arrived," she continued while stirring the cups, "he presented his badge and ID. Of course, I have never seen those things before. Looked real enough, I suppose. Had to go by what I'd seen on the tele. But he was a pushy young man, I must say. He went through all of Frank's things in the upstairs office and pretty much everywhere else."

"Did you notice if he took anything when he left?"

"No. I made sure that nothing was taken. Frank was the victim, so there would be no need to confiscate anything of his." She sat thoughtfully. "I don't think the man found what he was looking for anyway. After he was done tearin' the place apart, he started asking me more questions. His queries didn't really strike me as weird until later."

"What exactly did he ask about?"

She returned with a silver serving tray containing two large latte cups. "Well, he seemed very interested in Frank's work. While Detective Thompson had seemed genuinely concerned with who might have had it in for my husband, Detective Jurgenson only asked questions about his projects and anyone who may have been assisting him." There was a pause. Then, "It was almost as if he didn't care about finding Frank's killer at all."

Allyson and Sean gave each other an interested, momentary glance before graciously accepting their overly large cups of coffee with polite thank you's. Sean looked back at the lady, who now sat staring thoughtfully at her folded hands upon her lap. "Did this man happen to have any scars or an odd accent, just something that would set him apart?"

Her head cocked a few inches to the right. "You know, now that you mention it, I thought I picked up something odd in his voice. I didn't think much of it at first, but some of his words seemed to sound almost too controlled, like he was trying to cover up his accent." She paused for a moment, visibly realizing something was certainly out of place in this whole scenario. "But why would he...?"

"Mrs. Borringer," Sean answered before she could finish. "I don't believe that guy was a cop."

The statement struck her even though now it was becoming obvious. "I don't understand."

"Earlier this week, my friend Tommy Schultz was kidnapped. He had been working on a project with your husband."

Her face was dazed. "Tommy was here a few weeks ago." She looked down thoughtfully. The poor woman had been through too much in the last week. "And you think that this Jurgenson may have had something to do with my husband's murder and Tommy's disappearance?"

"I don't know, Mrs. Borringer," he leaned closer to her, setting his mug down on the wooden table in between. "Is there anything you can tell us about what Frank was working on? What Tommy and he discussed? If we can figure out what he was doing, maybe we can find Tommy. And if we find him, we find the guy that killed your husband."

Her face changed from confused to resolute. The look was a little scary to both of the visitors. "I cannot say for certain what it was Frank had found, but I do know what he was looking for." The older woman stood and started walking toward the stairs on the other side of the room. "I may know where we can find what you are looking for though." She smiled and motioned for them to follow.

Sean shared a skeptical glance with Allyson.

14

BLUE RIDGE MOUNTAINS

"Now, Thomas, this is how it is going to work." Ulrich circled the large desk like a big cat sizing up his prey. "You are telling me that you do not know where the chamber is." He stopped directly in front of Tommy, looking down at him with an almost pitying look. "You will figure it out."

"Why can't you figure it out yourself?"

Ulrich leaned back and smiled wickedly. He brought the side of his hand down hard across Tommy's face. Tommy grimaced for a moment from the quick strike. "Do not insult me, Thomas."

Pain and anger mingled in his brain. "That was unnecessary," Tommy managed through clenched teeth.

"Come now, Thomas," the voice had somehow grown even more sinister, "I know what you found. And I know that you have been working with Dr. Borringer on translating the code."

A horrific realization crossed Tommy's mind. "How did you... what have you done to Frank?" He struggled against the ropes in the chair, but he could barely breathe, much less escape. Thunder rolled outside following a flash of brilliant lightning not too far in the distance.

"You do not need to concern yourself with Dr. Borringer. I know what you and he were working on." Ulrich repeated the statement.

"If you did anything to Frank, I'll..."

"You will find the chamber for me, or you and the Wyatts will both die by this time tomorrow!" This was the first time he had heard Ulrich sound really angry. The tall man's face had turned red, his jaw tightening while he spoke. "You found the Stone of Akhanan! But you could not interpret the code. So, you took it to Borringer, the foremost authority in the Southeast on ancient languages."

Ulrich calmed momentarily and wiped a small bead of sweat from his forehead. "Now, I know that Borringer interpreted the code on the back of the stone. Unfortunately, I was unable to find the results of his work or even the stone itself. You can make this a lot easier if you just tell me what the code means."

"You're going to kill me either way," Tommy's face became twisted in rage. "You killed Frank, didn't you?" The question was direct, full of anger.

"I do what is necessary." Resolution now manifested itself in the man's voice. Ulrich stood erect and stepped to the window. "Sacrifices must sometimes be made for the greater good."

"Spare me your righteous speeches. Frank had a wife, you son of a..."

"Mr. Schultz!" Ulrich's voice thundered, "There is nothing you can do to help Dr. Borringer now." He thought for a moment, almost savoring it, before he continued. "It may comfort you to know that he died, unfortunately for me, rather quickly. The blade must have gone too deep into his back."

The chair strained against Tommy's adrenaline. Still, neither the rope nor the wood gave way. Moments later, his body relaxed, spent from the futile effort. His face blushed a bright red. Staring down at the ground, a sick-looking smile appeared on his face. In a quiet, matter-of-fact tone he said, "I *will* kill you."

"Now, Thomas, I seriously doubt that. The current situation would lead me to think otherwise." Ulrich had come back from the window to stand in front of his now-insane-looking captive. He walked around behind him, pulling a gun out from inside a holster concealed within his jacket. A second later, he produced a large blade in his other hand. "What you are going to do is exactly what I tell you."

"I don't know what the code means, you freak! Frank had everything. I gave him the stone and all the other stuff that I had been working on. He was going to return it to me when he finished. I'm not sure he even started working on it." The desperate sincerity was convincing. Of course, the man holding him prisoner had no way of knowing it was true. He might just as easily believe him to be lying.

"Don't toy with me," Ulrich stepped closer, holding up the blade, running the gun barrel down the side of it.

"Listen, why would I tell you I didn't have anything? If that's true, then I am useless to you. Unless..."

"Unless what?" He finished Tommy's sentence for him.

"There is one possibility..." His mind was running frantically. Truly, he had indeed given most of his work to Borringer, including the stone itself. If Sean could somehow get the stone and put together the clues, perhaps Tommy could leave a trail of the proverbial bread crumbs to where they were headed. That was a pretty big if considering Sean didn't know much about what he'd been working on. And it was doubtful that he would be able to find what Borringer had been working on if Frank had indeed begun his task. All of this ran through Tommy's mind as the blond man stared down at him, waiting. It was a long shot, but it was his only play.

"Well?" the accent was nearly gone with the question.

"The stone is only the first clue to the trail. It was dumb luck that I found it." He cleared his throat as Ulrich gave him a warning look to quit stalling. "However, I did make a copy of the stone. If we can get the copy, I may be able to decipher some of it. Even then, I don't know if I will be able to interpret enough to get us to the next clue. That's why I took it to Borringer in the first place."

"Next clue?" He leaned back a little, relaxing his menacing gaze into a questioning look.

"Yes. The legend claims that there is a path that must be traveled.

Only those who are worthy can interpret the code and find the path to the four chambers."

"How do you know about this?"

"Because of a riddle I came across a few years ago. It was written on an animal skin. An old man found it in a cave on his property. Said it was tucked away in a high place, sealed off with rocks and mortar to keep it dry. It was dated from the early 1800s. I'm pretty sure the stone confirmed the riddle and the location of the next clue, but I had to take it to Borringer for him to figure out the rest. Only God knows if he did or not."

Ulrich turned his gaze out the window in thought. He placed the blade down on the desk as he moved slowly toward one of the chairs facing his bound captive. Rain pattered on the glass as the storm reached the mansion. Thunder again pierced the moment of thoughtful silence.

Tommy could see the gears turning in the man's mind. His thoughts were interrupted by, "Why could you not decipher the entire code?"

He knew the question was coming. Fortunately, he had not had to lie so far, and he wouldn't have to start now. That would come later. "The text on the back of the stone is a mixture of languages. A great deal of it is hieratic, which I can figure about 50 percent of. The other parts are an ancient Hebrew and some kind of cuneiform, neither of which I can interpret. That left me with only about a third to maybe 40 percent of the riddle."

Crossing his leg over his knee, Ulrich asked, "Where is this copy of the stone?"

"It's at my house."

Ulrich was no fool. He looked skeptically at Tommy. "I'm sure that you would like for me to go to your house so the police can arrest me on sight, at the very least as a suspicious person."

"The thought crossed my mind." At least he hadn't lost his sense of humor. "But it's the truth. I left a copy there in my office. If there wasn't one, and you went there and couldn't find it, you would kill me as soon as you realized it was a lie or a setup."

"True," Ulrich agreed too easily.

"Look, I don't know who you work for or with, and truly, I don't care." Tommy was maintaining a surprisingly calm, matter-of-fact tone considering the circumstances. "All I care about at this point is the Wyatts not dying, hopefully myself as well, and never seeing you again. So if helping you find the Golden Chambers helps get us to that point, count me in."

Ulrich sat quietly for a minute, considering his options. His gaze pierced Tommy's eyes. He turned his head left, redirecting his stare to a stack of leather-bound books a few feet away near the desk. Some of them were typical of a wealthy person's study. A few first editions with rough bindings dotted the shelves in between some newer ones that seemed hardly ever touched. In fact, Tommy doubted many of them had been read. He wondered if this place even belonged to Ulrich. It certainly seemed like someone much older probably lived here. From his experience, décor like this came from years of trying contemporary things or chasing the mainstream but inevitably settling on something a little more classic. Ulrich had picked up the knife from the desk and had begun stroking it unconsciously with the palm of his hand.

"You certainly make a lot of sense for a man tied to a chair. And you understand that if you were lying to me, I would certainly kill you. But what makes you think that I am not going to do that once I find the Golden Chambers?"

Tommy swallowed hard. That thought had occurred to him. "Why would you do something like that? Once you have found the chambers, you will be able to disappear to anywhere in the world. Even if I did tell the police, not even Interpol would be able to find you. With the wealth the chambers would provide, you could live worry free forever."

Apparently, Ulrich had heard enough for now. "Fine then." He set the blade back down on top of the desk. "But if you try to cross me at any point, you and the Wyatts die. Understand?"

He nodded his acknowledgement.

"There will be police."

"I doubt there will be more than one guy watching the place. And I am guessing he will be at the front. You can park at the back and slip in through the neighbor's yard."

Inside, Tommy was hoping there would be more than one cop on the scene, but the reality was there might not be any at all. Still, he had to at least appear to be helping this guy for now to keep suspicion at bay. Ulrich seemed ruthless enough to kill him at the slightest provocation. And the last thing he wanted was to endanger the Wyatts. All he could do at this point was play along and hope that Sean was trying to figure out the clues.

The calm and logical way in which Tommy spoke seemed to convince Ulrich. "I will go to your house, but this better not be a trap. If it is, I assure you, the Wyatts will not receive a quick death from a fiery explosion." He laid the blade down on the desk again. "They will take a very long time to die."

15

ATLANTA

Sean and Allyson followed Mrs. Borringer up the carpeted stairs into a hallway with walls that were cluttered with family photos and reminders of years past. Though the Borringers did not have children of their own, they certainly had no shortage of relatives. There were pictures a plenty of boys and girls with what must have been siblings or cousins. A few black-and-white pictures that appeared to be quite old dotted the wall space, one of which was a wedding photo. In the corner of it, a date was written in with what looked to be faded black ink. It stated June 20, 19—something. He couldn't make out the last two numbers.

"A picture of my parents on their wedding day." She answered Sean's questioning glance at the wall. "That is my favorite one," she smiled, lost somewhere in the etches of time.

They continued down the hallway to the last doorway on the right. The door was open, leading to a small office. It was humbly decorated with a few simple black and white nature photos in dark wooden frames. The desk was colored a deep black but hardly posed as contemporary or trendy. It could have almost passed for an antique. A laptop sat quietly on the surface. A few letters, probably bills, and a lone candle accompanied the silent PC.

Next to the desk was a bookshelf, also black. There were only a few books filling its decks: the *Bible*, the *Torah*, the *Koran*, and a few books on ancient mysteries. Amid the collection of spiritual and historical reading was one book that seemed somewhat out of place. A collection of stories and poetry by Edgar Allan Poe, while considered an American classic, was odd sitting next to the works around it.

"Your husband must have really enjoyed studying religion," Sean broke the silence again. It must have been difficult for the newly widowed woman to reenter a room where her husband surely spent a great deal of his time.

"Yes," she replied. "He loved to read by candlelight. Sometimes, we would read together downstairs, but after I would go to bed he would come in here and continue. His search was tireless."

"Search?" Allyson queried.

"His search for God, dear. My husband did not accept the traditional views of God: an old man with white hair up in the sky. He wanted to know who God truly was. If he could find out what God was, then perhaps he could know his creator even better."

"Sounds like quite a heavy task," Sean continued.

"Most people spend their whole lives believing what they were taught since they were children. My husband did not simply just accept what was given to him. It was simple enough for him to believe in a higher power. He could never wrap his mind around the mathematical improbabilities that would produce a world full of species through mere chance. Believing in a creator was easy. The intricate way in which organisms work and behave is a delicate design, one which Frank had the utmost respect for."

"So he believed there is a God. He just wasn't sure which one was the right one?" Allyson's comment was uncertain.

"Not exactly, dear," Mrs. Borringer looked fondly at the books on the shelf, her gray-blue eyes weary. "You see, Frank believed that there was a small piece of truth inside each religion. At one point, thousands of years ago, we all came from one place. Most people know it as Eden. From there, the story of God mutated and changed as the population of the Earth migrated farther and farther from the epicenter and as the years passed. The many different stories you read in the *Koran*, *Bible*, and *Torah* came from what was at one point a single truth. Even all of the pagan religions had bits of the truth within."

"Like one of those team-building exercises," Sean said. Allyson and Mrs. Borringer gave him a similar look of confusion. He explained, "It was something I did once in college. The professor took the class of about twenty-five people and made us stand in a circle. He then went to one person and told them to repeat what he told them to the next person in line. After whispering the secret in the person's ear, that person leaned over and whispered to the next student in line. This process was repeated around the room until the last student had heard the professor's message. At that point, he asked the final student what the phrase was. Although it was similar to what he had told the first person in line, what he had whispered into the first ear had changed to something very different in mere minutes."

"That's exactly what my husband thought happened with the original religion," she smiled at him. "I am not sure what it is you are looking for, but if there is something to find, it would be in this room." Her hand waved carelessly toward the desk and the rest of the contents of the room.

The two guests exchanged a puzzled look. Sean said what they were thinking, "Didn't the police come look through this stuff?"

"They came up here and went through everything. The first group of officers was very respectful of Frank's things. They were thorough but were careful to leave everything the way they found it."

Her sweet face turned to a sort of scowl, "That Officer Jurgenson was quite the opposite though. He tore through everything, leaving books lying around all over the place. The garage was an even bigger mess. He went through our trash, leaving garbage all over the place. The house was a total mess after that fellow left."

Sean was feeling more and more certain that this Jurgenson character was not who he pretended to be. Cops could be insensitive at times, but not to an old lady who had just lost her husband to a brutal murder. No, even the biggest of blue-clad jerks knew how to treat a situation like that. He wasn't a cop but felt compelled to apologize anyway. Then he thought better of it.

She continued, "It took several hours to put everything back in its place, but it gave me a chance to look back on some fond memories."

This lady definitely seemed to be a glass-half-full type.

Her eyes returned from a distant gaze to the present. "Mr. Wyatt, you and the young lady may look through any of my husband's things that you wish. I trust you. If you are able to find what it is you seek, you may keep it."

"If we do find something..." he began.

"You may keep it," she repeated for him. "Whatever you find, I hope it helps you find Tommy and whoever killed Frank." She smiled again and disappeared around the door and into the hallway.

"Can she not just tell us what we are looking for and where it is?" Allyson pondered out loud.

Sean had to smile. Sometimes, historians could be a little socially awkward. He supposed this couple was no different. Those kinds of people spent their whole lives researching and analyzing the lives of other people from many different cultures and time periods. That was bound to have an effect on one's social skills. He couldn't help but wonder if Mrs. Borringer knew more than she was letting on. Sean considered the events of the last twenty-four hours. He had to help his friend. Apparently, the woman downstairs wasn't going to help any more than telling him that the first step to unraveling this mystery might be somewhere in this room.

"What are we looking for?" Allyson asked, interrupting his thoughts.

"I'm not sure." He began looking at the old religious texts, flipping through pages, scanning for some kind of bookmark that someone else might have missed.

Allyson, too, began looking through some the professor's things. She joined Sean at the bookshelf, picking up the copy of Poe's works. She opened it and looked through the table of contents. "The Fall of the House of Usher," "The Raven," "Black Cat," "The Gold Bug," and a plethora of other stories and poems, some she'd heard of and some that were beyond her memory of high school English. Most were probably never covered in class. Leafing through a few of the pages, she didn't recognize anything that should lead them to any kind of clue.

"Maybe it isn't here." She brushed against him slightly as she continued thumbing through the pages.

The touch of her skin sent an electric chill up and down his spine. He looked up and smiled at her. "I'm sorry you're involved in this." His gaze was sincere.

She smiled back at him. "I have to say, I don't enjoy being shot at," she paused, "but this is going to be one amazing story for the paper."

He snorted a laugh. Shaking his head, he continued his search.

Ten minutes went by, and still the pair had found nothing they believed to be what Dr. Borringer had been working on. It was starting to feel like a dead end.

Allyson interrupted his beleaguered thoughts. "I don't know much about Poe, but I don't think that he knew anything about the Golden Chambers." Sean spun the chair at the desk around and plopped down while she perused the pages as she paced the small room.

"It doesn't look like there is anything to help to us here," he broke the silence a few minutes later. If there had been anything there, the police or Jurgenson would have certainly found it. He hoped it wasn't the latter. Nothing seemed to point to any sort of clue, and frustration had settled in. Without a starting point, there was no way they were going to find Tommy.

Allyson had only begun to pace back from the window in the room when suddenly she stopped. Lifting her head, she smiled at Sean.

"What?" he asked and cocked his head curiously.

Her smile was joined by a nod. "I think I know what we're looking for."

She took a step over to the desk and set the book down on the shiny black surface. "Did you ever read 'The Purloined Letter'?" she asked him as her hand reached down for the envelopes on the table.

"Not that I remember. But high school English class was a long time ago."

"Well, in that story, Poe's main character is trying to hide a vital piece of information from the police and some other villains. The detectives and other investigators come to search his house, but they can never find what they are looking for. Essentially, they completely tear the house apart, but to no avail. Finally, the main character's friend comes over and asks where the letter is hidden. He is directed to a pile of letters that look like ordinary bills and correspondence. In fact, if I remember correctly, the protagonist of the story had gone to extra lengths to make the letter look old and unimportant."

"So, basically, the guy left it sitting right there out in the open where everyone could see it but where no one would think something secret should be. Pretty smart or really stupid."

"Yeah," she replied, pulling a very ordinary-looking letter from the small pile. "Sean, what is your middle name?"

"Matthew. Why?" His eyes narrowed in suspicion.

"I think we just found what we were looking for."

16

BLUE RIDGE MOUNTAINS

Ulrich left the car parked on the street in a parallel spot about a half block from Tommy's home. Bringing the captive archaeologist along would have been too difficult. Instead, leaving him behind in the care of his associates seemed the more logical thing to do.

As he approached the house, Ulrich moved stealthily from the open view of the street to the cover of a neighbor's home a couple of doors down. More than likely, if the cops were there, they would be stationed at the front and back of the house. He crept around the back porch of the first house, careful to stay low and in the shadows. Inside, an enormous flatscreen television was aglow with some late-night police drama.

Ulrich reached the corner and maneuvered to the house directly next to Tommy's. There, he crouched behind a wooden fence and waited next to a small gate. He reached up and cautiously unhooked the latch, careful not to make any noise. The last thing he needed right now was a dog to wake up. Fortunately, no canine appeared.

Keeping close to the back wall, Ulrich moved closer to his target. He could see the silhouette of what had to be a cop standing on the back porch, smoking a cigarette. Amateurs. Any moron could have seen the guard from a mile away. The man was pacing back and forth, obviously bored with his assignment for the night. As he turned in the opposite direction, Ulrich silently scuffed under the porch, squatting as he moved. Fortunately, the porch was about five feet high. Crickets chirped their night songs loudly. Hardly enough sound cover, but he didn't need much. To get in the house, he would have to take out the guard. Maybe he didn't need to kill the man. Knocking him unconscious could have the same effect. Ulrich preferred not to leave loose ends, though. Killing was something he'd been doing a long time, and through the years he had become quite proficient at it.

Above him, through the cracks of wood, the guard stopped his movement and spun slowly back the way he'd just come. His moment at hand, Ulrich was on the steps, flying up them in twos, careful not to trip. Unfortunately for the police officer, none of the planks made a sound, and in one swift motion, the long blade was pushed through the back of the cop's neck and out the front of his throat. A sickening gurgle was the only noise he made before falling to the deck, shock imprinted lifelessly in his wide eyes. Blood poured freely from the wound and oozed in between the gaps in the wood to the ground below.

Ulrich wiped the blade clean on the man's shirt then took a quick inventory, making sure there was no one standing directly inside. There wasn't. He stepped to the door. It was unlocked. He imagined if he had shown up thirty minutes later the *guards* might have been discovered passed out on the couch with ESPN playing in the background. Little wonder crime was so rampant in parts of the city.

Carefully opening the door, he slipped into what seemed to be the dining room. The house was dark with the exception of a fluorescent light in the kitchen casting a pale glow into the adjoining rooms nearby. Ulrich moved stealthily across the hardwood floor. Rounding the dining room corner, he could make out the shape of the other officer through the front window, standing, obliviously unaware to what had just happened to his partner. A few quiet steps up the stairs, and Ulrich was standing in Tommy's study.

He had to search quickly. It would only be a matter of time before the other police officer would go back to check on his partner. Schultz had said there was an envelope on his desk that contained what he needed.

Ulrich scanned the workstation for the parcel. He'd taken a big chance coming here. It was fortunate that Atlanta's finest had never received a level of training to deal with his skills. Still, had there been a larger force, things may have got sticky.

A stack of envelopes sat at the edge of the desk. Setting the blade down on the black wooden surface, he picked up the letters and shuffled them through his gloved fingers, not sure what he was looking for. He arrived at the bottom of the stack, having found nothing but ordinary junk mail and statements from various service institutions. Frustrated, he let the bunch fall back to the surface of the desk next to his knife.

Had he been tricked? He'd considered the possibility that Schultz had sent him here knowing full well there would be police around the area. Perhaps the archaeologist had underestimated the talents Ulrich possessed. Then again, surely his captive would not be so foolish as to trust that the police would be able to subdue him. No. It had to be here. He picked up the envelopes again and scanned them more meticulously. About halfway through the pile, he stopped at one that seemed peculiar. It was from a financial institution he'd never heard of. Granted, there were a million financial advisers out there, but this one struck him as odd. It had already been opened, whereas the rest were still sealed. Unconsciously dropping the other mail, he removed a piece of paper from within the frayed top. At the bottom of the correspondence he recognized the name of the professor he'd killed a few nights before. It was a letter from Dr. Borringer, and on it were the translations of the disc Schultz had found in North Georgia. The words were still in the form of a riddle: "The chambers will light your path." A chill went up his spine as he read the last few words. This had to be it.

Suddenly, a noise came from downstairs. The front door closed. Ulrich tucked the letter into a cargo pocket in his black pants as he shifted over to the door of the study. Below, he could hear the careless footsteps of someone who had no idea what had happened and what was about to. As the sound of the shoes on the hardwood moved toward the kitchen, Ulrich took a few precipitous steps downward, pressing close to the wall. Even though this flatfoot beat cop was surely no match for his level of talent, the blond assassin still preferred to always use the element of surprise if it was available, a policy that had probably saved his hide more than once.

In the kitchen, the refrigerator door opened, the light flooding the kitchen with a mixture of natural and florescent light.

"Hey, Billy!" The gruff voice of the cop froze Ulrich on the bottom step of the staircase. "This guy's got some Cokes in here. You want one?"

The Southern accent grated against Ulrich's European ears. The hapless cop, probably about five feet ten inches tall, looked more like a reject from a junior varsity offensive line. Ulrich judged his weight to be around 250 pounds and from the looks of him. He watched as the chubby man reached into the refrigerator and grabbed two red cans from the bottom drawer. Receiving no response from his partner on the back porch, he called out again, "Hey, Billy! You thirsty?" Silence.

Setting down the cans, the cop stalked toward the dining room where the door to the back deck was located. "Dadgummit, Billy! If you're on that cell phone again, I'm gonna kick your..." The officer stopped in midsentence as he stared out through the glass door at the prostrate body on the other side. "What the...Billy?!" Panic flooded his face as he reached for the handle of the sliding door.

Abruptly, he felt something thin and cold run across the breadth of his neck.

With fleshy hands, the blubbery cop clutched his throat and turned around to see a tall blond-haired man holding a knife. Blood gushed from the open artery and vein, his fingers doing little more than filtering the flow. The man's beady eyes quickly clouded, and the room began to spin. Finally, his heavy body crashed to the floor, torso and head leaning up against glass. After only a few seconds, the head toppled onto a shoulder, lifeless.

Ulrich simply stood for a moment watching the last few ounces of life spurt from the wound. Then, turning, he strode swiftly toward the front of the house, concealing the blade in its jacket sheath. He closed the front door of the house casually and returned to the quiet suburban sidewalk, unaware of the eyes that watched him from a black luxury sedan nearby.

17

ATLANTA

Allyson handed the envelope to Sean. "Would you like to do the honors?" She smiled at him like a kid who'd just found the last Easter egg.

What he took from her hand looked, on the outside, like an ordinary correspondence to a financial advisement company. The men who had come in to the Borringer house looking for something profoundly significant would have passed it off to be a typical everyday letter.

They would have no way of knowing that the institution to which the letter was addressed did not exist. In fact, the only people that might recognize the initials were the two people looking at it at that very moment. In the center of the envelope, the words *SMW Financial Advisers* were the send-to address.

Sean stared at the envelope. "That clever dog," he laughed. "A purloined letter with my initials on it, no one else would have ever realized."

Allyson smiled proudly.

He opened the envelope carefully and removed the contents. Inside was something that Sean did not expect. Instead of finding a translation of some ancient code, as he assumed, he realized it was a letter written specifically to him by Dr. Borringer.

The two exchanged confused glances. "How did he know you would come here?" Allyson seemed to read his thoughts.

"I don't know." Sean was just as confounded.

Both pairs of eyes scanned the letter as he laid it out on the desk.

Hello, Sean. If you are reading this, then I fear my suspicions were correct. But if you found this letter, you have taken the first step. Edgar Poe's "The Purloined Letter" trick is certainly a good one.

Recently, our mutual friend Thomas Schultz sent me a most interesting artifact he discovered in the northern part of Georgia . As you and I both know, Thomas has been searching that area and other areas in the state with a reserved, but notable interest for some time.

Until I received his request for help, though, I had no possible idea just how deep his search had gone. I hope that I have not failed him in his quest. It seems that someone else has learned of the artifact and has been watching me ever since it came into my possession. My first thought was that if I put off the translation and pretended that it was of no import, the man following me would consider the possibility that it was just another random piece from a dig somewhere else in the world. That strategy, however, did not work. He continued to follow me and watch my every move. The fact that this stranger and his cohorts did not attempt to steal the stone disc meant that they needed me to translate it just as much as Thomas did. There are only two others in the world who I believe could have performed this translation due to the rarity and the blending of the languages on it.

Unable to postpone the work any longer, I set about translating the mixture of languages on the back of the stone. I was shocked to discover that there were four different forms of writing inscribed into the ancient disc. The languages are rare to begin with, but having them combined together into a singular form of writing was most puzzling. It took many long hours to put together the combination of words and phrases. Almost more confusing than the languages were the pictures on the front of the artifact.

Eventually, I was able to decipher the message on the back, which proved to be interesting but less than helpful. Then, I realized that the inscription on the stone was only part of the message. What was written on the back worked in conjunction with the picture clues on the front. Even for someone as learned in ancient languages as I, it was very difficult, at first, to try and understand the meaning of the engraved scene.

On what I call the front of the disc is a picture of two birds. They are standing on some kind of perch, facing each other. In between the birds is a dividing line that looks like some kind of pole. I was not sure what the picture could possibly mean. Even now, I am not certain what the true purpose is behind it. I regret that I can be of no further assistance. But in relation to the message on the back, perhaps you and Thomas can unravel the puzzle that I could not. I wrote down the translation on the back of a separate piece of paper in this envelope. Good luck to you and your friend in this endeavor. I only hope that what has surely befallen me does not happen to anyone else.

Sincerely,

Frank Borringer

Sean finished reading the note, still puzzled. He set the letter down respectfully on the desk and removed the second piece of paper from the envelope. Its message was odd:

Ancient stones will mark your path and of the chariots of Heaven. The raven and the dove will guide you on your journey home. The key with sacred bones does lie. Make every step true, and unlock the chambers, for they shall light the way to the resting place of mankind.

"The chambers are real," Sean's voice was reverent, barely above a whisper.

"What does it mean?" Allyson was befuddled.

"I don't know." Sean's gaze went to the drawings of a circular object on the page. He examined what was labeled as the front and then the back, looking closely at the tiny inscription's remarkable detail. The picture of two birds facing each other was just as peculiar as the riddle. Indeed, they did appear to be sitting on some kind of railing with what appeared to be a rod in between them. "I have no idea what 'the resting place of mankind' could possibly mean. The letter from Dr. Borringer said that the message on the back and the picture on the front were both clues pointing to the same thing."

"So the stone points the way to the chambers. What do the chambers contain?"

"I suppose that whoever this stone was meant for would know the answer to that. But it seems like the chambers are not the final destination." Sean seemed to realize this last truth while he spoke.

"So, Tommy has been looking for this for several years?" she asked, looking at the translation. Her mind could not wrap around a possible meaning.

"I would say that one of the birds is a raven, and the other the dove, but they look similar." He looked closer at the medallion-shaped sketch. Then, realizing he hadn't answered her question, "Yes. Tommy has been looking for the Golden Chambers of Akhanan for some time now. I'd say these letters right here prove that they exist. At least, there was enough evidence for Dr. Borringer to believe they exist. The fact that he was murdered for this information makes me think he was on the right track." His fingers retraced the mysterious words on the paper.

She was leaning over his shoulder; her fragrant hair fell lightly onto his neck as her breath tickled his skin. Sean couldn't help but be momentarily distracted. It had been a long time since he had any kind of romantic contact. His job kept him out of the country a great deal, and when he was home, it wasn't for very long. Both facts made it difficult to meet people that way, much less maintain a relationship. For a moment, his thoughts drifted to a few years back to...he couldn't let himself think about that. Not now anyway.

"It would sure be nice if we knew what we were looking for," she commented, seemingly unaware of his thoughts.

"We know exactly what we are looking for," he corrected. "I just have no idea where to find it. I do have a friend, though, that might be able to shed some light on this little puzzle."

"Yeah?" She perked up. "Who?"

"A buddy of mine works at the Etowah Indian Mounds State Park. He lives near the site just outside of Cartersville. It shouldn't take us more than forty minutes to get there. The guy knows more about Native American history than anyone I've ever heard of. Plus, I'm sure he's heard some stories that never made it into the history books, and that is exactly the kind of stuff we need to find out about."

His mind was racing right now. Could this be the first real clue to finding the lost Golden Chambers?

"This friend of yours isn't one of those crackpot conspiracy theorists, is he?" She gave him a playful, suspicious glance.

"No...well, not completely. He's okay. We won't be looking for UFOs, if that's what you're thinking." Sean gave a reassuring smile.

Downstairs, the doorbell rang, and their smiles turned instantly to concern. Quickly, he grabbed the letters and stuffed them into his inner jacket pocket and stepped over to the door. Allyson leaned close behind him as he peeked around the door.

Around the edge, they could see Mrs. Borringer open the front door. Sean listened intently to a man's voice on the other side of the door. It sounded like the guy said something about being with the police. He wondered to himself if it were the mysterious Jurgenson, but these thoughts were answered as a black man in a tan jacket walked through the door, putting his wallet and identification into a coat pocket as he crossed the threshold.

Mrs. Borringer politely asked him if he would like something to drink. The lady must treat all visitors like friends. Sean pulled himself away from the door. He whispered, "We have to get out of here. That's gotta be Detective Morris, the guy that called me earlier from the Atlanta PD. If he is looking for clues, he will want to see this room."

"How are we going to leave without him seeing us?"

"Mrs. B is still talking to him." Sean paused for a moment to make sure he was right. Then he whispered, "Let's move across the hall to the bedroom. He won't have any reason to go in there."

Allyson nodded in agreement. Sean peered around the corner of the doorway again. Down below, the detective was saying something about Dr. Borringer's research. Silently, the two made their way across the hallway into the master bedroom. Upon entering it, they realized that it was much more tastefully decorated than the hodgepodge of the rest of the house.

The walls were painted a warm tan color with dark wooden nightstands and dressers. A large oak armoire rested in the corner, with intricate carvings of floral and forest themes on the front.

Sean motioned to the master bathroom, and the two of them quickly darted to the open door. Back in the hallway, the voices of Detective Morris and Mrs. Borringer grew louder as they climbed the stairs.

Tucking in around the corner of the bathroom, Sean inched his head forward to see across the hall.

"This is where your husband kept all of his research?" the detective asked.

"Yes, sir." She continued on, answering the man's questions the same way she had answered Sean's earlier.

"What are they doing?" The tension was too much for Allyson.

Sean motioned for her to be quiet with his finger while the two in the other room disappeared from view, apparently looking through some of the things on the desk. A few minutes passed. Suddenly, the detective appeared in the doorway again. Sean quickly ducked back behind the bathroom doorway, unsure if he'd been seen.

He heard the man comment on the nicely decorated bedroom, obviously looking inside. Apparently, Sean's and Allyson's presence was unknown because the cop was still talking with Mrs. Borringer about her late husband's work. The voices continued to move farther away and down the stairs.

Leaving their bathroom hiding place, the two fugitives went to the doorway leading into the hall. Downstairs, Mrs. Borringer politely escorted Morris to the door. He thanked her for her courtesy and invited her to call if she could think of anything he might need to know.

Sean and Allyson heard the front door close and looked at each other, breathing a sigh of relief. They'd caught a huge break not getting caught.

"We'd better get going," he stated.

"No argument here," she agreed as they stood and exited the bedroom.

18

CARTERSVILLE, GEORGIA

The gray sedan sped along the interstate, heading toward the rural town of Cartersville. Every few minutes or so, Sean would glance in the rearview mirrors to make certain no one was following them. A couple of times, he thought he had seen a car changing lanes with him, but then the vehicle turned off of an exit a few minutes later. He hadn't survived this long by being careless, and the people they were up against had to be considered extremely dangerous.

Even though Sean suspected the worst, something told him that his friend was okay for now.

Allyson interrupted his thoughts as if she could see inside his head. "I'm sure Tommy is still alive." A sincere smile accompanied the hopeful words.

He appreciated the sentiment. And most of him believed his friend was, indeed, alive. Still... "Logic would dictate that he is all right. If whoever kidnapped him wanted him dead, they would have already done it, like with Frank." Sean shook off the thought, "No, they need him for something."

"But what is it?"

"The only thing I can figure is whoever took Tommy can't decipher the clues. I guess they think he can. He knows more about the Golden Chambers than anyone else in the world. If anyone needed someone to help unravel the mystery, Tommy would be the go-to guy."

He clicked his left blinker and swerved around a minivan with a soccer ball sticker on the back. There was no hiding his cynical smile. She, apparently, didn't notice.

"I don't understand," she began again. "If these Golden Chambers do exist, why hasn't anyone ever found them? It's got to be hard to hide four giant golden rooms for so many centuries."

"Not really. I mean, think about it: Every single day there is a new historical discovery somewhere in the world. Entire cities that were once thriving metropolitan areas of the ancient world are being uncovered as we speak. Whole cultures that disappeared suddenly are found under the very ground people walk across every day."

"I guess." She was half-convinced, a smirk on her face.

He gave her an equally teasing look. "I'm just saying, there is a world of stuff out there that hasn't been found. That's why the IAA exists."

"So, let me get this straight, you guys look all over the world for random historical artifacts that no one else knows are there? That pretty much right?"

"Yep."

"But your organization does other stuff, too, doesn't it?"

Sean looked at her for a moment, at least glad that he didn't have to explain the whole story to her. "Yeah," he said as he turned the Maxima off the interstate and onto the exit. "We do a lot of charitable work, but one of our main functions is in the area of education." The car turned right off the ramp and onto a two-lane road heading into the foothills of northwestern Georgia.

"Do you go into schools and talk about ancient treasures and all that?"

A small chuckle escaped his mouth. "Sometimes. The kids certainly like to hear about those kinds of things. When you go into a school and tell young people about some of the things that we have discovered, they get excited about history. That's how we hook 'em." Sean smiled at his final remark.

"Everyone gets excited about treasure," she responded.

"Of course. But the more important part of what we do in relation to education has to do with the establishment of the Georgia Historical Center."

"It was quite an impressive accomplishment just to get the real estate for that in the middle of Downtown Atlanta." Now the reporter inside of her was coming out a little.

"Well, we had a few very generous contributors."

"Like Tommy Schultz?"

He gave her a curious glance but said nothing.

"Oh, come on. Everyone knows that Tommy inherited a ton of money when his family died, and shortly after, you guys started up the IAA and purchased the land near Centennial Olympic Park. That stuff is no secret."

"We had some generous donations from several contributors. That's all I am going to say about it. Of course, we did receive some large grants for the project, as well."

"Well, I think it's great that you have put such a strong emphasis on the unknown history of the world, especially the state of Georgia."

"It has been a really cool venture. Kids all over the state have learned about the history that surrounds them. Tommy has been looking for the Chambers of Akhanan for a long time. A find of that magnitude would put the whole region on the historical map. Up until recently, historians regarded the Native American history in this country as less important than European or Asian history. If we can find a connection to the Chambers of Akhanan here in the Southeast, all of that would change. The history of the world itself would change." The passion with which he spoke was mesmerizing.

Allyson admired the way that he talked. Maybe, if her history professors in college had been more like Sean Wyatt, she might have paid a little more attention in class, or at least not fallen asleep. Sometimes, she wished that she was in a line of work that she liked better. Journalism certainly had some positives about it, but there were times that she loathed her job. Long hours stuck in a cubicle could drive even the most avid writer to madness.

Realizing her eyes had been lingering for a few moments, she averted them to the dark passing countryside. If Sean noticed her look, he didn't say anything. Silence was blurred only by the hum of the car engine. Up beyond the road ahead, just over the distant Blue Ridge Mountains, the moon peeked out from behind the dark silhouettes.

"What a beautiful view," she broke the minutes of quietude.

Smiling, he nodded, "I love this part of the country. Been to a lot of places all over the world, but the Southeast just has something special about it."

"Are you so passionate about everything in your life, Sean Wyatt?" She laughed.

He thought for a moment, semi-pondering the question then replied, "I have no opinion concerning cats."

A full laugh erupted from her chest. "What?! Cats? What in the world are you talking about?"

"Well, I'm just saying, I can take or leave cats. I could have one or not. Doesn't matter to me." He cast a wry little smile at her. "You asked."

She continued laughing as the car whirred down the country road.

19

BLUE RIDGE MOUNTAINS

Tommy sat at a table situated in the corner of a cavernous kitchen. The ropes that had previously bound him had been replaced by two security personnel who were almost as large as the room. He'd been sitting there for almost two hours, waiting. For what, he wasn't sure. Ulrich had left quickly, determined to bring back what Tommy had said he needed from his house.

When he had received the correspondence from Dr. Borringer, there had been no explanation as to what the coded sentences meant. It was simply a translation of the ancient languages that had been combined to mislead and confuse those who would try to decipher it.

A nervous chill went up Tommy's spine as he considered the consequences. What his captors would do if he couldn't figure out the riddle from the stone? He figured they would surely dispose of him just as easily as they had done with Frank. Killing, it seemed, was not a moral dilemma for them.

He thought about his friend, Sean, and wondered where he might be at that moment. Internally, he shook the thoughts of uncertainty and fear out of his mind. His demeanor had to stay cool.

"You guys play football when you were in high school?" He tried to crack their stone exterior. They simply stared at him, cold and direct. "No?" Tommy continued, "Well, you should have. Couple of big rascals like yourselves, I know a lot of coaches that would have loved to had you guys playin' O-line or D-line."

Still no response.

After a few moments of awkward silence and thought, Tommy chirped up again, "You guys even speak English?" They still didn't respond. "Well, could one of you at least grab me a glass of water? I am freakin' thirsty."

Finally, something he said got a reaction. One of the large men turned his head slightly to the shorter one on his left and gave a quick nod in the direction of the sink. The neck-less behemoth resumed his stare at the prisoner while the other guy stalked over to the kitchen sink, grabbing a glass out of one of the overhead cabinets. After filling the glass, he clomped back to the table and set it in front of Tommy.

"Thanks. Much obliged." He truly was grateful and tried to act as natural as possible. The shorter giant had resumed his spot where he'd been standing previously.

Tommy took a big swallow of the water and set the glass back on the table. "So, you boys from around here?"

Apparently, he'd got all the interaction he was going to receive from the two guards.

"Yeah," he went on, as if they were listening, "I grew up just outside of Atlanta. Lived in these parts my whole life. Love it. Not a place on earth I would rather be." His friendly demeanor seemed to do nothing to crack the frozen exterior of the two suits. "Some people complain about the humidity, but I don't mind it. I always tell 'em at least it's a wet heat..."

Silence.

"So...you guys listen to music? Wait, let me guess. Techno? 'Cause you look like you would be into that. Me? I pretty much like it all. Rock, bluegrass, even some of that Euro-electronic stuff."

Tommy looked from one guard to the other, waiting. Then, finally, he said, "You boys heard of Jimmy Buffet?"

This time, the non-response was accompanied by the double

doors at the end of the kitchen bursting open. Ulrich had returned. He carried a letter in his hand. "I believe this is what you needed, Herr Schultz." The statement was calculated but not sinister.

Tommy's reply was sarcastically defiant. "Oh, good. You found it. I wasn't sure if it would still be where I left it, pesky police searching the premises and such after the kidnapping."

"The police were quite accommodating." The evil smile from earlier returned to the pale face.

Tommy wasn't sure what would happen when Ulrich went to recover the document. Part of him had hoped the police would detain the blond foreigner. Of course, if that happened, his own chances of survival might actually go down.

These two brutes in the black Secret Service outfits probably had a set amount of time to wait for their boss to return, at which point, they more than likely had execution orders. It was certainly a mixture of relief and disappointment as Ulrich stepped over to the table and laid the envelope upon it.

"Are you surprised that I returned?" His voice was sarcastic.

"No," Tommy's reply was quick. "I was just wondering what was taking you so long." He motioned to the two henchmen, "We were just talking about Jimmy Buffet when you came barging through the door.

Ulrich stood up straight and cast a quick glance at his employees, who were staring straight ahead. The shorter one had a somewhat dumbfounded look on his face.

"The time for your little wisecracks and games is over, Mr. Schultz." Ulrich leaned in close to Tommy's ear then added. "You have twenty-four hours to figure out this riddle. If you have not come up with the answer by then, I will remove one of your thumbs and will continue removing appendages once every two hours until all you have left is a torso with a head on it."

That old feeling of fear crept into Tommy. "How am I supposed to do that? People have been trying to figure this out for centuries, and you want me to do it in a day? I haven't even slept."

"That is not my problem. I have given you what you need. Just get it done." He turned and said something in another language to the guards. Tommy couldn't make out what it was. Then Ulrich strode back through the double doors whence he'd come a few moments earlier, dramatically extending his arms as he pushed them both open at the same time.

Under his breath Tommy whispered, "So, I'll just go ahead and take care of this then." His panic was masked by his characteristic dry cynicism. "Either of you guys experts in three-thousand-year-old dead languages?"

They looked at each other then both shook their heads simultaneously.

"Didn't think so."

20

ATLANTA

Trent Morris stood erect, disturbed by the scene before him. One arm across his chest, the other elbow resting upon it while he held his chin with a fist, he watched as the crime scene investigators snapped pictures and searched for evidence with gloved hands.

The call had come at 10:30, right after he'd got home for the night. He'd been so exhausted that a stop by a coffee shop drive-through had been necessary on the way over. The case that had started off as a kidnapping had taken a turn for the grim with three bodies lying in the wake.

Now, he stared at the carnage in disbelief. The portly body of one police officer lay bent against the sliding glass door amid a pool of thick, red liquid. Outside, an investigative crew was busy taking photos of the crime scene and searching meticulously for some kind of a clue.

Frustrated and angry, Trent rubbed his sleep-deprived eyes. "Anyone here know how this happened?"

The CSIs stopped what they were doing for a second to look at him with blank eyes that said, "Nope."

"Yeah. That's what I thought." At this point, they had no leads and no suspects. He turned and slowly walked toward the kitchen, careful not to touch anything. Weaving his way past more evidence collectors, he moved up the stairs. Upon entering the study, he found Will standing in the center of the room with a notepad in hand, busily jotting down notes. Another investigator was scanning the walls with a UV light, looking for heaven knew what.

"Hey, buddy," he greeted his partner with a half smile in an attempt to hide the emotional surge from the scene downstairs. "What a mess, huh?"

"Yeah," Trent sighed and ran his hand across his short hair. "Got anything in here?"

"Not really. But I do think whoever did our boys downstairs came in this room for something."

"Any idea what they were looking for?"

"No. But it looks like someone has been in here recently due to the shoe prints in the carpet. Seems like whatever they were looking for was on that desk over there. At least they thought it was anyway. Not sure what it could have been or if they even found it. All I know is that the footprints don't stray anywhere else away from the desk or the path to the door." Will motioned with his pencil and traced a line from the door to the workstation at the opposite wall.

"They didn't look through any of the books or in the closet?"

"Doesn't look like it."

"That means whoever came in here knew exactly what they were looking for and where to find it." Trent's mind raced.

Will finished his thought for him, "The guys who took Schultz?"

"Exactly." He turned his head back to the front of the study, analyzing the imprinted steps from the door to the desk.

"But why risk coming here? Surely, they had to know we would have somebody here watching the house."

"That can mean only one thing, Will. We're dealing with either someone very desperate or someone very dangerous. I'm inclined to believe it's the latter."

"So what are we looking at? Ex-military? Foreign?"

"Don't know. But my guess is they're pros. And they got no issues with killing."

"You think the same dude that did that professor over at KSU did this?"

Trent nodded. "Probably. Knife attacks in both instances. And Schultz and Borringer knew each other. Doubt it's just a coincidence."

He switched gears, "Neighbors see anything?" Trent knew what the answer would be. This killer would not let himself be seen by even the most innocent passersby.

"Nope. Most of the people around here were already asleep."

Not at all surprised, Morris took a couple of steps over to the workstation. A stack of envelopes and other unimportant-looking junk mail lay in a pile near a blank computer screen. Trent reached down and picked up the stack of letters, unconcerned about tampering with any possible evidence. He flipped through the correspondence without finding anything of interest and laid the papers back down where he found them.

No witnesses. No fingerprints. No weapon. No motive. The killer was a ghost. Suddenly, Trent twisted and took a step toward the wall opposite of the bookshelf. A few picture frames dotted the mocha-colored paint. One, in particular, caught his attention. It was a picture of Tommy and his friend, Sean Wyatt. The scene was of the two men at some archaeological dig in which they were each holding a statue of some kind. There was no date on the picture, but from the looks of it, it was probably five or six years old. Carefully, Morris lifted the picture off of its hook to get a closer examination. He flipped it over to check the back. There was a notation on the back that read, *Mobile Bay, AL. 2003. Mississippian-Era Statues.*

Will interrupted his thoughts. "You got something?"

Entranced for a moment, Trent snapped back to the present. "I don't know. But I think we need to talk to this Sean Wyatt."

"You think he's the one behind this?"

"Like I said, I don't know. But think about it. Who else would have known what Schultz was working on, much less have understood it?

The person who broke in here sure seemed to know where to look for what they needed. And Sean Wyatt is former special ops. It's the only explanation we got at the moment."

Pondering the theory for a moment, Will added, "We gotta find Wyatt."

"Exactly." Morris moved quicker now, dropping the picture carelessly on the desk. He pulled his cell phone out of his pocket as he and his partner swiftly went down the stairs and outside. Finding the number he'd saved earlier, he pressed the send button. The two men stepped out the front door and down onto the sidewalk as the phone on the other end went straight to Wyatt's voicemail.

"Sean, this is Detective Morris," he tried to maintain a calm tone. "Give me a call back when you get a chance. We just got some new information concerning Schultz's kidnapping, and we need you to come in to help us out. Thanks." Sliding the phone shut, he slipped it back into his pants pocket while he opened the door to his police-issue Dodge Charger.

"What you want me to do?" Will stood on the sidewalk, notepad still in hand.

"Make sure everything gets finished up here. I doubt the CSIs will find anything, but stick around for a couple of minutes just in case. Call me if they find anything, and if not, call me anyway."

"What about Wyatt?"

"I'm going to keep calling him. Doubt he'll answer." Then he added, "Get home, and get some rest. I'm afraid tomorrow's going to be another long day."

21

CARTERSVILLE

S ean and Allyson stood on the front porch of what appeared to be a rather large log cabin. The drive had only taken about fifteen minutes from the interstate to the wooden home, but it seemed like they were out in the middle of nowhere. Above them, the black sky glittered with more stars than Allyson had seen in a long time. Sounds of nature filled the night: cricket songs with croaking frogs and the melodies of nocturnal birds. The air was scented with a mixture of hardwood and pine.

She drew in a deep breath, filling her lungs and mind with the nature around her, melting away the stress of the day's bizarre events.

Lights were on in the house, but Sean had to knock a few times before they heard footsteps drawing closer to the door. Within the confines of the cabin, a dog barked and howled vigorously, announcing the visitors.

A moment later, the doorknob twisted, and the heavy wooden entrance creaked open. On the other side, a short man with beady eyes and a scruffy beard stared out at them. His brown hair laid in casual disorder atop his round face and head. Infrequent streaks of gray patched his facial hair. The man's flannel shirt and jeans completed the lumberjack look. He appeared to be in his midforties.

No more than three seconds after realizing who was standing in front of him, Sean and the smaller man were embraced in a friendly, back-slapping hug.

"Sean Wyatt. Where the heck have you been?" The voice was cheerful, accented by a heavy Southern drawl.

"I've been busy," Sean answered with a smile, releasing his friend. "Mind if we come in?"

"Mind? Get in here, wild man." He stepped aside to let the pair in, closing the door. "And who is your friend here?"

"Joe McElroy, this is Allyson Webster. She's a journalist for the *Atlanta Sentinel*."

She removed her hand from her pocket and offered it. "Pleasure to meet you. You have a lovely home here." Her eyes roamed the living room they had just entered.

"Thank you." Joe looked around at the timber-enclosed area. The cabin was rustic, with the exception of the flatscreen television near the fireplace and a computer workstation near one window.

"The floor is much older than the rest of the house," he said. "It came from an old knitting mill in Chattanooga, Tennessee. They were going to destroy the building, so I asked the city if I could take all of the flooring out before they did." His hands spread out across the breadth of the room. "I didn't have a place to install it at that time. I just knew I had always wanted to have a cabin like this, so I took the wood and put it in storage until construction began."

"Very cool." She seemed to be very impressed.

The bearded face beamed a big smile. "And this here is Roger." He pointed to a blue tick hound that had just plopped down on the floor next to the entryway.

Apparently, the dog was no longer interested in the visitors and lowered his head to the hardwood.

Sean interrupted, "Joe, I don't mean to ruin your HGTV moment here, but we need your help."

The smile never left the man's face. He just said, "Help? Sean Wyatt needs my help?" A chuckle escaped the grin.

"Yeah." Sean's serious tone sobered the moment.

Apparently, Joe understood and motioned to the couches, "Sit down, and tell me what's goin' on. You can always count on me for anything, Sean. Ya'll want anything to drink? Coffee? Water? A Coke?"

"Coffee would be good," Sean replied.

Allyson nodded in agreement.

While the two of them sat down on the voluminous brown couch, their host made his way into the kitchen adjacent to the living room. Inside, they could hear him turn on some water, presumably filling a coffee pot. A minute later, he reappeared in the doorway to the kitchen and joined them in the sitting area on a smaller tan couch.

"Coffee will be ready in a minute." Spreading his arms out across the back of the sofa, Joe continued, "So tell me what I can do for ya."

"Tommy's been kidnapped." Sean felt no sense in beating around the bush. "We don't know who took him, but we're pretty sure it has to do with something he found last week."

The grin disappeared from Joe's face, and the kind blue eyes went from relaxed to concerned in a matter of seconds. His arms dropped from the back of the couch, and he folded them, elbows on his knees as he leaned forward in thought. "Kidnapped? Why would...? Have they made any demands?"

"I don't think it's about money. The cops haven't received any contact. No," he stopped in midsentence and reached into his jacket. He produced the letter they had found at the Borringer home. "We think they are trying to find the Golden Chambers." As he finished the statement, Sean handed the letter to his friend, who reached out, curiosity covering his face.

"The Golden Chambers?" His eyes grew wide, and one eyebrow raised slightly. "I had my suspicions Tommy was still looking for that. But you say he found something?" Joe began scanning the letter while Sean responded.

"Yeah. That letter is from Dr. Frank Borringer down at KSU. Apparently, Tommy needed Frank's help with deciphering whatever it was he found."

"Oh? I haven't seen Frank in a long time. How's he doin'?"

"He's dead." Sean's tone was direct, almost cold.

Joe stopped reading the correspondence and looked up. "Dead? What happened?"

"Dr. Borringer was murdered a few days ago outside the library at Kennesaw State." He continued, "Nobody seems to know who did it. Apparently, whoever killed him was looking for something. We think it had to do with the information in that letter."

"Where did you find this?" Joe asked, holding up the paper.

Allyson chimed in, feeling like she needed to contribute, "In Frank's office. It was sitting on his desk."

"And the police didn't see it?"

"No," she said, glad to be included in the conversation. "It was in plain sight, but it was disguised as a letter from a financial company. If anyone searched through Dr. Borringer's desk, they would have just assumed that it was nothing important."

"Ahhh. Like a purloined letter, eh?"

She cocked her head sideways, impressed by Joe's literary knowledge.

"What? A country boy can't read Poe?" He cast her a playful glance to which she responded with a smile.

Joe went on, "That's a shame about Frank. He was a good man. I'll have to pay Gretchen a visit soon." He finished reading the letter as a reverent silence settled on the room.

After a few minutes, he set the note on the hickory coffee table. "Interesting." His face was thoughtful.

Sean had waited as long as he could. "So, what do you think?"

Joe answered with a question, "How much do you know about the Golden Chambers?"

"Not much. Just that it's one of those non-mainstream legends. There are only a handful of people on the planet who have even heard of the story. Tommy knows more about it than anyone I've met."

A big, mischievous smile returned to Joe's face. "Well," he paused, "I'm not so sure about that."

Allyson and Sean looked at each other in confirmation. They'd come to the right place.

22

BLUE RIDGE MOUNTAINS

The pale glow of the laptop illuminated the corner of the kitchen where Tommy sat. Frustration and exhaustion were written all over him.

He'd been working on the translation from Dr. Borringer for the last five hours with little success.

Tommy had relentlessly searched the Internet for clues, cross-referencing all of the words in the translation, but had, thus far, come up with zilch. This riddle wasn't something for which Google had an easy answer.

The guards had been trading off every couple of hours, taking turns watching the computer screen to make sure that their captive didn't try to send some kind of rescue email out. Their vigilance had proved to be without a crack, so he'd been forced to keep working, hoping that something would give.

Glancing down at his watch, he couldn't believe how late it was. He'd been awake so long. His legs were numb from sitting for such a long time. "Dude, I need to stretch for a second. Is that all right with you?"

The neck-less guard nodded, standing at an angle behind the prisoner. Tommy stretched out his arms over his head and tried to lean over to touch his toes just to get the circulation back in his legs for a few brief moments. Break time over, he slipped back into the wooden nemesis he'd been trapped in for the better part of the evening. The guy with the flattop haircut remained standing.

The nocturnal sound of a whippoorwill's song resonated from the darkness in a tree outside the kitchen window. As the hours plodded on, every little noise had become a distraction. Thoughts of sleep entered Tommy's mind and muddled his progress. His eyes kept begging to close as the drowsiness seeped into his brain. Again, the bird whistled its melody, communicating to another bird in some unseen tree in the woods. He let his eyes turn from the LCD screen to the glass and beyond. Outside, the night sky was clear, and the stars sparkled brightly against the black canvas. He found himself standing again, this time with his face pressed close against the smooth, clear surface. Flattop had a forlorn look on his face as the other security guy had come back for his shift. For the first time since arriving at this place, Tommy heard one of the men speak.

"What is the meaning of this?" A thick accent sounding like Russian made the words sound sharp and accusing.

The other guard didn't say anything. He just stood sheepishly to the side, eyes averted.

Looking back to the man who'd just spoken, Tommy said, "He was just letting me stretch my legs. I've been in here working all night."

"You sit down." Blunt and to the point, this guy had a severe lack of social skills. He turned his angry gaze at the apparently submissive sentry who had not done his job properly. Whatever was said between the two was in another language. Tommy was certain it was Russian. The exchange was brief and ended with the previous guard nodding in agreement, a defeated look on his face.

"Look, man. I'm not trying anything funny. My legs were going numb, and I just needed to stretch for a second."

"Get back to work, and be quiet. Mr. Ulrich will be returning soon, and if he finds you standing around not working, it will not be good."

For a second, Tommy contemplated the big man's words. He looked out the window again at the sky then said, "Can we please just go outside for thirty seconds? I'm getting sleepy, and I need some fresh air. I can't work like this forever."

The sentinel looked at the one who'd been standing watch for the last few hours, still sheepish in the corner of the breakfast nook. Stubbornly, he shook his head again as he would to a child reaching for a forbidden cookie.

"Listen, man," Tommy pleaded, "I'm not trying to get away here. And if I was, where would I go? If you guys want me to figure this riddle out, you gotta give me a little leeway here. I will work much better if I can get the blood flowing again."

Contemplating the circumstances, the guard finally caved, apparently seeing no harm in letting their captive go outside for a minute or two. "We give you one minute outside. But if you try anything, I shoot you in the knee." The humorless look on the man's face told Schultz he would do it without even thinking.

"Thank you," Tommy said with a grateful half smile.

The three of them left the laptop on the bistro table and made their way through a picture-laden hallway. All of them were photographs of places from around the world, some famous and some not: Saint Mark's Cathedral in Venice, the façade at the temple of Edfu in Egypt, a Grecian temple whose name he could not recall but which certainly seemed familiar. Turning left out of the corridor, the group entered a large antechamber. Even in the dark, Tommy could tell the room was elaborately furnished. The tapestries descended from windows that reached almost ten feet. In the center of the room were two high-backed leather smoking chairs placed in such a way that the sitters could enjoy the view of the hills below while discussing the ups and downs of the global financial markets.

The submissive guard stepped quickly to the French doors that led out onto a patio. The cool, autumn air felt refreshing as they strode across the threshold and into the night.

"You stop here," the larger guard crossed his arms forebodingly.

Tommy did as he was told, stopping at the railing of the large wooden deck they'd come to. Again, he stretched his arms and legs, letting the circulation get back into his extremities. Taking several large breaths helped too, filling his lungs with the invigorating night air.

The bird he'd heard before must have found a friend because now there were two of them chirping happily in the dark silhouettes of trees. Tommy's eyes drifted higher, beyond the treetops, into the dark sky. Seeing so many stars always gave him a sort of odd peace. With such a huge universe out there, he couldn't help but feel small, and yet in his heart he knew that the role he played in life was a significant part of some grander scheme.

He considered where his friend might be at the moment, hoping that Sean was looking for him. They had been through so much together...of course Wyatt was searching. Tommy would do the same for his friend if the circumstances were reversed. All of these things played through his mind while he continued to scan the diamond-speckled canvas above.

Suddenly, a shooting star crossed the face of the deep beyond, streaking quickly for only a second before disintegrating into invisibility. Turning to the two guards, Tommy said sarcastically, "Make a wish, boys."

They looked at each other with confusion, obviously not having seen the flashing meteor. The bigger guard simply said, "Time is up. You get back to work now."

Tommy started to turn around and follow the two hulking men back into the house when it hit him. He stopped in his steps and turned his head back to the sky. "I've got it!" His excitement surprised even himself.

"What is it?" The smaller guard asked, again receiving a chastising look from his superior.

"The chariots of Heaven! Did you guys see that shooting star?" Tommy's exhilaration overpowered his fatigue, causing him to sound like a raving madman.

This time, the larger man grabbed Tommy by the arm and yanked him back to the house. Even though the guy was a mountain, he'd underestimated the strength the guard possessed.

As they forced the hostage back through the double doors, he took one last look up in the sky. Another space rock appeared, burning brightly as it soared through the blackness, then disappeared. Being dragged backward by his arms, Schultz didn't struggle. Instead, he started laughing.

The whole time that he had spent searching for the chambers, Tommy believed that the ancient rooms might be located somewhere else in the world, that he'd been wrong to hope the magnificent find was near. Sure, there were a few clues scattered throughout Georgia, but surely a treasure of such amazing significance couldn't be there. Yet he and others, like de Soto and Ponce de León, were convinced that the entire chambers were located somewhere in the southern United States. Now, after searching for so many years, the riddle was starting to come together. And Tommy started thinking that maybe, just maybe, de Soto had been right all along.

There was only one place that he could think of anywhere that could contain the description in the riddle. He just hoped that Sean would come to the same conclusion.

23

CARTERSVILLE

After serving the coffee, Joe had left his guests alone in the living room for a few minutes, not explaining where he was going. When he returned, he had a somber look on his face and was gripping something in his worn fingers. He opened his hand, revealing something that astonished both of the visitors.

"Is that what I think it is?" Sean couldn't believe what he was seeing.

"It is."

"But how did you get it?"

"I received a package from Frank earlier today. This stone was inside." Joe carefully handed the disc to Sean.

He continued while Sean inspected the medallion. "When you told me that Frank had been murdered, I was initially shocked. Frank and I have known each other a long time. But if Frank had figured out the code on this stone, it could be the first step toward finding the most incredible treasure in history. And if someone found out about this stone and that Frank was working on it, that certainly explains his murder and Tommy's disappearance."

Sean and Allyson were both still looking at the ancient medallion.

"How much do you know about the chambers, Joe?" Sean looked up at his friend, trying to piece all the information together.

Joe's lively eyes lingered briefly in thought then darted up, perched above a wide grin. "I'd be glad to tell ya. But first, I want to know what you know about them." He wagged his rough finger at the air in Sean's direction in a playful gesture.

"Well," he replied, somewhat unsure of himself. He took a look at Allyson and then back at the curious face staring at him from a few feet away. "According to most of the mainstream legends, seven priests left their parishes in Spain when they came under attack by the Moors. No one is sure about the timeframe, but it could have been somewhere between 800-1000 CE. These priests sailed west and constructed a city of gold, El Dorado, Cibola, whatever you want to call it. Again, I'm not sure why. Down through the centuries from around 1150 CE to the present, explorers have searched for the lost city. Francisco Coronado was perhaps the most famous to try and find it. There were rumors that Cortez believed it to be Mexico. De Soto was relentless in his quest throughout the Southeastern United States. Ponce de León was also said to have been trying to locate it. Of course, Ponce de León's more well-known search was for the fountain of youth, but some say that was only one of two reasons he came to the New World."

McElroy smiled at the last statement.

"Anyway, the lost city was never found, so, throughout history it has simply been regarded as myth. To most historians, it still is." He took a sip from his steaming cup of coffee as he finished.

"As well it should be regarded that way," McElroy chimed in. "Even though the legend was originally a European folktale, the Indians learned that by retelling the story and embellishing it, the invaders were pacified, at least temporarily, by the thought of finding a city of unimaginable wealth."

Joe took a gulp of coffee then went on, "There is another story that Tommy and a handful of others came across that bears a small resemblance but has different details."

Allyson sat quietly, completely out of her element. All she could do was listen, her eyes wide with curiosity.

"Which is the story that I believe to be far more valid," Joe added.

Sean nodded and went on, "A few people, Tommy being one of them, believe the core part of the story about large quantities of gold in several places is correct. So, to them, the question isn't whether or not the gold exists. It is where and in how many locations. These researchers do not believe the part of the legend that talks about seven golden cities. They also don't give any merit to the seven priests sailing west to escape Islamic persecution or that Europeans even built these mystical places."

"But if the Europeans didn't build them, who did?" Allyson found the topic spellbinding.

"Native Americans," Sean answered in a matter-of-fact tone. "But some of the facts became twisted and removed so that the white settlers would never find the true locations. There were never seven cities built from gold, but there was a number that Tommy kept coming across in many places all over the Southeast. Through the years of his research concerning the lost cities of gold, he kept coming across the number four. He found many clues in ancient Native locations that led him to there were four compartments or chambers. So, it was four golden rooms built by ancient Native peoples, not seven cities built by European settlers."

"What did they use these golden rooms for?" she had to ask.

"That's just it, no one really knows," Sean answered. "There are some ideas, but nothing really adds up. They must have been used for ancient ceremonies or rituals. Native Americans did not put a great deal of import on the material value of gold. It was more of a sacred metal to them than anything else."

"Perhaps, this is where I may be able to shed some light on the story," Joe interrupted.

Sean set his cup down and listened intently, glad to be out of the spotlight in the conversation. He had a feeling Joe McElroy was about to enlighten them far more than he ever could on the current situation.

The older man's face looked like he was ready to explode. He started by saying, "There are several local legends that have been passed around for the last fifty or so years that revolve around a constant theme: Indian gold." After pausing for a second, Joe went on, "Now, you won't find these stories in any history books. In fact, they're probably more like family tales than local legends." His eyes moved dramatically from left to right as he spoke, peering at his audience.

"Most of what I've heard came from my father, stories he'd heard from friends or relatives. The first legend supposedly took place not too far from here, up in the mountains where there is a small river that leads to a waterfall. This waterfall is probably around seventy feet high. One day about thirty years ago, some rock climber was scaling the wall behind the falling water. Not sure how you do that without slipping on the wet rocks, but this guy did it. When he got up near the top, he found himself at the lip of a shallow cave. After pulling himself up onto the ledge, he crawled back into the dark space. His eyes fell upon something quite peculiar sitting on the ground in the corner of the small room. What he had found was a stack of gold bars."

McElroy let what he believed to be a small climax set in with his audience. "The climber picked up one of the heavy bars and took it closer to the edge of the rock face so he could get a better look at what he'd found. Once in the light, he discovered odd characters carved into the shiny yellow bricks."

Allyson and Sean cast each other a surprised look. "What was it?" she asked, mesmerized.

"An ancient Native form of writing that used a combination of symbols and pictures, much like hieroglyphics," he replied. "Of course, the man who found the gold was not permitted to keep it since it was discovered on government land." His tone had become cynical.

Sean laughed, "Naturally."

"Indeed," Joe chuckled. "Have to say the Natives were right not to trust our government." Taking one last gulp of the coffee, he returned the empty mug to the wooden surface. "Now, legend number two spans about two hundred years and contains many fascinating implications.

"Right around the end of the eighteenth century, in the 1790s, there was a wealthy Cherokee businessman named James Vann who lived in the area near Chatsworth, Georgia. He was a powerful leader in the Cherokee Nation and ran one of the most profitable plantations in the state. In 1804, he completed construction of an elegant brick home on his large estate. To this day, it is Georgia's best preserved historical site."

Joe stood up and walked over to the fireplace. The flames that had been crackling vibrantly before had died down to just a flicker. He grabbed another log from the stack next to the hearth and placed it in the fire before stoking the coals with an iron poker. The two visitors looked like children sitting around a campfire, listening to ghost stories, so he went on, "James Vann had a charmed life for an Indian, right up until 1809 when he was mysteriously murdered."

"Murdered?" Allyson chimed in.

"Yes. Murdered. They never found the killer, and no one knows why they did it. Oh, sure, there were suspects. Rival Cherokee leaders, jealous white settlers, even his son, Joseph, was a suspect."

"His son?" Sean asked.

"Uh huh. In fact, his son stood to gain the most from the death of his father. When James died, Joseph inherited the entire estate. And over the next thirty years after the murder, Joseph became even more prosperous than his father. He owned more land and had accumulated more wealth than any other Cherokee tribesman in the state, and possibly in the nation."

Allyson had an inquisitive look on her face. "So, what does this have to do with our scenario?"

Joe smiled. "I'm getting to that. In 1838, Andrew Jackson and the federal government ordered the relocation of all Cherokee Indians. They were forced to move to Oklahoma. The Creek Indians had already been removed ten years earlier to separate reservations in the West."

"The Trail of Tears," Sean's voice trailed off. It was one of the most sombering and despicable events in America's history.

Joey nodded, "One of the most appalling things our government has done in our country's history. Men, women, and children forced to march through the fierce winter, given little food and even less shelter." He looked down, seemingly touched personally by the thought of the grim tale. "It was such a strange turn of events. There were around seventeen thousand Cherokee in western Georgia in the 1830s. John Ross, the principal chief of the Cherokee Nation, fiercely fought the notion of relocation for nearly three decades. In fact, there were white members of Congress who tried to prevent the removal from happening. Most notably was the Tennessee congressman Davy Crockett. By siding with the Cherokee, Crockett's political career was ruined, and we all know what happened to him soon thereafter." Pausing in his story, Joe plopped back down on the couch.

"I just don't understand how the United States government could do something like that," Allyson's voice was full of empathy.

"Well, it was a weird sequence of events," Joe sighed. "Ten years before the Cherokee were relocated, the Creek Indians were taken from their lands when one of their acknowledged leaders, Chief McIntosh, signed the Treaty of Indian Springs. All the U.S. government needed to move the Creek was that signature. Less than a year later, McIntosh was found dead, stabbed by one of his own people.

"By 1832, there was a division among the Cherokee. John Ross held sway over the majority, but there was a small contingent of about five hundred Indians that supported three other leaders: Major Ridge, his son, John, and Elias Boudinot. These three men met with Congress behind the backs of John Ross and the rest of the Cherokee nation and signed the Removal Act as representatives of the tribe. That was all Andrew Jackson and the feds needed. Daniel Webster and Henry Clay, two notable figures in history, pleaded that the act not be ratified. It happened, nonetheless, and Gen. John Wool was ordered to invade the Cherokee lands. Wool was a good man and knew to do such a thing was morally unjust. He refused and resigned his post. So, replacement Gen. Winfield Scott went in with seven thousand troops and did the job.

"Almost a third of the Cherokee, including John Ross's wife, died on the way to Oklahoma in the bitter winter of 1838-1839." Joe gave a grim chuckle, "Ironically, the three men who signed the Echota Treaty allowing for the relocation were later murdered the same way McIntosh was by the Creek ten years prior."

Allyson looked perplexed. "Why did the Indians need to be moved in the first place?"

Leaning back, he crossed his legs and folded his hands. "Excellent question. The Cherokee had, essentially, become a part of society in the United States. They lived in homes designed like the whites, dressed in the modern European styles, and ran a system of government much like a democracy. The Cherokee were a civilized part of America. But the white settlers had discovered something for which conquistadors and explorers had searched for centuries."

"Gold," Sean realized aloud.

"You got it. A vein of the stuff was found down in what is now Dahlonega, 'bout an hour from here. Once that was discovered, the young government needed no other reason. Of course, they claimed that the area was overcrowded to justify their actions, but the plain truth of it was that those innocent people were brutally murdered and herded out of their homes like animals so that the search for more gold could continue."

"And once the Dahlonega mines had been found, the probability of the El Dorado legend became much more viable," Sean rationalized.

"Bingo," he replied, spreading his arms out across the back of the couch. "And there is one more piece to this legend that you should know about.

"When my dad was just a boy, he and a few friends were playing in the woods forty-five minutes northeast of here, about ten miles from the Vann house. They were running around in the hills when suddenly, they happened upon a cave. Boys never really have a good sense of fear, so the three of them decided to go inside and take a look around. What they discovered was astounding. The cavern wasn't natural; it had been carved out of the rock by human hands. Within the giant chamber, a large stone table sat in the center. As the boys' eyes adjusted to the darkness, they could see carvings in the stone that encircled the room on the wall just below the ceiling."

Mystified, Allyson asked, "What did the carvings say?"

"Well, the boys ran back into town and told their parents about what they had found. The kids took their families back to the cave to show them the strange sight. A few *experts* were brought in to investigate, including an old Cherokee man who had returned to the area decades before. He was brought in to see if he could interpret the writing on the stone.

"As the old man read the inscription, his eyes grew wide, and his face took on a troubled look. He urged the families to leave the premises quickly and claimed they were all in great danger. After exiting the cave, the group stood around outside the entrance, uncertain what was going on. My grandfather was there along with my dad. Grandpappy asked the old Indian what the carvings meant and what the danger was.

"The Indian's reply was grim, 'It says the white man will never take our gold, and for those who try, death awaits.'"

"What does that mean?" Sean interrupted the story. "What was going to kill them?"

"I'm not sure. All I know is that old Indian was scared out of his wits. Musta been something pretty bad."

"So what did everyone do?" Allyson rejoined the conversation.

"Well, Allyson, they went back to their homes and started making phone calls. Many of the locals wanted to excavate the site and bring in archaeologists to study the room. The funny thing is the whole area was fenced off about a week later by the government. Even stranger than that, the following year, a dam was built nearby, and the land was flooded. That cave is somewhere at the bottom of what is called Carter's Lake now. "

"What happened to the Indian translator? Did he stick around long?" Sean asked.

"He died a few months later; I think they said it was a heart attack or something like that. Can't remember. It's a little odd, but the guy was old, so it was bound to happen at some point, I suppose."

Silence fell on the room as the facts and the strange sequence of events settled in. Suddenly, the telephone rang in the kitchen, disrupting the moment and startling all three of them. "I should get that. It's probably Evelyn. She went to her mother's tonight. I'll be right back. Ya'll need anything else?"

"No, we're good, Mac," Sean answered for the both of them as his friend jumped up and took off toward the kitchen.

In the other room, they heard him answer the phone, "Hey, honey." Then his voice trailed off in a discussion about her staying at her mother's for the night.

Sean turned to Allyson as he lounged farther into the soft material of the sofa, "What do you think?"

"The whole story is fascinating. It's a lot to digest." She looked thoughtfully into her empty cup.

He couldn't help but stare at her for a moment; then, as her head lifted slightly, he caught himself and averted his eyes.

"Yeah, I just hope Joe can help us find Tommy." He picked up the conversation again.

"All right, what were you saying about me? I know I just heard my name." Their host returned to the living room with a smile on his face. Sean was glad his friend had come back in time to end the awkward moment.

Allyson smiled. "Sean was just saying that if anyone could help us find Tommy, it would be you."

His face took on a serious expression. "We'll find him, buddy, and whoever is behind all of this." He gave his friend a sincere nod.

Another thoughtful moment went by before Allyson spoke up again. "So what happened to Joseph Vann and his family when the Cherokee were moved to Oklahoma?"

"Glad you remembered." Joe collapsed back into his spot on the couch. "Vann and his family relocated to Oklahoma and picked up right where they left off. Of course, losing all of their land in Georgia hurt, but it needs to be noted that the forced move did not hurt the Vanns nearly as much as the rest of the Cherokee population. The family prospered in Oklahoma almost as much as it had in Georgia."

"How is that possible? Was Joseph just a better businessman than the rest of his fellow tribesmen?" Sean was interested.

"Possibly. There isn't anything concrete, but there is an interesting end to the Vann story. A hundred and twenty years later, in 1958, the Vann house was turned into a state historic site.

"A year or so after that, four dark-skinned men walked into the old manor one day. The park's curator offered to give them a tour, but they said nothing. They simply walked by and went directly to the fireplace. The park ranger watched as the men knelt down and started removing some of the bricks from the back of the chimney. Mesmerized, he stared as the strangers reached into a secret compartment and began removing gold bars from the hole."

"Gold bars like the ones at the waterfall?" Allyson could barely contain her curiosity.

"Exactly the same, and with similar carvings on them as well. We can only assume that the symbols the state worker saw as the men walked out were identical to the ones that were discovered in the waterfall cave."

Sean piped in, "So you think that the Vanns had some of that gold when they left?"

"It would certainly make sense as to how they were able to keep up the type of lifestyle to which they had become accustomed."

Allyson wasn't sure. "If the Vanns did have a bunch of Cherokee gold, how did they transport it to Oklahoma without it being seized by the army?"

"You really must be a great journalist, Ms. Webster, to ask all the right questions like that." Joe gave her a quick wink, causing her to blush momentarily.

"To answer, yes, transporting any amount of gold would have been a difficult task not only from the point of keeping its existence unknown to the army, but also from a logistical front. They had few wagons and were certainly under constant supervision from the soldiers who were escorting them west."

"Well, how'd they do it then?" She was on the edge of her seat.

"I think most of the gold remained right here in the state of Georgia, hidden in a secret location. Only a select few would be able to interpret all of the clues that would lead to the larger deposits. That being said, the Cherokee still must have taken quite a bit of the loot with them as they went west."

"Yeah." She was becoming impatient, so she asked the question again. "So, how did they move so much gold without getting caught?"

McElroy scooped up the empty coffee cups and started to make his way to the kitchen with them. "Tell me something, you two. How much do you know about Mormons?"

24

BLUE RIDGE MOUNTAINS

Tommy sat defiantly at the breakfast table, arms crossed. His two guards stood on either side of him, anxious and uncertain. It had been about thirty minutes since the bigger guard had called Ulrich and requested that he return to the mansion immediately. After being dragged inside, Tommy had refused to do anything else except for pulling up a website about lost worlds. Once that was done, he simply sat there until they had telephoned their boss.

"You better not be toying with us," the smaller guard remarked in his almost unintelligible accent.

Tommy replied with a sarcastic smile, which only seemed to anger the man even more.

Sounds of dogs barking came suddenly from somewhere else in the building. A few moments later, the tall blond man burst through the door, dressed in an expensive-looking suit like he had just stepped out of the pages of *GQ*. "Jeez, man!" Tommy laughed, "You just come from a wedding or something? Kinda late to be dressed like that, isn't it?"

Ignoring the question, Ulrich strode purposefully toward the table. He stopped a few feet away, produced a black handgun from his pocket, and pointed it at the insolent prisoner. "Why are you not working?"

Having a gun pointed at him seemed less unsettling every time it happened. Apparently, Tommy was getting used to it. "Put that thing away, man. Last thing you need right now is to accidentally shoot the guy who just figured out where the next clue is." His demeanor remained cool as Ulrich's icy-blue eyes searched him for the truth.

Ulrich didn't lower the weapon. "If you are lying to me in the hope that someone is going to come to your rescue, you will be sorely disappointed."

Unwavering, Tommy unfolded his arms and spun the laptop around so that the screen faced the man with the gun. "Track Rock near Brasstown Bald," he said triumphantly.

He lowered the gun slightly as he glared at the computer screen that displayed photos of some large boulders, each one riddled with odd symbols and shapes painted on them. The giant stones were surrounded by crude, steel cages. Eyebrows furrowed, Ulrich inquired, "What am I looking at?" His voice had grown slightly less menacing.

"What you are looking at is a place called Track Rock." Tommy repeated the name then added, "It's the only spot that makes sense."

"You are certain?" The gun lowered a little more, though the killer was still alert.

"Dude, I'm sure."

"How are you so positive this is the right place?"

"Okay, let me explain it to you," Tommy said in an exasperated voice. "First of all, I've been sitting here all night with the Cosmonaut twins searching every friggin' possible place in the world." The two Russians turned their heads giving each other a confused shrug. "Secondly, you have to understand the context of the riddle."

"Tell me," Ulrich said as he came around the edge of the table, leaning in closer to the monitor. The gun was now hanging unthreateningly at his side.

Tommy was a little put off by the man's lack of awareness of personal space, but he went on nonetheless. "The riddle says that the stones will mark your path and that of the chariots of Heaven, right?"

A quick nod was all he received.

"Right...So, we went outside for a minute," Ulrich's head turned quickly to the guards, eyes flashing in anger. The two subordinates didn't offer an excuse. They just stood there trying to look professional.

"Take it easy," Tommy came to their defense. "I was getting sleepy, and I couldn't keep my eyes open. I just asked them if they would take me outside for some fresh air for a minute. They were both with me the entire time."

His explanation seemed to be satisfactory, and Ulrich's attention came back to the matter at hand. Tommy began again, "So we were outside when I saw a shooting star. That's when I realized the answer."

"A shooting star?" Ulrich sounded unsure.

"Yeah, a shooting star. You know, a meteor? Streak of light that goes across the sky?"

A nod again told Tommy that the guy knew what he was talking about. "Anyway, that's when I realized what the riddle meant by chariots of the heavens. The real meaning behind that phrase comes from many different pagan mythologies. Chariots were considered to be not only a powerful weapon, but an honorable mode of transportation. Kings and generals used them not only for ease of movement, but as symbols of their greatness. In many ancient cultures, it was considered an honor to be in the chariot corps of a royal army. So, it was only natural that the religious leaders of the time wanted their gods to look both powerful and yet relate them to a high human position. Imagine if you were a child growing up in ancient Egypt and you saw a shooting star flash through the sky. Every single child was probably told that it was one of their gods on his chariot, coming to aid a human on Earth. It was a better story than Santa Claus."

"Interesting, Thomas. But what does any of this have to do with the place you are showing me on the computer?

"It has everything to do with it." He pointed to the screen with an open hand. "Brasstown is the only place on the continent that even comes close to having anything remotely similar to what is described in the riddle."

"And why is that?"

"Because it's the only location in this part of the world that has large stones with what many historians believe to be a significant celestial event recorded on them." He threw up his hands.

His hand moved back to the computer screen in an effort to describe the picture the man was seeing. "These symbols right here are constellations. But the other stuff that appears all over the rock face, those are some kind of anomaly. The only explanation would be some kind of occurrence such as a meteor shower. Seems like the early settlers in the land felt the need to document whatever it was that happened."

"Where is this place, this Brasstown?"

"It's a little over an hour northeast of here, up in the Blue Ridge Mountains."

Ulrich seemed to contemplate what Tommy had presented. Schultz was a renowned historian of ancient cultures. Surely, he had found the answer to the riddle. Still, something made him hesitate. "What about the birds in the riddle, the raven and the dove? Do you have an explanation for that?"

For a moment, Tommy thought about making up some kind of story with the birds, but he decided to go with the truth for now. "Honestly, no. Best I can figure is that the raven and the dove are a separate part of the puzzle."

"Separate?" It was a good sign that his captor wasn't too upset by the lack of an answer.

"Yeah. You see, throughout history, most riddles, maps, clues, whatever you want to call them, have all had one thing in common: duality. At least, every single thing like this that I have ever come across has had that feature. There is either more than one meaning to a riddle, or it is two separate mysteries combined into one."

"So what do you suggest we do?"

Finally, a little respect. "I say we go up to Brasstown and check out the site. My guess is, whatever is there will point us in the right direction."

Ulrich sat, considering what to do for a minute. "Get the truck ready," he finally said to the shorter guard.

The man nodded and quickly exited the room.

"I hope, Thomas, that you are correct." He raised the gun back up until the cold, black barrel was pressed firmly against Tommy's temple. "Because if you are trying anything funny, you know what I will do."

25

CARTERSVILLE

"Mormons?" Sean blurted out. "What do they have to do with this?"

Joe's head turned from side to side as Allyson continued Sean's line of thinking, "Yeah. Are you talking about the Latter-day Saints...those Mormons?"

"The very same."

"All right," Sean jumped back in. "Enlighten us."

Again, their host took on the look of an avid storyteller. "You see, right about the same time the Indians were moving west, the newly formed and heavily criticized Mormon Church was facing an exile of its own. Their founding leader, Joseph Smith, along with his brother, had been murdered by an armed lynch mob.

"Brigham Young and other church leaders, seeing that the denomination was faced with a great deal of prejudice due to their unconventional beliefs, decided that moving west to a place where they could govern themselves would be in the best interest of all their members. So that is exactly what they did."

"And by west, you mean Utah?" Allyson knew a little about the history of the Mormon Church. One of her best friends was a Latter-day Saint.

"Eventually, yes. Of course, Utah now has more active members than anywhere else in the world. That is where their headquarters is located, as well as their great temple." Gaining momentum, Joe went on, "However, early on in their migration, they had intermittent periods in the Midwest, settling briefly in Missouri and Oklahoma."

Sean had to interrupt. "Wait a minute…Oklahoma?" He paused for a second, putting the pieces together. "Are you saying that the Mormons helped the Indians move their gold out west?"

"That is exactly what I am saying. And all you have to do is look at the history of the two groups of people to understand that it is not only plausible…it's dang well probable!"

"Really? You honestly think that the Mormons took the risk of helping the Natives move all that gold?" Sean couldn't buy into this new idea. "What would keep them from turning it in to the authorities or just keeping it for themselves?"

"Look at the facts, my friend. First and foremost, the Indians didn't take all of it at once or to one location. The only thing we do know for certain is that no one has found it since the Cherokee were removed from the area. Fact number two: If the gold *was* here, and we are assuming it was, there was no way those Indians could have removed it without some kind of assistance. And who better than a group of Christians who themselves had nothing to lose?

"Mormons could come and go as they pleased for the most part, ministering to the Cherokee, helping them with their ailments, or trying to comfort them. The soldiers escorting the Natives would not even think that the *innocent* church members would be trying to aid the Natives in sneaking their gold out of the South. It was the perfect cover."

"So," Allyson cut in, "how did the Cherokee people know they could trust the Mormons? I mean, who's to say that these *Christians* that were helping them wouldn't just take the gold and run?"

"Excellent question, Allyson." He raised his finger in acknowledgement. "First of all, John Ross, the leader of the Cherokee nation, knew several Mormons as personal friends. He had even briefly studied the religion while in Washington, D.C., after hearing some congressmen talking about the Mormon group being dangerous to the true Christian morals of the country. So, Ross knew a little about their belief system."

Joe twisted open a bottle of water he'd brought from the kitchen and lifted it to his mouth to take a swig. After screwing the cap back on, he resumed. "Now, one of the most interesting ideas the Mormon Church has presented to the world is that the Native Americans were, and still are, the lost tribe of Israel."

Sean and Allyson looked at each other and then back at McElroy. It was Sean that spoke up. "Lost tribe of Israel?"

"Yep. They believed that the Cherokee were part of missing tribe of Israelites, lost Jews, if you will. Apparently, the tribe had left the kingdom at some point and had traveled west. John Ross knew about this belief. He also knew the troubles that this group of radical Christians was having. So, in a last-ditch effort to save the ancient tribal fortune, he contacted some of the leaders of the Mormon Church and made them a deal."

"What kind of deal?" Allyson poked.

Nodding, Sean agreed, "Yeah, the Cherokee hardly seemed in a position to make a deal with anyone, Christian or otherwise."

"True, but don't underestimate religious values of the zealous. The Mormons held the Indians in the highest regard. They were treated almost like living saints." He stood and walked over to the fireplace and stoked the flame with the black metal poker a few more times before saying, "And let's not forget, the Cherokee had something that every church in the world seems to crave: money."

"So, you are saying the Mormons helped siphon off millions in gold right under the noses of the federal government?" Sean was still skeptical.

"Absolutely. But there is something you need to remember about the relationship between the Mormon Church and the Native Americans."

"Which is?"

"They both needed each other. The Indians were treated like animals, and the Mormons were outcasts. Without the Mormons, the

Cherokee would not have survived the journey west, nor would they have been able to salvage their treasure. Likewise, the Mormons would have faced annihilation at the hands of other tribes as they moved farther west had they not possessed something that would ensure their safe passage."

"What do you mean by that last sentence?" Allyson was intrigued. "What did the Mormons have that would keep them safe from other tribes?"

Joe persisted, "Look at the history of all the white settlers that went west. There are literally hundreds of stories of Indian attacks on the wagon trains. Everyone knows about them. But there is not a single recorded incident of any tribe ever attacking a Mormon settler or a group of Mormons. Why do you think that is?"

Allyson and Sean looked at each other again, wondering what the answer was.

Joe answered the question for them, "Remember the local stories I told you about the gold bars? There was a symbol on each yellow brick, right?"

They both nodded.

"John Ross told the Mormon leaders that if they would use that symbol in their wagon trains and show it to any Indian they came across, their people would be granted safe passage."

"So, there was a universal symbol that every Native tribe in the country knew and acknowledged?" Sean still wasn't convinced.

"Look through the history books, buddy. I can't make this stuff up. There was not a single recorded Indian attack on Mormon settlers, ever. Seems a little odd, doesn't it?"

"So the gold that the Mormons were smuggling kept them safe from being attacked by all tribes?" Sean still didn't see how it was possible.

"It wasn't the gold that was so important. What every tribe respected was the symbol on the gold."

"And what exactly was this symbol?"

Joe smiled as he replied, "It was the same one that is on that medallion."

26

ATLANTA

The phone on the other end rang another time before the voicemail came on the receiver. Morris had attempted to call Sean Wyatt's cell phone three other times without success. Sean was either ignoring the call, or he was in a place where wireless service was poor. He doubted it was the latter.

Tired and frustrated, Trent had left the scene of the double homicide hoping that he could at least talk to Wyatt. The voicemail beeped after a short message. "Hey, Mr. Wyatt. Trent Morris here from Atlanta PD. Please give me a call back as soon as you get this. I have a few more questions I want to ask you. I appreciate your help. Thanks."

He flipped his phone closed and tossed it into the empty passenger seat. The Charger veered from the middle lane of the interstate over to the far right lane as his exit approached on the right up ahead. Fatigue was starting to get to him, and his eyes seemed to get heavier by the second. Fortunately, other cars were sparse at this time of night. He maneuvered up the exit ramp leading toward home.

As he turned at the stoplight, a thought occurred to him. Reaching over, he picked up the phone again and pressed some numbers. A few seconds later, someone answered on the other line, "Homicide."

Recognizing the voice on the other line, he said, "Lynch, it's Trent Morris. I need you to do me a favor. You busy?" He imagined the young detective sitting alone at his desk, the rest of the police department having long since disappeared for the night. They always kept someone on hand, though, for emergencies.

"Nah, Trent. You know the routine. Pretty much just sitting here playing solitaire. What's up?"

"Hate to interrupt you," he replied with a laugh, knowing he'd done the same thing ten years ago. "There's something I want you to take a look at."

"Hit me."

"Look up any known associates that Sean Wyatt might have, other than Thomas Schultz. I'm trying to figure out where this guy may have gone today."

"You want me to just look up people he knows within a certain radius?" The young cop was efficient. Morris liked that.

"Yeah. And see if you can get any outgoing flight information from Hartsfield International." He added, "I know that the IAA has their own private jet, but it could be that they decided to take a commercial plane. It's unlikely, but check it out anyway."

The other end of the line was quiet for a second as Lynch was busy jotting down all the information that Morris wanted. "All right, sir. Anything else?"

"I think that about covers it." Then he had another thought, "Oh, Lynch, go ahead, and check to see if his cars have LoJack. We might get lucky and be able to trace exactly where he is."

"Okay. Anything else? Fries? Milkshake?"

Trent released a forced laugh. "No. I'm good."

"Sir, if you don't mind me asking, why are you so interested in Sean Wyatt's whereabouts? Do you think he might be connected to the Schultz kidnapping?"

Deciding that it would be okay for the younger cop to know a little, he simply answered, "Possibly. Just get me that info as soon as possible. You have my cell number?"

"Yes, sir. Got it right here."

"Good. Call me when you get something."

"Okay."

"Oh, and Lynch..." Morris added.

"Yeah?"

"Don't mention this to anyone. I'm not sure what is going on, but I don't want too many people to know where we're snooping."

"Ten four."

Morris hung up the phone as he pulled the car into his driveway. A few moments later, he was stumbling through the door like a drunk on a binge. He laid his keys down once again on the counter in the kitchen. "What a day," he sighed, making his way into the bedroom without even turning on any lights. He let the softness of the mattress take him in as his body collapsed onto the bed.

27

CARTERSVILLE

Allyson looked skeptical, squinting her eyes slightly.

"There's something else you need to realize about the Mormons' relationship to the Indians," Joe went on. "Remember, I mentioned they believed that Native Americans were actually the lost tribe of Israel."

"What do you mean by lost tribe?" She was apparently unfamiliar.

Sean turned to her to explain. "The Church of Latter-day Saints believes that American Indians were actually a lost tribe of Israel from Biblical times. Although there are only a few vague scriptural references to such a group, the founding fathers of the church believed this firmly."

Joe nodded in agreement. "Joseph Smith, the man who created the Mormon doctrine, claimed that while he was out in the woods one day, an angel came to him and told him to dig a hole. The angel said that he would find something amazing if Smith would do as he was told.

"Smith said that he eventually found two golden plates with strange inscriptions on them. On these plates, were supposedly the lost scriptures about Christ's ministry to the Americas."

"So what happened to these golden plates?" She asked.

"No one knows," Joe replied. "In fact, Smith claimed that only he was allowed to see them. Many people were suspicious of such a claim. Smith had been a known charlatan. But some did believe him and supported his new ideas. This was essentially how the Church of Latter-day Saints came about."

The picture was becoming a little clearer. Still, neither Sean nor Allyson was certain.

Joe could tell they weren't sure, so he nailed home his main point. "You see, whether the Mormon beliefs are correct or not doesn't matter to us. What matters is that they basically revered the Native Americans, almost as if they were gods among men. Some Mormons even believed that the Indians were actually angels."

Sean put it all together to make sure he understood. "Ah. So if the people of the church helped the Indians or angels, as was believed, they would be rewarded by God."

"Correct." Joe smiled as he saw the realization on both of their faces.

"Now, the final piece of the puzzle is also the first piece," he went on. "You see, it all comes back to the four Golden Chambers. Thousands have fought and died, searched and sacrificed, all to find the lost rooms of Akhanan. I would say that you two are probably closer than anyone has been in two thousand years. But before you can take the final step, you have to learn why it is that the chambers exist."

"I thought you said they were ceremonial, used by the ancient Indians of the land," Sean stated.

"Nope," the grin never left the scruffy face. "I only said that was what everyone else believes. The real reason they are here goes much deeper."

He turned all the way around, facing his computer. "How do you think the Native Americans got to this continent?"

The guests waited, unsure if the question was rhetorical or not. Sean decided to answer. "The mainstream historical theory as to how the Native Americans arrived is that they came across an ice bridge up in the Bering Sea." He felt no reason to ask any more questions since there was a creeping feeling answers were coming soon anyway.

"Correct," Joe said, a mischievous look on his face.

Sean continued, "But Tommy never believed that. In fact, when he discussed it with me several years ago, I had to agree that story did not make a whole lot of sense."

"And why is that?"

Allyson leaned in closer to listen.

"Well, it would take extremely low temperatures, even for an ice age, to cause that amount of sea water to freeze over to the point where those two particular land masses could be connected."

"Good point." Joe took a sip from his fresh cup of coffee. "And it hardly seems that anyone would have been living up in Siberia at that point, much less have been able to survive the temperatures in that area during an ice age. And then, of course, the crossing of an ice bridge in itself would have posed many dangers. It is much more probable the Natives that settled in this part of the world would have arrived by a different means than some fanciful frozen ice overpass."

At this point, Allyson had to speak up, "What exactly are you saying? If the Indians didn't arrive that way, then how did they do it?"

"Sean, you want to take this one, or should I?" The man's voice had somehow become even livelier with the current discussion.

"By all means, you're the expert." Wyatt motioned with his hand, telling his friend to go ahead.

"First of all, we need to ask ourselves, why would a group of people from such a far-off land come here to begin with?" He waited for a second before continuing. "Throughout history, there have been many reasons people left their home countries. However, persecution is one of the primary reasons. Heck, the United States is here because colonists from Europe wanted religious freedom. So, they loaded up their boats and sailed west."

"Are you saying the Indians came here to escape religious tyranny?" Allyson interrupted.

"Not at all," Joe stated quickly before moving on to his next point. "The other main reason that people have left their Native lands throughout history was to establish larger kingdoms. Empire expansion was a necessity. Manifest Destiny has essentially been the motto for every major nation since the dawn of time."

"So, were the Native Americans settlers from an empire across the sea?" she continued the questioning.

"You got it. And it's going to blow your mind which empire they came from." Joe looked at Sean and then back at Allyson. "The crazy thing is, our biggest clue has been sitting right here in our back yard for nearly four thousand years."

Turning back to the computer, he pulled up a website that apparently had information about the history of the ancient Native Americans. After entering a few words, a new page came up under the heading of Fort Mountain. "Now, this place is fascinating. Sean, I know you have heard of it."

Wyatt nodded in agreement.

Joe pointed to a picture on the screen of a rock fortification, "This stone wall stretches for about 795 feet on the top of a mountain near the town of Chatsworth, Georgia. It isn't a wall in the sense you might think because there was no mortar used; the rocks were just piled on top of each other."

"Why is it there?" Allyson inquired.

"That's the funny thing about it. It's like our very own Stonehenge. For decades, no one has been able to understand its purpose. It isn't a defensive wall because it's linear." Pointing at the computer screen, he showed the two of them an overhead diagram of the wall stretching like a crooked snake across the top of the mountain. "No one would build a wall like that if they wanted to defend themselves. With no cliffs or precipices on the sides, the enemy could just walk around behind it."

"So, it had to be used in some kind of ceremony then," Sean inferred.

"Well, that is one of theories. Some historians think that the wall was used as some kind of sun worship temple. Since it stretches from east to west, they supposed that it was built to track the movement of the sun.

"Others hypothesized that it was a sacred matrimonial place for Cherokee newlyweds. That story suggests that the couples would go there to spend their first night of marriage together."

Stopping to zoom in the overhead picture, he went on, "Another oddity of this site is the two dozen pits that dot the landscape within the wall. Most of the experts agree that these exist as a result of looting or people excavating the area throughout the centuries."

"Let me guess," Sean said, "you don't buy that. Do you?"

Joe smiled up at him from the desk. "Of course not, buddy. All right, getting back to the wall, you see the outline of it on this overhead, right here." His rough-skinned finger traced the outline of the wall on the screen. "Now, when I first saw this, the pattern completely slipped by me. I never realized what it was until I was researching something on another website." He opened up a separate window on the Internet and typed in the web address for the British Museum of Ancient Egypt.

Sean started to ask why the man was showing them something about Egypt when it suddenly hit him like a lead ball. On the museum's intro page an outline of the Nile River appeared. His eyes grew wide at what his friend was implying. "No," he stammered. "That's not possible..." his words trailed off in disbelief.

"Not only is it possible, it's exactly what you think it is."

Allyson was unfamiliar with the geography of Egypt and didn't seem to realize at what Joe was hinting. To make certain they both understood the implications of what they were looking at, Joe took the topside map of the wall at Fort Mountain, and flipped it vertically. Then, using an overlay transparency tool, he moved the outline of the wall over top of the window containing the map of the Nile. It was nearly a spot-on match.

Abruptly, she grasped the magnitude of what she was seeing. "I don't understand though. Why would that wall in North Georgia match a map of the Nile River?"

Joe looked at her with patient, brown eyes. "Because Allyson...Egyptians built it."

28

NEVADA

The black-and-gold antique telephone rang loudly. The old man wondered who would dare call at this hour of the night.

Annoyed, he rolled over and clumsily pulled the device from its cradle, ceasing its painful noise. "Hello," he answered in a sleepy voice.

"Sir, things are progressing as planned."

Instantly, the gray head shook away the drowsiness. "What is your status?"

"We are holding for the moment, sir." There was a pause. Then, "What would you like me to do?"

After a few thoughtful moments passed, he answered, "Wait until morning. Then eliminate the problem. Accidents happen all the time on country roads." The final sentence was layered with insinuation.

"There are...other factors."

No hesitation, "They are expendable."

"Understood." The younger voice on the other end was direct, methodical. "What about...the other asset?"

"For right now, simply observe." The old man had grabbed his glasses from the nightstand and placed them on his nose. There would be no going back to sleep for a few hours now. "Make certain everything is proceeding according to plan."

"Yes, sir."

"If the other asset deviates in any way, you know what to do."

"Of course, sir."

"Anything else I need to know?" It was time to wrap up this late-night conversation.

"Not for now, sir."

"Good." With that, he placed the phone back down. With both hands, he rubbed his eyes under the metal-framed glasses. Everything was going according to plan...so far. Still, he knew there were dangerous elements in play, and everything had to be properly managed.

He was close now. Nothing could be taken for granted.

29

CARTERSVILLE

Sean's head was spinning. During the last hour he'd heard it all, or so he thought. He listened patiently while Mac went on about local legends and parts of American history that few others knew about. All of which paled in comparison to this last little bit of evidence with which he had been presented.

"What does it all mean, Mac?" he posed.

Joe had turned around to face the two, who stood a few feet away, dumbfounded by everything they'd been told. He still smiled, though his words carried some gravity. "Essentially, in a nutshell, ancient Egyptians were the first true settlers here in the New World. They came over between 3000 and 2500 BC, as my best calculations indicate."

"But how?" Sean couldn't wrap his mind around the idea. "Don't get me wrong, I don't believe that Christopher Columbus was the first person to sail here, but Egyptians?"

"Well, it is much more likely than crossing some ice bridge in the middle of the coldest period in Earth's history. Wouldn't you say?" He turned back to the computer and entered another search for the words ancient Egyptian navy. After a moment, an article popped up on the screen in which a renowned archaeologist described finding an ancient fleet of Egyptian seafaring vessels.

"Surely, you have read about this tasty little find," Joe said with an implying tone.

Sean and Allyson both shook their heads, clueless about what their host was saying.

"Really? I'm surprised you didn't know about this one, Sean." Joe cast his friend a chastising glance. "Anyway, there are two fascinating things about this discovery. One, the place where the ships were found is in the middle of the desert. At first, no one understood why ancient boats would be there."

"Maybe they were really ancient tombs," Sean blurted out.

"Could be," Joe agreed. "Except that they found none of the usual artifacts that would accompany something like that. It is now being learned, though, that thousands of years ago, a vast waterway penetrated deep into the land in that area. The second interesting fact was that the boats in the desert were not like other boats discovered in Egypt. Up until they had been unearthed, it was generally agreed upon that the ancient Egyptians only navigated the Nile River and the shoreline of the Red Sea. These ships, however, were designed for long-range sailing and were built from much sturdier material than the reed-and-pitch ferries that were used in fresh water."

"I actually did hear something about that," Allyson chimed. "But then again, I work for a newspaper." She was unsure about the significance until the man continued.

"You see," he explained, "this is the only theory that makes sense. And you can see the evidence right here in front of you." Joe pulled up the cross-reference screen of the Fort Mountain wall and the Nile River. "And if you are still not convinced...remember the pits I was telling you about that seemed randomly located near the wall?"

Sean nodded while Allyson just listened.

Joe pointed to the computer screen at some little dots along the stone wall. "Each place there is a pit at the rock barrier, there is a dot on the map of the Nile. At first, I thought that they may have just been fire pits marking random areas. Then, when I looked closer, I found that every single dot indicates the location of an ancient Egyptian temple or city along the river. Pretty cool, eh?" His hands were open in a gesture as if he'd just done some kind of magic trick.

What they were being shown was pretty amazing stuff. Sean still had doubts though. "I see the similarity between the wall and the river. And I get what you're saying," he answered. "But Egyptians from 3000 BC here in America? I don't know, Mac."

"Okay. Let's forget the wall for two seconds and look at the similarities between the cultures. Something that a lot of people don't even think to look at is the comparable design of Native American pyramids with Egyptian ones."

Allyson butted in, "Wait a minute. I know they have pyramids down in Mexico and Central and South America, but we don't have anything like that here in the States."

"Oh, contraire," Joe's Southern accent sounded funny saying a word rooted in French. "We have pyramids in three separate locations right here in the state of Georgia."

"How come I've never heard of them?" Skepticism covered her face as she inquired.

"Sean, I know you know what I am talking about," he answered her, looking at his friend.

"Actually," Wyatt began, "he's right. In fact, you probably have heard of at least one of the three locations here in the state. Etowah Indian Mounds State park is a few miles from here, where Joe works. Then, there is Kolomaki down in southwest Georgia and Okmulgee a little south of here in central Georgia."

"I know about Etowah, but aren't those just big mounds of dirt? I always thought the Indians just buried their dead there or something." She still looked doubtful.

Joe was enjoying the interaction, just happy to be an observer for a minute.

"Not exactly. Archaeologists have never been permitted to excavate the areas completely, but with ground-penetrating radar and other instrumentation we have been able to identify that underneath the dirt, the mounds are concealing pyramids built from rock and gravel powder not dissimilar to the ones down in Central America." Sean continued, "Also, if you look at the mounds from a distance or from the air, you can see the shapes of the pyramids more definitively."

While he was talking, Joe pulled up a website featuring pictures of the pyramids. He pointed to them so she could get a visual as they talked.

"Unbelievable." Her voice was barely a whisper.

"Yeah," their host responded. "It kinda is."

Sean decided to play devil's advocate for a moment. "Unbelievable...except for the fact that the pyramids at Giza and most of the others in Egypt were used as burial sites. The ones in the Western Hemisphere were mainly for rituals of state religion." His statement was blunt. "If they were built by the same people, wouldn't they be used for the same purpose?"

"Right you are," Mac responded. "But excavations of many of the newly discovered pyramids of Central America have revealed large burial chambers. These rooms were filled with the remains of what are believed to be priests and royalty."

After a minute of quiet contemplation, Sean asked, "How long have you known about all this?"

"I learned about some of it before I started working at the park. In fact, that's partly why I took the job and left the forestry service. When I discovered the legends and saw the similarities, I had to do it."

"You said there was other evidence suggesting this?" Allyson pressed him.

"Absolutely," Joe agreed. "In the areas I mentioned, the Cherokee and ancient Mississippian villages and towns were designed exactly like those in Thebes, Luxor, Hathor, take your pick. The streets and city plans were extremely close from the looks of them. Another interesting fact is that the Indians in the Americas used totem poles, which are very similar to some structures in Egypt, save for the fact that the ones here were primarily made from wood. And last, but not least, the gods that the ancient Nile dwellers revered were very much like the animals held in high regard by the American Indians."

She didn't know much about what these two guys were saying, but from what they'd shared so far, she was convinced. "So, how does this play into finding Tommy and the Golden Chambers?"

"I like her," Joe commented. "She's direct. I hate beatin' around the bush." He winked at Sean and went on. "I would guess that whoever took Tommy is trying to find the Chambers of Ahkanan because it would be the most significant treasure discovery since Tut's tomb. That's a significant amount of gold, and as history shows us, people will do almost anything for money.

"As the story goes, when the early Egyptian explorers came here, they were sent by one of their leaders, Prince Akhanan, to establish a new empire. Now, gold was something the ancients revered as powerful and sacred. To them, the value of the yellow metal was more spiritual than material. Of course, down through the ages, people's perception of it became perverted through greed and the concept of supply and demand. But in the beginning, gold was believed to have supernatural powers, and it was treated as a gift from the gods."

Joe stopped for a second to let the information settle in before continuing. "You know what reason these settlers could have had for constructing giant golden rooms?"

The visitors stared at the floor for a moment, deep in thought. Then Sean said, "My first thought would be that such a structure would show potential newcomers or enemies that their tribe was powerful, like a symbol of strength."

"And..." Mac persisted.

"And not only were they a strong people, but they were blessed by the gods as exhibited by the amount of gold they had. The thinking being that no enemy would dare attack a city that was protected by the gods."

"Very good, my friend; both excellent points. But there are two other reasons for the rooms. One of the purposes we can extrapolate is that of religious control. The ancients understood that if they could not maintain some form of crowd management, the ensuing chaos would destroy them all. As the old saying goes, 'He who owns the gold makes the rules.' There is, however, another power behind the gold."

Again, Joe returned to the desk, his fingers flying over the keyboard. "I'm a big fan of the History Channel, ya know. Can't get enough of it." He turned his head for a second, grinning at Allyson. On the screen appeared the home page for the History Channel. After entering a few more words, some pictures popped up of golden boxes under the heading, *Ancient ark technology*.

Allyson tilted her head quizzically. "That looks a lot like the ark from the Indiana Jones movie. Don't tell me you're looking for that."

Joe had to laugh. "Not at all, Ms. Webster. But I do believe the technology behind the ark may play into what we are looking for.

"A couple of months ago, I saw a program on the History Channel about how the ark worked. I was fascinated about how they discussed the design and purpose of it. Many Christians around the world would give credit to Moses designing it. But, as the show pointed out, these people forget where Moses spent at least a decade of his life before going into the wilderness."

"In the courts of the pharaoh," Sean said, citing the Old Testament.

"Exactly," his old friend gave him a smirk. "Down through the centuries, many arks have been discovered in Egyptian temples and burial sites. Until recently, their purpose had been thought to be ceremonial. However, as HC pointed out, there is an amazing science behind the purpose of the gold boxes. Have either of you read about the power of the Ark of the Covenant in the book of Genesis?"

They both shrugged. "Maybe a long time ago," she said. Her expression was as bland as cardboard.

"Well, it is fascinating," Joe didn't let their ambiguity slow him down. "There are several instances where the people of Israel bore witness to the great power the ark possessed: Uzzah was killed instantly when he reached up and touched it to keep it from falling off a cart, the walls of Jericho crumbled before it, and the Philistines were struck with what seems to be some kind of radiation sickness after they stole the box from the Israelites. The program on the History Channel said the reason the ark had such amazing power was that it was essentially a superconductor for static electricity.

"Researchers discovered that there are certain points on the surface of the earth that collect more of this electric energy than others. Not coincidentally, most of the hotspots for this geostatic power are where Egyptian temples were built. It seems the Egyptians had discovered a way to harness electricity. To what ends is still a mystery."

Sean was starting to understand, "So these arks were designed by the Egyptian leaders to control the people with displays of electric power. To the ordinary citizen, the arcs of *lightning* they produced would appear to be some kind of divine power."

"Yep," Mac agreed.

Allyson was also starting to draw the connection. "Do you think that these Golden Chambers were designed for a similar reason?"

Joe shook his head. "I honestly don't know. But I do know that Egyptians had a far greater understanding of gold and its uses in science than we could have ever imagined. Just makes me think that if they constructed four Golden Chambers, there must have been two reasons."

"Two reasons?" Allyson's eyes scanned him curiously.

"Most definitely," Joe chuckled. Then he said, "If we find one chamber, we should be able to find the next one."

"Why is that?" she wondered aloud.

His voice grew a little quieter, "The other reason the chambers were built was to point the way home."

30

CARTERSVILLE

McElroy's dog perked his head up for a second and turned toward the back porch. His brown ears twitched, probably hearing a raccoon or some other nocturnal animal in the woods. Whatever it was, he lost interest a few seconds later and laid his head back down on the floor.

"Home?" Sean asked. "You mean Egypt? That home?"

Joe had presented an enormous amount of information over the last hour, and it was all starting to come together in a way that Sean would never have imagined.

"Egypt," Mac confirmed with a matter-of-fact nod.

"So the chambers are some kind of beacons," Ally said more as a declaration than a question.

"Yes. And if someone can find the first one, there should be a clue that will point to the next one and so on until eventually, the final chamber is located."

Reaching down, he scratched behind the hound's ear. The dog tilted its head slightly in appreciation. "Naturally, the people who placed the chambers in their locations would have found it simple to find the way home. This could only mean that they were ordered not to return until an appointed time."

"But the appointed time and path were lost to antiquity," Sean pointed out.

"Until now." Joe had picked up the stone disc and was examining it again. His eyes were mesmerized by the object. "Amazing that such a remarkable treasure has been hidden for thousands of years without anyone ever coming close to finding it."

Allyson interrupted his thoughts, "So, what's the next step?"

His tone was direct. "We figure out the riddle, of course," he replied. "That's the reason you came here."

Taking the sheet of paper in his hand, Joe began reexamining the lines. His finger traced the passages a couple of times before he looked up from the page. "It is so simple, and yet it is immeasurably difficult to figure out."

"Do you have an idea of what it might mean?" Sean had hoped his friend might know something in relation to the key words used in the clue.

"Not really." Then he corrected himself, "Well, I mean, the chambers make sense. That part we get," he forced a quick laugh, "but the raven and dove, chariots of Heaven, stones? It all seems pretty random."

Allyson sighed. Her brain was on information overload. She paced her way over to the back door of the cabin and looked out the large window onto a darkly stained deck. Deep forest awaited just beyond the moderately sized yard behind the house. At the edge of the woods, twisted ancient trees stood hauntingly silent in the faint lights of the house like something out of a horror film. "You mind if I step outside for a minute, guys? My brain needs a break."

They looked over at her, startled from staring at the disc. "Sure," Joe responded, "go right ahead. Take a look around." He made a passive motion with his hand, turning immediately back to the round piece of stone in the other palm.

Allyson eased the glass door open and stepped onto the planks of the patio. Her ears filled with the sounds of the forest, and, as when she arrived, her nose enjoyed the sweet smells of nature. In the clearing where the house was situated, the cloudless sky that opened up above was absolutely breathtaking. With no moon visible, the number of stars dotting the canvas of night seemed infinite. After walking across the porch, she stopped at the railing, spun around, and leaned back against it so she could just gaze at the sky.

There were many advantages of living in a big city like Atlanta, but there was something very cool about being out in the middle of nowhere. All of the day-to-day stuff just seemed to melt away. Well, except the current situation. That was hardly something day to day. She found herself thinking about what they might find. What would a golden chamber even look like? Certainly, the events of the past twenty hours were unfathomable. On the other hand, though, she felt a sort of calm at the moment.

Was she a closet action junkie? Or did she have a secret passion for history that had never been explored until now? There was one other thought that entered her mind, but she dispelled it quickly.

A shooting star burst through the black sky above, shaking her from her thoughts. It only lasted a couple of seconds before burning out. Allyson closed her eyes, just like she had done as a child whenever she had seen a falling star. Abruptly, she opened her eyes at the sound of the sliding door opening.

Apparently, the two men had decided to join her for a bit of air as well.

"What were you doing?" Sean asked, a little curious.

"Nothing. Just saw a shooting star." Her response was lighthearted.

"Did ya make a wish?" Joe smiled playfully.

"Of course," she said, returning the grin.

"And what did you wish for?" There was hint of flirting to Sean's question.

"I can't tell you that. Then it won't come true." She twisted her body around and propped her elbow on the wooden rail.

The group stood on the platform, staring up into the universe. Constellations and random clusters of stars all blended together in the elaborate cosmic tapestry.

"Yeah," Joe began, "you can sure see a lot of shooting stars out here. No lights from the city to blur out anything. On a clear night like tonight, I bet you can see half a dozen an hour."

Out of the blue, Sean exclaimed, "That's it!"

"What?" The other two were startled by the sudden excitement and spoke in unison.

"The falling stars!" Sean said hurriedly. "Chariots of Heaven. You see?" He held out his arms wide, reinforcing the question.

Allyson didn't understand, but Joe caught on immediately. "Dadgummit, boy, I think you're onto something. I didn't even think of that."

Sean tried to clarify what he was saying, "Meteors, or shooting stars, as we call them, were sometimes called the chariots of the gods in ancient times. There are several myths in which a deity's arrival on the Earth to visit mankind is by means of a falling star. The chariot was a common conveyance, so whoever created the myths simply applied it to the story as a necessary detail for the ordinary citizen."

"Oh," she said after hearing the explanation. "I see. Sort of like those pictures of a Greek god riding a chariot."

"Exactly!" the two men answered in tandem.

"So what does ancient mythology have to do with a golden chamber in the United States?" She placed her hands on her hips, still not seeing the big picture.

Turning his attention to their host, Sean said, "Mac, check on your computer to see if there was a significant meteoric event ever recorded anywhere here in America. I'm talkin' cave drawings, stone carvings, anything you can find."

Joe was already walking back to the door. "Way ahead of ya, bud."

Still confused, Allyson followed the two of them back to the computer. The dog looked up curiously from his spot on the floor near the fireplace.

Once again, they huddled around the computer, Joe busily typing in different key words to find anything he could that might give them some kind of indication as to where they should go next. After about ten minutes of turning up nothing, he had an epiphany. "I think I know where the next clue is," he said, looking up. "Have you ever heard of a place called Brasstown Bald or Track Rock?"

Allyson shook her head while Sean responded with a slight nod. "I think so. I've never been there though. You think it has something to do with all this?"

"Yep. At this site there are a few large boulders with very odd markings on them. They're ancient petroglyphs," Joe was on a roll again.

"What do you mean, odd?" Allyson didn't want to be left out.

"Well, the shapes of the drawings are not like anything that has ever been discovered on the planet. There has never been a single documented find of cave drawings or carvings anywhere in the world that even closely resemble what is on those stones." He held up his finger to make the point firmer. "And that is exactly what the riddle tells us to look for, 'ancient stones.' Along with finding these ancient stones, it also suggests that they mark not only the path of those who are seeking the chambers, but also the path of the chariots of Heaven. One of the theories that I had completely forgotten about says that the markings on the boulders at Track Rock are actually recordings of celestial events. That has to be the place that will show us where to go next."

"How are we going to be able to decipher the symbols if there is nothing like them in the world?" Sean hated to be the downer in the conversation.

"I don't know. Haven't figured that part out yet." Joe looked at both of them gravely. "We have to try. We can take my car and leave first thing in the morning," he said as he rose and walked toward a hallway that led to a spare bedroom. "You two can sleep in here tonight if you'd like."

"I'll stick to the couch," Sean insisted.

"You don't have to do that," Allyson looked at him with a smile. "I won't bite."

"No, the couch is fine for me. I might snore, and I don't want to keep you up."

Joe stared open-mouthed at the interaction. "I don't care what ya do or where you sleep. I'm going to get some shut eye. We got a big day ahead of us tomorrow."

"Mac," Sean turned away from the previous conversation, "you don't have to go with us." As he spoke, Sean saw the look in his friend's eyes. There would be no keeping Joe McElroy from at least seeing where this next clue might lead. The man had, seemingly, spent more time than Sean had imagined researching and learning about the four chambers.

They had most certainly come to the right place. "All right. But don't tell your wife I let you do this. She already doesn't like you hanging out with me." Sean passed him a wicked grin.

"That's because you get me in trouble." Joe laughed then said, "You think I want her to know what we're doing? She'd go friggin' nuts. I'm just glad that she's at her mother's tonight. There'd be no end to the grief I'd be getting right about now."

"Sounds like you have a good relationship," Allyson said sarcastically.

"Oh, I love my wife," he answered. "She just doesn't want me to do anything crazy."

"Wonder what would make her think you would do anything like that?" It was Sean's turn to be sarcastic.

"Why do I feel like there is an inside joke going on right now?" Allyson stabbed.

The two old friends exchanged knowing glances as Joe headed toward his own bedroom. "That is a whole other story, my dear," he replied.

"Yeah," Sean continued, "maybe later."

"I hate inside jokes," she pouted and shut the door in Sean's face.

He couldn't help but laugh. "Good night then." The smile was still on his face five minutes later as he drifted off to sleep on the sofa.

31

ATLANTA

Detective Morris woke from some of the deepest sleep he'd ever had. Sunshine poured through the bedroom window of his condo as his eyes struggled against the bright light. On the nightstand, his cell phone was ringing and vibrating in the odd, circular dance that phones do when they're on hard surfaces. He reached over and grabbed it, glancing at the caller ID to see who'd awoken him at such an early hour. Whoever was calling him was doing so from a number he didn't recognize.

"This is Morris," he answered groggily.

The voice on the other line sounded extremely fatigued. "Hey, Trent. It's Lynch."

"You been working all night?" The sound of Lynch's voice woke him up a little.

"Yeah. I'm actually on my way home. Just didn't want to call from an office line at this time of morning. A few too many ears around, if you know what I mean."

Smart kid. A common misconception was that cell phones were monitored more closely than land lines. When cell phones were monitored, it was usually specific suspects who were already being watched by the police. The lines in the office, however, could be permanently tapped. Trent had asked Lynch not to let anyone know what he was investigating, and so far, the young cop had done well. A simple phone call the night before put everything in motion. Lynch was thorough and more importantly, he was honest.

"So, what you got for me, Lynch?"

"A couple of things," he answered promptly. "First, Hartsfield said the IAA jet is still in its hangar and has been for nearly a week.

"Also, all the airlines report not having a Sean Wyatt onboard. It is possible that he has some kind of fake passport or documents as an alias, but I doubt it."

"That means he probably didn't leave the country." A good sign, but the fugitive could still be anywhere. "What else did you get?"

"There are a few people here and there that he runs with, but for the most part, he's a loner. I guess when you live most of your life in foreign countries, looking for ancient artifacts, you can't have much of a social life."

Trent rubbed his face. "So no real associates other than Schultz? No girlfriend? Nothing?"

"No." The voice on the other line paused. "Can't say I blame him for the girlfriend thing though."

"What do you mean?"

"Well, several years back, when Wyatt was in college, he was in a motorcycle accident. His girlfriend was on the back. She died on the spot. He only had a few scrapes and bruises. That's gotta mess with your mind for a long time."

This was new information. "What happened in the accident?"

Lynch was glad he at least had something to share after working all night. "Apparently, they were on their way to the movies and passed through a busy intersection. Some moron shot right through a red light and smacked into the bike."

Morris contemplated the story. "How was Wyatt not hurt?"

"Just one of those weird things. The car barely missed hitting his left leg, but hit her square on. Wyatt was thrown about twenty feet but left the scene with only minor injuries. The report said she was killed almost instantly."

"Ugh. That's rough."

"Yeah," Lynch went on after yawning. "At any rate, Wyatt finished college and disappeared for a few years, as I'm sure you know."

He did. "So, there's no one else connected to this guy?"

"Nope. Except some guy up in Cartersville. He's a park ranger up there at that Indian mound state park, Etowah or something like that. Found a few pictures of them together and looked him up. Name's Joe McElroy, in his mid fifties. He and his wife have a cabin in the woods up there about twenty minutes from the park."

Trent's mind snapped awake instantly. "You have the address of that cabin?" His voice had lost its scratchy sound.

"Yeah. I got it here somewhere." There was a silent moment as the cop on the other end of the line was busy looking through what Trent imagined to be a small pile of papers in the passenger seat. A few seconds later, Lynch came back on, "You ready?"

Morris wrote down the address quickly with a pen and notepad from the nightstand. "Anything else I need to know?"

"No. I don't really think that this McElroy had anything to do with what's been going on though. He was on duty at the park all day yesterday."

"You checked?"

"Of course." The young cop's tone of voice made it sound like it was a routine thing. Good kid.

Lynch continued, "From what I can tell, McElroy is probably your best bet."

"Probably," Morris agreed while getting out of bed and heading toward the bathroom. After a quick shower, he would be on his way north.

"Should I get a unit out there to the McElroy place?" Lynch broke into Trent's thoughts.

"No. I'm already on my way there. Just get some sleep."

"All right. Sorry I couldn't find anything else, sir."

"You did great, Lynch. Thanks." Trent hit the end button on his phone while he turned on the water.

He showered quickly and threw on some clothes, barely drying off. A few minutes later, he was out the door and in his car, flying down the street toward the interstate.

32

BLUE RIDGE MOUNTAINS

The highway from Cartersville to the Track Rock Gap Archaeological Area is a rolling and twisty stretch of road, bending in and around the Blue Ridge Mountains. During the warmer months, motorcycle enthusiasts frequent the area in search of the fantastic mountain views and curvy asphalt that make for a spectacular ride. Autumn in the area also provides some of the most vibrant colors in the country with trees of red, orange, and yellow spiking the normal green of the forest.

Joe, Allyson, and Sean had arrived in the mountainous region only thirty-five minutes after leaving his cabin, and the sun was shining brightly in the midmorning sky. Joe got up earlier and made an enormous pancake breakfast for his guests. Sparing no thought to gluttony, he made eggs, a bowl of fresh fruit, hot maple syrup, and turkey sausage to accompany the flapjacks.

Allyson and Sean had barely taken the time to chew the delicious food. They'd been extremely hungry, not having eaten a meal since the previous day's breakfast. Sean had slept well on the soft couch, insisting that Allyson take the guest bed. Of course, Joe had said he would sleep on the couch, but Sean couldn't allow his friend to follow through with that generous offer.

Most of the drive so far had been spent in silence; the three companions were either too tired to talk or still in a post-breakfast coma. After looking out the window at the passing countryside for a while, Allyson broke the quiet. "Thanks again for the food, Joe. It was amazing."

"You're more than welcome." He grinned across the center console at her.

Joe continued guiding the truck through what the locals called, "God's Country." With the amazing views, the passengers in the truck could understand why. "I wonder why more people don't visit this area," Allyson remarked.

"We do get a fair share of visitors coming through here, but it certainly doesn't get a lot of the publicity state parks in the West get, or even as much as the ones in the Northeast. Can't say that I mind that though," Joe looked over at her in the front passenger seat. "I kinda like it quiet up here. Too many people comin' and goin' might take away from the beauty of the place."

"I guess," she returned to staring out across the rolling valleys from their high vantage point.

In the backseat of the truck, Sean had been checking his voice-mail messages for the last few minutes. Odd, he thought, that Detective Morris had called several times trying to get ahold of him. Morris should have got the hint.

Looking in the rearview mirror, Joe noticed the perplexed look on Sean's face. "What's goin' on, buddy? You okay?"

"Yeah," Sean slid his phone closed, "just checking my messages."

"You sure everything's all right?"

"Everything is fine. A detective from Atlanta PD called a few times. Said he wanted to ask me some more questions." Sean stared at his phone. "Not sure what's going on."

Allyson turned around. "Was it the same guy you talked to the other day?"

"Yeah."

Joe had a serious look on his face. "I wonder if they heard something from the people that took Tommy." His country accent seemed to get deeper with the grave tone that accompanied the statement.

"Maybe," Sean contemplated. "Or he still thinks I had some part in his disappearance."

"I can't believe this cop thinks you had something to do with it. Tommy's your best friend."

McElroy listened to the conversation patiently. He understood exactly what Sean was saying, and it made sense. The thought that the police were probably looking for them caused him to speed the truck up a little.

"I know," Sean said with resolve. "But right now, I guess I am the most logical suspect to the cops. That just means we have to figure this thing out so we can find Tommy and whoever has done this."

Behind the wheel, Joe was increasingly becoming more nervous. Maybe it was paranoia from the thought that he could be aiding fugitives, but he could swear that the silver sedan behind them was tailing them.

Allyson had turned back around to face out the front of the truck. She ended the conversation by saying, "Well, I don't think you as a suspect makes any sense."

Sean appreciated the confidence she had in him. He decided not to continue the talk. It was probably better that he not mention some of the other evidence that the police were inevitably looking at. The main motive the cops probably had was that if Tommy died, Sean inherited control of the entire IAA and the enormous fortune that went with it.

Detective Morris had more than likely thought of that before anything else.

Looking up in the front seat, Sean saw that Joe was noticeably uneasy. He leaned forward and put his hand on the driver's shoulder. "What's the matter with you?"

McElroy was busy checking both mirrors. The sedan that he'd thought was following them had got closer and was only a few car lengths behind. Sean didn't need a response. His friend's eyes told him exactly what was going on. Just as he was turning around, he saw a black barrel held by a gloved hand extend out of the passenger side of the silver vehicle.

Instantly, his mind cleared of all other thoughts, and his years of training kicked in. "Get down!" he shouted at Allyson, who had certainly not seen the danger in the car behind. To make sure she obeyed, Sean grabbed her head and shoved it downward.

"What are you doing?" Allyson started at him, angry at the gruff behavior. Then she saw him pulling the gun out of his jacket. She risked a peek in the side mirror just as the glass exploded. The sudden blast brought a scream from her mouth.

"Stay down!" he barked again. This time, she did as told while another round of bullets thudded against the tailgate of the pickup truck. Then, two hit the back window, sending a spiderweb across its surface.

Joe didn't say anything. His focus was on the curvy road ahead. He swerved the truck back and forth across the lanes, trying to give the attackers a more difficult target.

With the chase speeding up, both vehicles were reaching speeds that were certainly unsafe on the dangerous, tight turns of the mountain road. Guardrails ran along the side of the highway, but they hardly seemed enough to stop a few tons of metal from blasting through and into the chasm beyond.

Sean rolled down his window and bent his body sideways, bracing his back against the front part of the door. With two arms extended, he squeezed off a salvo of bullets at the pursuers, sending a few through the hood and another grouping into the windshield. The driver of the car slowed down slightly and duplicated the maneuvers Joe had used a few seconds before instead of keeping the car steady.

"You get 'em?" Joe yelled as Sean climbed back into the seat, ejecting the empty magazine and replacing it with a practiced ease.

"No," Sean's breathing had hardly changed at all. He'd no sooner spoken than the clinking sound of more bullets hitting the truck interrupted him.

Allyson remained tucked away in the front passenger seat, unsure of what she should be doing.

Sean slid across the bench seat to the other side and lowered the window. He shoved the weapon out the opening and squeezed the trigger again. The shots he fired this time were at the gunman, shattering the mirror at the man's waist. Sean had hit his thigh. Momentarily, the assailant leaned over, grasping his now-bleeding leg.

Pulling himself back into the cab, Sean shouted at Joe. "Mac, I got an idea!"

"Do I wanna hear it?" Another volley of projectiles pounded the truck, one missing Joe by mere inches, piercing the windshield. He reacted by lurching the truck to the right.

"When I tell you, slam on the brakes, and let them hit us!"

"What? Are you crazy?!" His beady eyes were wide with doubt.

"Just do it," Sean insisted.

"All right," Joe mumbled. Then he raised his voice, "But you're buyin' me a new truck!"

Without acknowledging the comment, Sean reached back out the driver's side rear window again, this time only peppering a few shots at the car. He turned his head around to look at the road ahead, the wind blowing hard in his face. Joe steered the car around a sharp corner, edging over into the other lane; the force nearly pulled Wyatt out of the window. The road straightened out briefly, but another curve approached rapidly about a hundred yards ahead.

"Mac, just before you get to that turn, hit the brakes!"

Joe didn't say anything. He didn't need to. Sean arched his body out the opening again and launched a few more bullets.

"Hang on, buddy!" Joe shouted back. He looked over at Allyson, who was bracing herself for the collision.

Joe slammed on the brakes. Sean braced himself against the back of the seat as the truck quickly lost velocity.

The driver of the pursuing car did not expect the brash move and swerved immediately to avoid the stopping pickup.

Instantly, Sean turned out the window unleashed a flurry of bullets into the exposed and now-off-balance gunman in the passing car. Crimson liquid erupted from his neck as he slid back in through the window, grasping pointlessly at the wounds.

Suddenly, another gunshot resonated from the front seat of the truck. Sean saw the bullet hit the driver in the shoulder, causing the attacker to jerk the steering wheel left.

The feeble guardrails gave way easily to the head-on force of the speeding vehicle. There was a brief sound of metal grinding on metal as the car vaulted over the edge of the mountain and disappeared from sight.

Joe eased the truck to a stop, feeling very awkward at the moment.

Sean's face was stunned as he peered into the front seat. What he saw was Allyson sprawled across his friend's lap, arms extended out the window, holding a Glock 9 mm.

"Journalist?" he asked with an eyebrow raised.

She was busy trying to pull herself off of Joe, who just stared at her with his mouth agape.

"Well," she said, sliding her gun back into a concealed jacket pocket, "I may have hidden a few details." She shrugged and gave a flirty smile.

Sean just shook his head. "You mean, like, all of them?" He couldn't help but chuckle as he reached for the door handle.

The three simultaneously opened the doors, got out of the bullet-riddled vehicle, and stepped over to the now-mangled railing. Just beyond it, the mountain dropped off down a steep cliff. At the bottom, probably five hundred feet below, the undercarriage of the smoking car lay motionless, facing the sky.

Mac snorted, "In the movies, don't those things usually blow up?"

"Yeah," Sean said without a smile. He holstered his gun back inside his jacket.

Allyson stood calmly, looking down the mountainside at the wreckage.

Joe was still very confused. "I think you have some explainin' to do, young lady."

Sean turned and looked at her as well. "Yeah," he agreed, "exactly who are you working for?"

"I work for the same agency you used to work for, Sean," her demeanor had changed dramatically from vulnerable to stalwart.

"You work for Axis?" Sean was skeptical, one eyebrow raised.

"Yeah. Sorry I had to lie to you. It was necessary."

"I'm used to women lying to me," he replied sarcastically.

"I was just following orders. They gave me permission to fill you in if and when necessary."

"I had those two handled," Sean motioned to what was left of the sedan in the ravine below.

She smiled and cocked her head to the side, "Just thought you could use a little help. No need to thank me."

He snorted a few laughs and shook his head. "Wow. It's like that, huh?"

"I don't mean to interrupt," Joe cut into the interaction between them, "but we should probably get out of here."

The two acknowledged his assessment and headed back toward the truck. Joe looked back one last time at the gaping hole where the gray metal barrier had stood. Then he got in the cab and revved the engine to life.

Sean closed the back door then asked, "So is your real name Allyson Webster?"

She looked back at him playfully with a wicked grin, "Maybe."

33

BLUE RIDGE MOUNTAINS

Normally, Tommy didn't sleep well in cars. In fact, traveling in airplanes, buses, and even the occasional train made it difficult for him to get any kind of real rest. For the last hour, however, he'd slept like a log in the backseat of the Hummer. Unfortunately, the nap was over.

"Wake up, we're here." The accented voice startled Tommy.

During the brief sleep, he'd hoped that the man called Ulrich had just been a figment of some nightmare. With waking came the realization that he wasn't. "Where is here?" He asked, still half-asleep.

"Track Rock," Ulrich reminded him from the front passenger's seat. Apparently, the guy running the show preferred to be driven when possible. Or maybe he just wanted to keep an eye on the prisoner, not fully trusting the guard in the back with Tommy.

"Oh, yeah. Right," he feigned forgetfulness. "So, is there a Waffle House around here? I could use some scattered, smothered, and covered hash browns right about now."

The response he got was a cereal bar hitting him in the chest from the front of the vehicle.

"Thanks," Tommy replied sarcastically with an upward nod.

Outside the truck, the sun was bright coming up over the mountains in the early morning sky. He was glad the windows were at least tinted.

The hired gun driving the SUV pulled into a parking spot near an open field that led uphill and into a forest that stretched another thousand feet higher.

Ulrich spoke up again as he opened the back door, "Move."

Tommy opened his own door, stepping into a vastly different world than he'd left in the city. All around them, the hills of the Blue Ridge Mountains were patched with the vibrant colors of autumn. No other cars were in the parking lot at this time of day, save for the white-and-green truck of whatever ranger was on duty. A light breeze brushed over the group, making the air cooler than normal. The elevation also dropped the temperature several degrees. Tommy was glad he had put on his jacket the morning he'd been kidnapped.

A solitary cloud wisped through the sky high above them as the entourage walked from the parking area through the grass. Short Guard was carrying a black book bag on one shoulder. "What's with the bag?" Tommy asked.

The stocky man in the black trench coat did not answer. He just kept walking with his eyes focused forward.

Up ahead, perhaps only a hundred feet from the parking lot, four large cages sat at the trailhead of the woods. The iron bars had been fastened around the rocks to keep graffiti artists and vandals from disturbing the integrity of the site.

Tommy thought back to the research from the night before and shook his head, realizing that the number four appeared again with these four boulders. Apparently, the number four had something to do with the solution. Maybe it was a coincidence. There was no way to know for sure at that moment. He just hoped there was something to find at that site, anything. If he was wrong about the boulders having an answer to the riddle, there was little doubt what these killers would do.

As the small group arrived at the cluster of caged stones, Ulrich said something in Russian to the guy with the backpack who nodded and set the bag down at Tommy's feet. He turned and skulked his way back toward the car, head down.

"Where's he going?" Tommy asked.

"To watch the car." The answer was short. "Now tell me, Thomas, how are these stones going to show us anything?"

That was a question that had puzzled historians and tourists alike for centuries. What their eyes stared at was like nothing else they had ever seen in any history book. Every boulder had snakelike lines drawn on them. Along with the linear designs were circles and ovals in what looked like random placement all over the soft soapstone surfaces. There were also different types of animal tracks and even human feet drawn on the rocks in between the other designs.

The native Cherokee had called it *Degayelunha* meaning painted place. Amazingly, the mysterious petroglyphs had resisted translation for thousands of years.

Tommy took it all in. He'd been here about a year ago. The view from the top of the mountain top was absolutely breathtaking. A visitor's center was open there from Memorial Day until October. With a summit elevation of 4,784 above sea level, it became one of the colder spots in the Southeast during winter.

When he'd first heard the idea that ancient Indians had drawn constellations and meteoric occurrences on the hefty rocks, he'd been skeptical. Surely, a primitive people like the original Native Americans were unable to document such an elaborate celestial map. Yet when Schultz had arrived on site during his previous visit, his mind had changed.

He had spent hours scouring over the detail of the drawings, analyzing them and taking photographs. After returning to his office in Atlanta, he spent days trying to compare the site to other ancient carvings and paintings all over the world. Nothing could be found that was even remotely similar.

Of course, Tommy had intended to return to the location to study the stones further. He'd even hoped that there was a link between the area and his ongoing search for the lost chambers. Caught up in a whirlwind of other discoveries that took precedence, he'd been unable to come back. Now, he stood on the ancient site again, wondering what it all meant and how everything connected.

"Do you have a camera?" he finally asked, shaking loose his thoughts.

Ulrich nodded toward the black bag that was sitting at Schultz's feet. "Everything you need is in there."

Tommy acknowledged the answer by squatting down and unzipping the backpack. Inside, he found a small digital camera, a notepad, and a laptop with an Internet card lying next to it. "Wow, were you guys Boy Scouts?"

Both the guard and Ulrich gave him puzzled look, apparently not appreciating the sarcasm.

"Never mind," he mumbled back.

Tommy grabbed the camera and fiddled with a few of the buttons to get the settings the way he wanted them. Ten minutes later, he was finishing up taking pictures of the last boulder. Ulrich and the remaining guard had walked around the area with him keeping a careful eye on his every move. At one point, Jens had asked, "Why do you need so many pictures?"

Tommy sighed. "Are you going to let me do what I do or not?"

He replied by moving his jacket to the side to expose the pistol underneath.

Uninspired, he continued speaking at his two captors, "Look, hundreds of experts over thousands of years haven't been able to figure out what these glyphs mean from looking at them. How will I do it with just a few pictures? We have a much better chance of succeeding if we use technology to our advantage. Taking shots from every possible angle should help."

Ulrich let his jacket fall back to where it had been covering the gun, apparently satisfied with the response.

"Did you guys happen to bring a USB line for this camera?" They'd thought of everything else up until this point.

"It's in the bag," the guard said, speaking for the first time since leaving the mansion.

With that, Tommy moved quickly back over to where he'd left the backpack on the ground. First, he took the laptop out and laid it on top of the nearest stone with a flat area. He then dug around in the inner pockets of the bag until he found the cord he was looking for. A few minutes later, he was busy transferring the photographs over to the computer.

"Now what are you doing?" Ulrich demanded as he watched over Schultz's shoulder.

Tommy answered directly, "I am putting all of these pictures on one screen. If I can look at them all at once, maybe I can make more sense of the entire layout than if we just look at them individually."

"Do it." Ulrich approved.

Nodding, Tommy finished setting up the pictures so he could see all of them on the screen. "This may take a while," he remarked while giving them an annoyed glance. Then he started shuffling the pictures around with the mouse.

Doubt crept into his mind as he meticulously scanned the drawings on the screen. What if they were in the wrong place? It was entirely possible that the glyphs on the boulders were not drawings of constellations at all. No, this had to be the place. There was nowhere else that would fit the clue's description.

Minutes went by with zero recognition of anything even vaguely familiar. Tommy was about to go back over to the steel cages for another look when something on the screen finally caught his eye. His pause caught the attention of his watchers.

"What is it?" Ulrich prodded.

"Give me a second," he answered, maneuvering a few more pictures around. Then, "Wow. Now, that's interesting."

"What?" Ulrich was impatient. "What do you see?"

"I really don't understand how so many people could have missed this before, including myself. I suppose it was because of the randomness of the patterns."

"Missed what?" The blond man was beginning to remind Sean of a five-year-old.

"Okay," Tommy began, "the Cherokee nation was built on a political system similar to what we have today. Their leaders became the heads of the tribe and nation a little differently, but they ran their tribal council much like a parliament or a congressional meeting."

The blank looks from his audience told Schultz they were not sure what this had to do with anything, so he sped up his explanation. "However, there were some major differences. In ancient Egypt, and several other cultures, even today, the people of the country were/are divided up into a caste system. Groups like rich and poor, priests and governors, royalty and peasants." Their eyes were still narrowly watching while he talked. "Essentially, the Cherokee in this area adopted the same system, most likely because they were from Egypt themselves!"

"So, what does any of this have to do with what we are looking for?"

"Everything!" Tommy was brimming with excitement. "The animal, bird, and human tracks on these rocks represent the different castes in all the clans of the Cherokee Nation. It's pretty friggin' cool."

"I still don't understand what all of this means." Ulrich was growing more impatient as the minutes went on.

Sighing, Tommy pointed at the screen again. "It's so simple. Look here. The key to the whole thing is finding the middle first, which is the opposite of the normal way to put a puzzle together."

"So what is the middle?" Jens asked.

"It's right here." The image his finger touched was a drawing that looked like a double circle or a circle within a circle.

"What is that? Why is it so important?"

"Because there aren't really any other glyphs that look like it, for starters. But the other thing you notice when I start arranging the photos around this double circle is that a pattern begins developing. See?" As Tommy placed the different pictures in the order he believed they were meant to be in, Ulrich started noticing the trend. The drawings of the animals and human footprints began spiraling outward, alternating every three spots.

After all the photographs had been arranged on the screen, the entire scene made sense. The double circle was in the center of everything, and the subsequent forms followed after, working their way farther and farther from the middle. He tapped the center of the spiral with his fingernail. "This is where we have to go next."

"And where, exactly, is that?" Ulrich was still not convinced.

Tommy responded with a question of his own, "When you look at any map, country, state, etc., what is the thing that stands out the most?"

The two foreigners looked at each other dubiously.

"Ugh. Do I have to do all the work here?" Sighing again, Schultz continued.

"I know when I look at a map the thing that always jumps out at me is the capital of a country or state. Right?"

A nod told him that they were following along so far.

"Right. Usually, it's marked with a star, or sometimes it even looks like a dot within a circle, similar to what you are seeing right here."

"So, you are saying that this symbol represents the capital of what? Georgia?" At least Jens was trying.

"Not the capital of Georgia," Tommy corrected. "The state of Georgia wasn't formed until the late 1700s. These petroglyphs are pre-Columbian. I'd say even further back, more like pre-Babylonian."

"Egyptian?"

"Sort of. Probably several decades removed from the original settlers, but yes, a crude form of it. That would explain why no one has been able to determine what it all means."

He went on, "At any rate, the place I was talking about is called Red Clay. It was the capital of the Cherokee Nation until the council was dissolved completely in 1838."

Ulrich was interested. "Where is this Red Clay you speak of?"

"It's close to Chattanooga, Tennessee."

"What are we looking for when we get there?"

Tommy smiled. "Probably for something with very similar markings on it. I'd say there must be something at the council grounds that will point us to the next marker. It could be another stone, a piece of pottery, I really don't know for sure."

"And how will you know what this next *marker* is saying?" Ulrich was still doubtful.

"I think I can manage," Tommy replied with a sarcastic grin. "We've made it this far."

TWO FIGURES STOOD by the damaged guardrail, staring into the gorge at the wreckage below. One of them, a tall, brunette woman in a black, ankle-length jacket, was holding a cell phone to her ear. Her shoulder-length cocoa hair was pulled back into a pony tail.

"Yes, sir. I'm certain they are dead," she spoke with no emotion. "No. They left. We know where they are going though."

She paused a moment, listening to the voice on the other line, then nodded. A moment later, she had finished her conversation with an "Understood" then closed the phone and slid it into a jacket pocket.

"What did he say?" The man accompanying her was dressed similarly, but his appearance was strong, like a rugby player, and he had short brown hair. He had been examining the debris of the crash site with binoculars.

"He wants to move ahead."

"What about them?" The man turned his head back down toward the destroyed car at the foot of the mountain.

"Leave them." She regarded them with a flick of the head. "Only a matter of time until someone sees this mess and calls the authorities. I'd rather not be around for that."

He nodded in agreement, and the two slipped back into their black sedan and sped up the mountain road.

34

BLUE RIDGE MOUNTAINS

The red Silverado looked like it had been on a mission through Afghanistan. Bullet holes were scattered across the back window, and a few more were dotting the windshield.

Sean looked at Allyson with a quizzical face from the backseat. "So when were you planning on telling us about this little gem of information?"

She returned the glare with a smile. "I already told you, I was just following orders. That information was on a need-to-know basis."

"Heck," Joe cut in, "it might be handy to have another gun around. Seems like she's pretty good with it."

Allyson raised an eyebrow and grinned at the driver. "Thank you, Mac."

"It's not that I mind you helping out," Sean explained. "I just don't like surprises. Better to know what I'm dealing with. You know?"

"I understand," she replied. "Don't worry. No more surprises."

"You sure about that?" He looked dubious.

"Pretty sure." She squinted her eyes at him.

Sean averted his eyes to the passing countryside for a moment before returning to the conversation. "How long have you been with Axis?"

She turned around and faced forward while she answered him. "I've only been working there for two years. They recruited me just before I finished college. It sounded like a good opportunity. It's fast-paced with a lot of travel and student loan forgiveness."

"One that can become very dangerous," he added. "It's a gig that can get you killed."

"I'm aware of the dangers, Sean. But I do appreciate the concern," Allyson twisted her head back around to face him. "I'm a big girl, and a well-trained girl at that. I can take care of myself."

His face blushed a bright red. "I'm sure you can. But it's a fine line that you walk all the time when you're an agent."

"Is that why you quit?"

"Mostly," he replied. "I got tired of looking over my shoulder, wondering if there was a barrel aimed at me from the shadows. Sleeping was almost impossible. Every little noise made me pop up with my gun drawn." He paused. "I don't miss those days."

"I never have trouble sleeping," she said defiantly.

Sean let out a laugh and turned his head back to the window. "Give it time; you will."

The next few minutes passed in silence. Trees blurred by as Joe guided the truck through the twisting highway. "It's just up ahead," he finally broke the silence. "I doubt anyone is here at this time of day except for the ranger."

As the truck rounded a curve going up a slight hill, a black Hummer H2 came into view. A stumpy-looking man in a black trench coat and a flattop haircut was standing in front of the grill.

With quiet calm Sean said, "Mac, they're here."

"What?" Joe's demeanor was not as composed.

"Take it easy. Just drive by, and don't do anything brash. Let's just keep going, like we're going to the visitor center."

Understanding the situation, Joe continued on past the black SUV. The man standing in front of it had noticed them, but once they had passed, he paid them no mind.

After the pickup rounded the next curve, Sean again spoke

evenly, "Tommy's back there with two other guys. They're looking at the stones. Looks like they brought some backup."

"What should we do?" Allyson and Joe thought out loud, simultaneously.

"Turn around up there," Sean directed, pointing at a gravel turnoff next to the road.

Joe did what his friend asked and pulled the truck off to the side of the little street.

"Okay," he continued as he loaded another magazine into his Ruger. We're only going to have one chance at this. Mac, here's what I want you to do…"

35

CARTERSVILLE

The police-issue Charger came to a crunching halt on the gravel driveway in front of the log cabin. Trent looked through the windshield, trying to detect if there was any movement inside the dwelling. His partner, Will, had met up with him at the exit off of Interstate 75 and followed the road from there into the national forest a few miles from Cartersville. He pulled his unmarked vehicle into a spot next to Trent.

Will rolled his window down and asked, "You think anyone's here?"

A silver Nissan Maxima sat off to the side of the house near a carport. Under the outdoor roofing, a white Subaru wagon was parked next to the wooden dwelling. Trent motioned over to the two empty cars. "Not sure, but we're going to find out," he said.

After taking a brief look around the back of the house, the two detectives marched up the front steps and knocked on the door. From inside, a dog howled the long, bellowing barks of a hound. A few moments later, they heard a woman's voice call from inside, "Just a minute."

They adjusted their stance and tried to look professional,

removing their wallets to show their identification. There was a sound of a deadbolt turning before the door opened to a short, pretty woman who looked to be in her late forties. Her hair was brown with a few streaks of gray. Her clothes were simple: blue jeans and a snug-fitting T-shirt that accentuated her slim physique. She smiled at the two strangers and held back the hound that seemed to be a little on edge with the unexpected visitors. "What can I do for ya, fellas?"

Trent spoke first, "Hello. I'm Detective Trent Morris, and this is Detective Will Anderson. We are with the Atlanta Police Department." The two men raised their badges simultaneously while he talked. "We were wondering if you could help us."

Her face curled in confusion. "What's this about? You boys are a little far from home for Atlanta police, don't you think?" She spoke with a thick Southern accent.

Will answered politely, "We just need to ask you a few questions, ma'am." He put his wallet back into a jacket pocket. "Your husband home, too?"

She eyed them suspiciously. "He's out of town today. Should be back later tonight though."

Morris continued, "You happen to know where he went?"

"Didn't say. Just told me that he would be back tonight."

"Does he go off like this a lot?" Trent scoped out the surroundings while he talked.

"Just depends. He might have gone huntin'. I assumed that was what he was doin'. I stayed at my mother's last night about thirty minutes from here. His truck was gone when I got back this mornin'." She waved a hand carelessly toward the carport. "Ya'll can come on in and have a seat if you want to. I was just about to have a cup of coffee."

They nodded and followed her into the living room of the enormous cabin. She directed them to some deep couches in the center of the room while closing the door behind them. The rustic feel of the interior meshed well with the natural surroundings of the woods. "Would either of ya'll like a cup of coffee?"

Morris raised his hand and shook his head politely, "No, thank you, ma'am. I appreciate it though."

Will shook his head, "I'm good."

"So your husband does a lot of hunting, Mrs. McElroy?" Trent asked as she sat down in a soft-looking, dark brown seat.

"Depends on the time of year, but he doesn't really go very often," she took a sip of her coffee. "But you boys didn't drive all the way up here from Atlanta just to talk about my husband's hobbies. Why don't you just cut through the bull and ask me what you came here to ask me?"

Trent smiled at her frankness. "Fair enough, Mrs. McElroy. Are you familiar with this man?" He produced a picture from his jacket pocket and handed it to her across the coffee table.

She smiled, "Of course. That's Sean Wyatt. He's been a friend of ours for years. Joe's known him since they were boys. Sean's about eight years younger, but they have always had a good friendship. I suppose it's on account of their families bein' so close for so long."

"Their families?" Will interrupted.

"Yep. They've known each other for decades, going all the way back to their grandparents. Joe's parents got married at an early age and started having kids shortly thereafter. Sean's parents wanted to travel the world and see everything before they had children, so that's why the boys are so many years apart."

"Have you seen Sean recently?" Will continued.

"Nope. Can't say that I have. He was up here a month or so ago, but he's always so busy with work and all." There was a pause before she said, "Now that you mention it, I guess it's time he got his butt up here to say hello."

Trent pressed her, "So, he hasn't called or anything in the last couple of days?"

She looked at him like he had just asked a stupid question. "I just told you I ain't heard from him for nearly a month." Looking from Trent to Will and back she asked, "What does the Atlanta PD want to do with Sean Wyatt anyway? He ain't never done anything wrong. One of the nicest guys I've ever met."

The two cops looked at each other as if to ask permission to tell her. Trent spoke up, "Mrs. McElroy, we have reason to believe that Sean Wyatt was involved in the murder of Frank Borringer two days ago. There is also suspicion that he murdered two police officers at the residence of Thomas Schultz yesterday."

If they had slapped her across the face with an iron skillet she could not have been more surprised. "Are you two out of your minds?" Her voice raised. "The idea that Sean Wyatt could be implicated in a murder, much less three of 'em, is the most ridiculous thing I have ever heard. What would make you think something crazy like that?"

"Wyatt is our only suspect at this time. We have reason to believe that he is somehow involved. That's all I can tell you at this time." Trent tried not to be insulted.

The stare she gave him could have melted steel. "You have reason?"

These guys were just doing their jobs, but the idea that Sean had murdered someone was overwhelming. After taking a second to calm herself down, she spoke again, "Gentlemen, I am sure that you have got something that is making you think that Sean was the one who did these things. But I can tell you right now, you're wrong about it. Now, I haven't seen or heard from him in nearly a month, like I told you. But I will say this, if my husband is helping him, then I don't blame him. I'd a done the same."

It was Will's turn to speak again, "Would you help him if he had betrayed his best friend?"

She looked at them both, not sure what the younger detective was talking about.

"You see, ma'am," Will explained, "Tommy Schultz was kidnapped a few days ago, just before a press conference he had scheduled at the Georgia Historical Center. Apparently, he had found a new artifact that was going to be put on display at the center, but he disappeared a few hours before it took place."

At this, she stood up. "Now I *know* you two are crazy. You're insinuating that Sean killed three men and kidnapped his best friend who, by the way, he's known since childhood?" Her head shook violently. "I've heard enough of this." She waved a dismissive hand.

"Mrs. McElroy, we just need to know where your husband is," Morris pleaded. "I promise, if Sean is innocent, we will clear his name and let him go. We just need to know where they might have headed."

For the last thirty seconds, she'd been pacing back and forth behind the sofa. The dog stared at her with big, droopy eyes, wondering what was going on. After another few steps, she stopped. "I don't know where he is." Her face was one of resigned honesty. "But I do know this, if I did know, I wouldn't tell you. My husband hasn't done anything wrong, and neither has Sean Wyatt."

"Your husband is aiding a fugitive of justice and..." Will started in angrier than Trent had ever seen.

"Mrs. McElroy," Morris cut off his partner, "we thank you for your time. If you do find out where your husband might be and you change your mind, please let us know." He produced a business card from his wallet. "Just call my cell phone if you need anything. We're just trying to figure this out. Okay?" Will slunk back a little, understanding Trent was pulling rank.

This seemed to settle her down a little; she took the card and nodded.

"Thank you. We'll leave you alone, ma'am. We really would appreciate any help you can give us."

The two men stood and walked toward the door. As Will opened it and walked across the threshold, she stopped them. "Officers," her voice was firm but had become pleasant again, "I didn't mean to be rude. It's just that we've known Sean a long time. And I know that he wouldn't do anything like what you're sayin'. But if I had to guess, knowin' him, I'd bet Sean was tryin' to find his friend."

The two detectives looked at each other, then Trent said, "You mean trying to find Schultz?"

She gave a quick nod. "Those two have been like peas in a pod since the day they met. If something happened to one of 'em, it happened to both. Know what I'm sayin'?"

Trent acknowledged the statement with an understanding smile as the two of them turned and ambled back down the steps to their cars. Mrs. McElroy stood in the doorway to the cabin with the floppy-eared dog standing by her side watching the men as they got in their cars and took off down the driveway.

36

BLUE RIDGE MOUNTAINS

J oe guided the pickup truck back up the street toward where
the Hummer was parked. As they slowly rounded the curve,
he could see that the three men who had been over by the
caged boulders before were nearly back to their vehicle.
Walking casually toward it, they were completely unaware of any
possible threat.

Sean held down his emotions as he saw Tommy escorted by a tall
blond male, probably mid- to late thirties and a tree trunk of a man,
shorter, but much thicker.

"I see 'em," Joe confirmed what Sean was thinking.

No response came from the back as they approached where the
four men were now standing together in the parking lot. They looked
startled as Joe slowed the truck to a stop right behind the black SUV.
"Excuse me, fellas," he said in what was definitely a deeper Southern
accent than he normally used. "Ya'll don't happen to know where the
Apple Festival is, do ya?"

Tommy stood absolutely still, recognizing the face of his old
friend Joe McElroy. Where was Sean? If Joe was there, then Sean had
to be close by.

The two muscular guards looked questioningly at the tall blond, who was apparently in charge of the whole operation. No one said a word. Finally, the blond man simply shook his head.

"I think we might have taken a wrong turn," Joe went on, trying to stay cool. He reached down and pulled up a sheet of paper. "These directions are a little vague."

All four of the men standing on the asphalt were staring at the paper in the driver's hand when suddenly, the loud pop of a gun erupted from the direction of the truck bed. Four more shots followed almost instantly. The short, flattopped man at the front of the entourage collapsed backward, three bullet holes grouped in the center of his chest. The surprise on the faces of the other three disappeared quickly as the larger, suited man jerked his weapon from its holster and dropped the bag he'd been carrying.

Another two shots fired from around the front of the truck, one striking the big man in the arm. He seemed unaffected as a volley returned from his black firearm, drilling holes into the side of the truck.

Joe ducked down below the window just seconds before a bullet zipped over his head.

Allyson risked popping around the grill of the pickup to squeeze off a few more shots at the tall guard. The man noticed her too late as he took a round in the chest and stumbled backward into the open passenger door of the big SUV.

The blond man had grabbed Tommy as soon as the bullets started flying and was holding him around the neck as a human shield, gun extended toward the attackers.

Upon seeing his subordinates taken down, he fired off three quick shots at the driver of the pickup truck. The bullets thudded into the door as the man behind the wheel stayed down to avoid the barrage.

Instantly, the blond man turned toward the truck bed where the initial shots had been fired and launched a brutal retaliation, sending more rounds pinging into the metal. As he backed up toward the front of the SUV, he sent two bullets at the woman who jerked back behind the cover of the pickup's engine.

Sean knew he'd taken down one of the three men but wasn't sure if Allyson had been able to take down another. Shots were hammering into side of the truck, and there was no way he could risk a glance over the edge. He looked in the direction of the rear window of the truck and saw that his friend was out of sight. For a split second, he worried that Mac had been shot. Then the truck lurched forward and turned into a position where the rear was facing the back of the Hummer, now about twenty-five feet away.

Sean raised his head slightly over the tailgate and caught a glimpse of the blond man shoving Tommy into the backseat of the SUV. Amazingly, the shorter henchman was slowly getting up, and crawling into the opposite door.

After pushing Tommy into the vehicle, Ulrich slammed the door and, leaning around the back quarter panel, squeezed off four more rounds. Three of the bullets thumped harmlessly against the tailgate, but one found its way into the back left tire of the truck. Instantly, the rubber gushed white air from the wound.

Sean felt the truck sag and knew exactly what had happened. He heard the Humvee rev to life and squeal its tires. He risked another look over the edge of the truck bed and watched as the four men in the SUV tore past the pickup. He fired off his remaining few bullets at the tires of the escaping truck, but the shots missed.

Allyson also emptied her remaining magazine at the accelerating vehicle, but it disappeared over the hill as the clicking sound of her gun signaled it was on empty.

Lowering his head in disappointment, Sean realized he might have just missed his one chance at getting his friend back.

37

CARTERSVILLE

T rent and Will sat quietly, eating the breakfast they'd ordered. After leaving the McElroy place, they had driven into the nearby town and stopped at a diner. Both of them had left Atlanta in a hurry earlier that morning so by the time they were seated, they wanted one of everything on the entire menu.

The restaurant was nice enough for a cliché 1950s-type place. It had the traditional jukebox in the corner, checkerboard tile floors, and pictures of celebrity icons from the golden age of Hollywood. Cushiony booths were upholstered in the traditional glossy vinyl with black and white stripes down the center. Even the waitresses dressed the part with the cute little skirts and red-and-white striped shirts. Their particular server's blouse was unbuttoned at the top and sported a nametag that read, *Wanda.*

Neither cop had said much to the other since arriving at the eatery. After they'd nearly devoured their meals, Will finally spoke up. "I'm sorry I lost it back there, man. I didn't mean..."

"Don't worry about it." Morris cut him off. "You're all right."

"It's just that...people with disregard for the law...it gets me angry, that's all."

"Believe me, bud. I understand completely. Why do you think so many police brutality cases come up? It's not that cops have problems with rage or anger issues, necessarily. The way that people disrespect us *and* the law can get anyone pissed off."

"Well, I'm sorry. I appreciate you handling the situation back there so I could settle down." The younger officer looked up from the now-empty plate. His eyes squinted as he smiled with gratitude.

"Like I said, it's done. Let it go. *I* did."

Will looked up from the table with questioning eyes. "So, do you believe the lady?"

Trent looked out the window at an old pickup truck driving by, his thoughts somewhere else. "I don't know." He turned his attention back to his partner. "I think so. If I was McElroy and I was helping a fugitive from the law, I wouldn't want my wife to know either."

He let out a few short laughs, which made Will smile. Morris continued, "Yeah, I suppose I do believe her. My guess is that she really was at her mother's last night, and by the time she got home this morning, her husband and Wyatt were long gone."

A look of determination came onto Morris's face. He'd been a police officer for a long time. Sometimes, it seemed like too long. One of the biggest things he hated about detective work was that sometimes answers were hard to come by.

"What we gotta worry about now is where to go next." He dropped the fork he was holding onto the plate and wadded up the napkin next to it. "Looks like the trail has gone cold."

"Maybe we're missing something." Will stirred his coffee, his eyes staring into the brown liquid while he considered the problem.

"Every crime scene has been searched thoroughly. Every possible witness has been questioned. We went to Wyatt's house, Schultz's house. And we got nothing. I just can't think of where else we could turn."

Five minutes passed as the detectives sat in quiet frustration, drinking their coffee and turning over every proverbial rock in their minds.

The only thing in the diner that wasn't circa 1950s was the flatscreen television that hung over the kitchen area. Two older gentleman who looked like stereotypical truck drivers with trucker hats and jacket vests sat at the counter watching a news report on CNN.

Trent looked up at the screen to see what they were watching. An aerial shot from a helicopter displayed a deep ravine in a mountain range somewhere. The headline on the bottom of the television read, *Tragic accident in Blue Ridge Mountains.*

Rescue crews could be seen at the top of the drop-off, working vigorously to get to what looked like the remains of a car resting upside down at the bottom of the mountain. Trent stared at the scene. He could make out that the wreckage was a late model Mercedes-Benz. The news anchor was busily describing the rescue team's efforts but continued emphasizing that officials believed there were no survivors. No identification had been made on the vehicle or its passengers, and the authorities were expecting the worst.

Will had stopped gazing out the window at the passersby and joined his partner in watching the news story. Curious, he grabbed the waitress's attention as she was walking by. "Excuse me. Do you know where that is?" He pointed at the screen.

Her head twisted around, and she noticed what everyone in the diner seemed to be gazing at. "Oh, yeah. That's up near Brasstown, 'bout forty minutes from here. Looks like somebody went through the guardrail up there. They been sayin' fer years they was gonna put a stronger railin' on that road. I imagine they'll do it now. Too bad that someone's gotta die before things get changed in this country. I suppose that's how the government works though." Her deep Southern accent was typical for the region. She stared at the television. "Such a shame."

"You say that place is forty minutes from here?" Will seemed curiously interested in the accident.

"Yeah," she answered, turning her attention back to the table. "If you get on the highway out there past the light, it will take you straight there. Don't believe I'd want to go up there right about now though. You can see from the pictures that they's turnin' people around."

"Is there anything of interest up in that area? Historical sites, campgrounds...?" His voice trailed off. Trent wasn't sure what his partner was up to.

"No...well, I mean, yeah." Her face displayed consternation. "There's a ton of campin' up there, but nothing super interestin'. It's pretty and all. I like driving through there this time of year just to look at the leaves changin' colors."

A gruff voice interrupted from behind the counter with the clearing of a throat. The cook had, apparently, been listening to the conversation. "There is one interesting place up near that area."

Will and Trent both tilted their heads toward the man. "And what would that be?" the younger cop urged.

The older man, probably in his late fifties, was busily scraping the grill clean. His brow eked out a little sweat underneath his paper hat. The belly that stretched out his white T-shirt seemed to suggest he'd not only been working, but also eating, in the diner for a long time. "Up about twenty minutes past that area right there is a spot called Track Rock. It's down below Brasstown Bald." Even though the cook had started talking, he didn't let that get in the way of his work as he tossed a couple of sausages and hash browns onto the hot surface. His hands busily scattered and mashed the potato strips and flipped the patties.

"Track Rock?" Trent was interested.

"Yeah," the cook continued, glad to have someone new to talk to. "It's fairly well known around these parts. There are four large boulders there at the trailhead leading to the top of the mountain. The big rocks have some kind of ancient writing on them that nobody's ever been able to figure out."

"You mean, no one has been able to translate it?"

"Exactly. I reckon about a half-dozen or so history experts and scientists come up here throughout the year to try their luck at interpreting the drawings, but no one's ever been able to do it."

"What kinds of drawings are on these boulders?" Will questioned.

The cook stopped shuffling the sizzling food for a minute and angled his head as if trying to visualize something he'd seen a long time ago. "It's been a while since I been there. But I can tell you this, ain't nothing like it anywhere I ever been. All kinds of weird lines and symbols and animal tracks painted all over four big soapstone rocks."

Trent and Will gave each other an understanding glance. Will spoke. "It's worth a shot. We got nothing else."

Considering the option for a minute, Trent finally nodded in agreement. "What have we got to lose? If this guy is looking for something, where else around here would he have gone? It's at least worth us checking out the wreckage. Maybe he got in a hurry and went off the cliff."

Will snorted. "I doubt we'd be that lucky."

They both dropped a few dollar bills on the table next to their empty plates and stood to leave. "We appreciate the information," Trent offered to both of the diner workers, who simply nodded their acknowledgment as the two detectives hurried out.

38

BLUE RIDGE MOUNTAINS

Allyson stood quietly nearby with hands in her jacket pockets, watching the two men. Sean and Joe had been working on changing the flat tire. The work was slow, though, due to the flimsy jack that they were using to lift the heavy vehicle off the ground. Unfortunately, it was all they had.

Swapping out the old tire for the skinny doughnut had taken longer than it should have. Now, Mac was lowering the back end of the truck down, nearly finished with the chore.

His assistance unneeded at this point, Sean had walked back over to the parking area where the shootout had occurred earlier.

"Where are you going?" Allyson asked. Her tone was direct, emphasized by her hands on her hips.

"The only way that we are going to get another chance at saving Tommy is to press on and figure this whole thing out." His jaw clenched mirroring the resolve in his voice. "Maybe we can figure out the symbols on these rocks and catch up to him."

"Do you think Tommy solved it?" Her eyes narrowed with concern.

"He must have." Sean forced a grin. "That rascal shows up here this morning and unravels a mystery that has been unsolvable for hundreds of years." He shook his head, "No, they wouldn't have been leaving if Tommy hadn't put it all together. How he did it, though, is a whole other matter."

She had joined him, and the two of them were walking in the direction of the caged boulders when his eyes caught sight of something lying near the curb next to the concrete parking barrier. The spot was where the Hummer had been parked during the shootout. Curious, he stepped over to take a look.

"What is it?" she asked, following him closely.

"Looks like a camera bag." He reached down and picked up the small black case, confirming his suspicions. "Yep. It had likely been dropped during all the chaos." Flipping the case over, Sean examined it more closely then opened the zipper and removed the digital device. "Tommy must have taken pictures of the stones."

"Why would he do that?"

Joe had finished up with the tire and was loading up the meager tools in the large metal box in the front of the truck bed. "You guys find something?" he yelled across the lot.

"Yeah," Sean answered his buddy's question first.

He returned to her question, "I'm not sure why they would need pictures." His mind was racing, wondering what his friend was up to.

Cautiously, he pressed the power button on the camera and turned the selector so they could view the pictures. Sean's eyes scanned the images. All of them were of the four rocks from different views and positions. None of it made any sense. Every one of the scenes appeared to be nothing more than random shapes and lines.

Joe had caught up to them and was curiously looking over their shoulders at the pictures on the little LCD screen.

"Doesn't make much sense to me," he commented. "I've been to this place several times and can't make heads or tails of it."

Sean nodded, looking at the last photo. "Whatever it all means, Tommy figured it out, and he must have done it quickly."

Several minutes passed while the three stood there, bewildered. The morning sun peeked over the mountain treetops to the east, bathing their little group in beams of soothing warmth. A crow cawed loudly from a nearby branch while other birds carried on their conversations under the cover of the colorful leaves.

The three flipped back through the pictures again, trying to understand what it could have been that Schultz had noticed that would have given him something, anything, that pointed the way.

Allyson snapped out of her trance by saying, "I wonder if he used a computer."

"You mean, like, a laptop?" Sean tried to follow her train of thought.

"Yeah."

"Maybe the problem all along has been that everyone who has tried to figure out what the glyphs mean has just been looking at them as they are. If he had a laptop, Tommy could have transferred the pictures onto it and shuffled them around all on one screen." He pondered the idea. "Mac, where could we find a computer?"

"There's a town about twenty minutes from here. I'm sure the library has a computer we could use."

"Let's do it," Sean said, turning to head back to the truck.

Upon arriving back at the hobbled vehicle, he opened the front door for her. "Good thinking, Agent Webster," he said with a smile.

"Thanks." Her eyes were playful.

"I think you're beginning to get the hang of this," he quipped and closed the door after her.

As Sean climbed into the backseat, Joe turned the ignition. "I just hope we can put this together as quickly as Tommy did."

39

BLUE RIDGE MOUNTAINS

U lrich had stopped at a gas station near a small mountain town that seemed to have been forgotten by time. Having to fill up was something too frequent with the giant SUVs his employer had provided. They could go anywhere in the world as long as *anywhere* was within close range of a fuel pump.

The guards took turns relieving themselves in the outdoor restroom while the other watched the prisoner. Ulrich was careful to make sure the convenience store manager didn't take much notice of the peculiar situation.

The man behind the counter inside was an older fellow with a six-day-old scruff of gray on his face. Even if the geezer tried anything, it wouldn't do much good. Still, better to be careful than stupid. They'd been caught completely off guard by Sean Wyatt earlier. And apparently, he'd brought help. That could not be allowed to happen again.

He glanced around again, still paranoid after the gunfight on the mountain. There was no way that Sean Wyatt knew which direction they were headed at the moment. But if Wyatt had been able to find them before, it was possible the man could do it again.

Jens Ulrich hadn't checked in with the old man for a while now. With normal clients, something like that would not be a problem, but the old man was known to be intolerably impatient. A great deal of money and resources had been invested in this operation, and results were expected more quickly than was reasonable.

Now was as good a time as any, he thought, and pulled the phone out of his pants pocket to make the call. It only rang twice before the voice of the older man on the other end answered with a curt, "What is our status?"

Ulrich imagined the mysterious man sitting in his giant leather chair at his oversized desk, staring at the phone, waiting for the call.

"We are making progress, sir. Schultz is far cleverer than we anticipated." His answer was as direct as the question. "Our next destination is a place called Red Clay State Park about twenty miles from the city of Chattanooga."

"I have heard of it."

Ulrich was a little surprised by this statement. "You know about this place?"

The older man replied as if he were talking to a child, "Of course. It was the location of the capital of the Cherokee Nation for hundreds of years up until the relocation began in the late 1830s. Their people believed it to be a sacred land, full of mysterious power. They thought that the ancient dead inhabited the forests surrounding the area and that those spirits would protect them."

"Schultz believes we will find something there that will point the way to the first chamber," Ulrich added.

"Was he specific about what it was that might be found there?"

"No. Only that the area was where we should be able to find the next piece of the puzzle."

"Is he being cooperative?"

"Yes, for the moment. He has not given us any trouble. We should be to the next location in a half hour or so." Ulrich waited a few seconds, trying to decide on whether or not he should tell his employer about the shootout that had occurred earlier.

Before he could begin again, the Prophet cut in. "I have some concerns, Jens."

This was an unexpected statement. "Such as?"

"Your methods are getting sloppy," remarked the voice coldly.

"What do you mean, sir?"

"First, the professor. Then the two police? There are too many body bags lying in your wake. I must encourage you to be more discreet."

Ulrich clenched his teeth in an effort to control his emotions. "I do what I deem necessary to complete the mission, sir."

"Understood. Just make sure you do complete it." Then he added, "But it cannot be done in a way that will draw attention to our purpose or to me. Do I make myself clear?"

"Perfectly." There would be no telling the man on the phone about what had happened earlier that morning.

"One last thing, Ulrich," the voice in the earpiece interrupted his thoughts.

"Yes," he replied, irritated.

"A body was found near a church yesterday. From the description in the police report, it sounded like one of your operatives. Should I assume that was your doing?"

The question was an insult. He knew the police would find the incompetent assistant he'd shot the day before and didn't care. The man had no identification that could be connected to anyone in the operation.

Ulrich took pride in being very good at what he did. Now this ignorant man had the gall to insinuate he was incapable. "I assure you, sir, the situation is completely under control. Will there be anything else?" His tone was sarcastic.

"No. But do not fail me, Jens. If at any time I need to bring in someone else, I will not hesitate."

With that, the call was disconnected.

Foolish old man, he thought. The wealthy always felt that with money came power. They push people around like pawns on a chessboard. "I am no pawn," he said quietly as he slid the phone back into his pocket.

Jens peered down the road against the glare of the sun and adjusted his sunglasses on his face. An eighteen-wheeler rumbled by. "You will see, old man. I am no one's pawn."

40

BLUE RIDGE MOUNTAINS

Morris teetered on the edge of the steep slope amid the mangled remnant of the guardrail. A few bits of broken glass and plastic were strewn about on the dirt shoulder next to the road.

Will was busy talking to one of the accident site investigators, trying to figure out what exactly happened. It had taken the rescue crews more than an hour to get down to the bottom of the ravine where the wreckage of the Mercedes lay. Upon arriving, they discovered the two occupants were, as they suspected, dead.

The driver's body was crumpled against the upside-down windshield, his neck broken from the impact. About twenty feet away was the body of the passenger. His twisted body was riddled with bullet holes.

Who they were, though, was a total mystery. Neither of the two dead men had any kind of identification. And the fact that they both had gunshot wounds was indeed bizarre. The car itself had at least a dozen bullet holes riveting the metal and windshield.

Trent took a step back from the precipice and sauntered back to where his partner was finishing up with the lead CSI. The short gray-haired man in the traditional navy blue jacket with yellow lettering walked away, being called over to another marked spot to examine something.

"What did you find out?" Morris asked.

"This is nuts." Will's voice was half in disbelief and half-excited. They have found bullet casings all over the road for the last mile or so. One of the bodies in the car down there has a round in the arm. The other one has a couple of bullet wounds, one of them to the neck." He looked down the road, contemplating the scenario. "There must have been quite a shootout here."

Morris took a swig from a bottle of water he was holding. "Any ideas who or what these guys were shooting at?"

"The cops here don't have a clue. All they do know is who lost." He finished this last sentence by jerking a thumb toward the torn railing. Then his voice lowered, "But if you ask me, I think it was Wyatt."

So it would seem. These kinds of things didn't just happen out in this part of the country. Even in the worst parts of Atlanta, car-to-car shootouts were a rarity. The whole scenario brought up more questions than answers. Why would someone other than the police be chasing Wyatt?

After a few moments of careful thought, he said, "If Wyatt was here and he was involved, that means somebody was chasing him. But who?"

Will only responded with an ignorant shrug.

Trent scratched the back of his head, trying to understand what was going on. Things had just got a lot more complicated. What if Wyatt was innocent after all? The dead guys at the bottom of the canyon wouldn't be much help. He doubted the weapons that were found near the wreck would give them any answers either.

Suddenly, one of the radios on a nearby police officer came alive with a voice from dispatch.

"What's going on?" Trent asked the officer who was about to respond to the call.

The man did not seem bothered. "Got a call from a ranger station up near Track Rock. Someone said they heard gunshots a minute ago." He spoke into the radio, letting the dispatcher know a unit would be on its way immediately.

Morris gave Will a quick nod that told the younger detective it was time to leave.

"Mind if we tag along?" he asked, following the cop toward a set of parked police units.

"Sure. Never a bad thing to have some backup." The man opened the door to his squad car and added, "Shouldn't take us too long to get there, fifteen, twenty minutes tops."

"Lead the way," Trent replied.

41

BLUE RIDGE MOUNTAINS

S ean felt horrible about Joe's truck. The vehicle had basically
been totaled from the two firefights it had endured thus far.
How the thing had kept running boggled his mind.

"Aw, heck Sean, I appreciate it. But I ain't worried about it," Joe
had replied to Sean's apologies with a huge grin and a pass of the
hand. "Now my wife on the other hand..."

They both laughed, imagining the scene when they returned to
the cabin with a truck full of bullet holes. The look on Joe's wife's face
would surely be one for the record books, followed by a fairly certain
divorce filing, or at least the threat of one.

No, Sean would definitely see to it that the truck was replaced
with one that looked exactly the same. The less Mrs. McElroy knew,
the better.

The group got out of the truck and made their way up the short
set of stairs into the old looking brick building. It seemed the library
was in keeping with the town aesthetic. In the small Main Street
district, most of the other buildings were very similar.

There had been a time, long ago, when the area was booming.
During the Georgia Gold Rush in the early 1800s, people had moved
there seeking fortune. But the vein of gold that had been found

locally did not last long. A lasting tribute to the city's past was the gold dome on top of the town hall, plated with metal from a mine nearby.

After passing through the security sensors, the room opened up into a much bigger space than seemed possible from the outside. To their right was a spiral staircase that led up to a second floor where it appeared many of the books were located.

On the ground floor, there was an open area in front of the librarian's long checkout counter. Several computers were set up at one end. Through large, wooden doors behind the main counter was a large room with at least ten rows of reference books. Every ten feet there was a large window that looked into the reference room, perhaps to monitor patrons while they worked.

Beyond the staircase, a section for periodicals contained dozens of magazines and newspapers. A few empty couches that looked as old as the building itself sat unused in front of the shelves.

A skinny librarian, probably in her late fifties, was standing behind a computer and asked, "May I help you with something?" Her face seemed pleasant and honest behind the wire-rimmed glasses.

"Yes, ma'am," Joe replied. "We just need to use one of your computers for a minute or two."

She continued smiling. "Help yourself. Right over there," she replied, pointing at the machines before going back to pecking at the keys on her own computer. The three visitors quickly stepped over to the computer nearest the door. Its screen was already on, as were the other six computers stationed in the little area.

Sean removed the digital camera from its black hard case and laid it next to the monitor. It was then that he realized they actually would need something from the lady behind the large counter.

"Ma'am," he interrupted her politely. "You wouldn't happen to have a camera USB cable would you?" Her eyes raised just above the glasses that were situated on the tip of her nose. The woman was still smiling as if her face were frozen permanently that way.

"Of course." She clicked her mouse a few times, evidently saving what had been on the screen. Turning from the computer, she languidly moved over a few feet to her right. Seconds later, she had removed the needed cord from a drawer in the long counter. "Here you go," she said, stepping toward the visitors. "Just be sure you give it back to me."

Not like they would be able to escape the building without her noticing. She was the only other person there.

"Thanks," Allyson offered to her. They certainly had to look awkward, the three of them coming to the library in the middle of the afternoon on a weekday. Even though the librarian was still smiling, she had to be thinking something wasn't quite right about the crew that had just walked through her door.

"You're welcome," the kind voice replied. She went back to her computer, minding her own business. They must not have seemed like too much of a threat. A minute later, Sean had connected the camera to the computer and was pulling up the images they had viewed earlier.

"So, now what?" Allyson asked.

"I'm going to pull up all of these images on the screen and see if they make any sense together. If they don't..." he was already busy lining up the pictures from left to right, "...then we move them around until they *do* make sense."

"Like a jigsaw puzzle."

Joe stood behind them, looking between their heads as Sean continued to arrange the photos. Once he had finished, the entire layout was even more confusing than when they had been looking at the actual boulders, if that was possible.

"I gotta say," Joe started, "I don't see how you are going to make any sense of this."

No reply was offered. Wyatt had to admit he held little hope that once the pictures were on the computer it would all come together. Unfortunately, it still seemed like a bunch of jumbled, meaningless drawings of animal tracks, lines, and circles.

After staring for a minute or two, he began rearranging the images on the screen. Another problem that presented itself was that looking at the boulders as entire units did not work. Essentially, Sean was now breaking up the large rocks into chunks in order to separate the symbols themselves. He spent a few more minutes sliding the pictures around and then stood still, befuddled.

"I just don't know what to do," he said finally. "Everything is so random." He began again, moving the digital photo squares around on the screen, looking for something, anything, that might help.

Allyson leaned closer, trying her best to assist, but she was way out of her depth.

Joe appeared equally perplexed. "Sorry, bud. It is a several thousand-year-old mystery, you know."

Sean ignored the comment and kept working. After ten more minutes of trying, though, he stepped away from the computer, frustrated. "I can see why no one has been able to understand these drawings. Makes me wonder if whoever drew this was just some ancient graffiti artist leaving a bunch of meaningless art on some rocks."

He sighed deeply and ran his hands through his hair, holding them on the back of his sandy-colored head for a few seconds before dropping them down to his side.

Allyson stood aimlessly at the computer, wishing there was something else she could do.

Joe's eyes were wandering now, looking around the old library as if the answer might come from the old brick walls. His head stopped as he focused on a large painting attached to a column rising all the way to the ceiling. In the picture, a Native American warrior stood on a hilltop, overlooking a valley. His eyes were staring with a stern look into a scene of majestic, green mountains in the distance with a fiery sunrise in the backdrop.

Across the Indian's back was a bow accompanied by a quiver of arrows. His arms were muscular and even more defined by the colorful bands of cloth that were snugly wrapped around his biceps.

What caught Joe's eye, though, wasn't necessarily the beauty of the picture or the Indian's impressive physique. It was something smaller, fairly obscure. On the young brave's arm was a kind of tattoo. To the casual observer, the mark would probably go unnoticed. But at that moment, the little tattoo in the picture made everything much clearer to the middle aged park ranger.

"Sean," he said, interrupting his friend's discouraged thoughts. "I think you should come take a look at this."

He pointed up at the painting as Wyatt walked over to see what it was that had got the man's attention.

"See the Indian?"

Nodding, Sean continued looking at the picture, not fully understanding what Joe had thought to be so important. Allyson joined the two of them looking at the scene on the column.

"Look at his arm," he said finally after giving his friend a minute, "at the tattoo."

Sean's face indicated that he was still not connecting the dots.

"Do you not see it?" Mac seemed to think the answer was obvious.

"I see the tattoo. Looks like a bird claw. But what does that have to do with anything?"

"There are some bird claws just like that on the rocks in the pictures," Joe was talking frantically now. His demeanor had even got the stoic librarian's attention as she looked up from her computer monitor, apparently annoyed with the volume of the discussion.

Then Sean and Allyson realized the connection he was trying to point out.

"What does it mean though?" Allyson asked confoundedly.

Joe explained, "In ancient Native American society, there were many different classes, or castes, similar to what exists in several present-day cultures. Here in the United States, we have upper, middle, and lower classes, but they are divided by socioeconomic status. We don't really have divisions of people into groups like artists, doctors, military, clergy, etc. But in the Native societies, they did divide things up that way." Again, he pointed up at the arm of the Indian in the picture. "This young man in the picture was obviously a warrior or a hunter because of the bow strapped to his back."

The other two nodded, following along so far.

"But the bird claw tattoo is the real clue as to who this guy was. Those types of tattoos were used as markings of the warrior class.

Interestingly enough, the United States still uses a touch of that symbol on many government emblems."

Joe reached into his back pocket, removing his wallet. He produced a dollar bill and pointed at the image of the eagle for the small audience. "You see there? The claws are holding an olive branch and the arrows. Eagle claws were a symbol of strength. And only the strong can wage war or create peace. That's how it has always been."

Now Sean understood what his friend was getting at. "So, the claws on the rock represent locations of where the warriors dwelled in the ancient times?"

"It sure looks that way. I would imagine if we take a closer look, the other symbols will also have some kind of significant representation of the ancient Cherokee cultures."

The two men quickly moved back over to the computer station with Allyson in tow. Joe took control of the mouse and began moving some of the pictures around. He moved the pointer arrow over one of the claws in one image. "Okay, we have a claw that looks a lot like the one in the picture."

He continued as he positioned the arrow around another picture. "Here we have a bear paw. That would probably indicate a scout or tracker group. And here," his hand moved the mouse again, "we have a bird with its feathers spread out, probably the religious order of the area."

Symbol by symbol, the two analyzed each figure until most of them had been appointed to a Native caste. When finished, they gave each other a look of satisfaction.

"Not bad, Mac. Not too bad." Sean slapped his friend on the back.

Smiling, Joe responded, "Yeah, but that's only half of the puzzle. None of it makes sense unless we know where all of these people lived. We identified who dwelled there, but this settlement could, literally, be anywhere."

The mood that had, for a moment, been upbeat turned sour again.

Again, silence took over the group as they stared at the screen, understanding part of what they were looking at, but not enough to know where to go next.

Allyson broke the hush after a few minutes of thought. Her arm extended out as she pointed at something on the screen. "What does that symbol mean?"

Sean and Joe looked as her finger indicated a drawing that looked like a circle within a circle on one of the rocks.

"The two circles?" she clarified. "What did they use that for?"

The two men looked at each other, uncertain. It was one of the few things left on the screen that they could not decipher.

"Because," she went on, "to me it looks like something you would see on a map, like a city marker, or maybe even a state capital. Did the Indians use anything like that back then?"

Both guys stared at the screen in disbelief. "Unbelievable," they said in tandem.

"Of course," Joe said exuberantly. "All this time it was right here in front of us. I can't believe we missed that."

Sean's face also lit up. He grabbed the mouse and started moving some of the photos around.

Allyson was lost again. "Hello? Are you going to tell me what's going on?"

"Pretty sure you figured out the solution," Joe answered with a grin.

"I did?"

"Yeah," Sean added, moving the picture of the double circle to the middle of the screen. "The answer was so simple all along. I don't know how so many people could have missed it for such a long time."

"Missed what?" She was becoming irritated.

"The capital of the Cherokee Nation," Joe finally gave her an answer.

"The Cherokee Nation?"

"Mmm hmm," Sean hummed, as he arranged some of the pictures around the centerpiece. "The Cherokee Nation's capital was located in a place called Red Clay. It was considered a sacred land

and was the site where their government council met to decide important issues."

Allyson raised an eyebrow. "Government council? You mean, like a democracy? I thought their chiefs made the decisions."

"Of course, they did. But they acted more like our president when it came to the manner in which their government operated." Sean stopped moving around the pictures. Waving a finger at the screen, he went on. "The capital was the center of their society. Around it were located the homes and workplaces of the citizens. Their organizational methods were simple but very effective. I'm not certain about the order or the exact places where their castes were located, but usually, the religious and political leaders of the tribe were located closest to the center. Then, it appears that they spiraled out, working through the community of medicine men, warriors, farmers, hunters, etc."

"So this is the place that we are going next?"

Looking at each other, the two men responded with a nod.

"It would seem so," Sean replied.

"And what are we looking for when we get there?"

A look of concern crept back onto the thirtysomething-year-old face. "I have no idea. We'll try to figure that out when we get there."

She looked at Joe, but he responded with a questioning shrug, arms flung out to his sides.

"So we're going to drive to this place and hope that the next clue will just jump out at us?"

"We don't really have a choice," Sean affirmed. Then he added, "But it seems to be working so far." His boyish smile was contagious. "Of course, you don't have to go with us…"

She gave them both a chastising look, "Are you freakin' kidding me? Sorry, boys, but, like I said at Joe's place, you're stuck with me."

"No use in trying to get rid of her at this point, Sean." Joe shrugged again.

He knew his friend was right. And, after all, she had actually been helpful a couple of times so far. Inside, though, old feelings crept into his mind. Over the past few days, he had found himself glancing at her when she wasn't looking. There was certainly an attraction there, but he kept reminding himself not to allow such thoughts. Those kinds of things were what got his heart ripped out so many years before. For a moment, he forgot he was standing in the library of a small mountain town in Georgia, and he was suddenly back in college, lying on the grass near the promenade of his university. Laughter filled his ears as visions of someone he'd not seen in a long time scorched his mind's eye.

"Sean?" Joe interrupted the flashback. "You okay?"

"Yeah. Sorry. Just trying to piece things together."

"We should probably get going. Red Clay's another hour from here at least. We'll need to get there to see what they have in the museum, maybe talk to the ranger there to see if they can give us any information that might help."

Sean nodded, agreeing to the plan. He detached the camera from the computer and returned the borrowed cord to the pleasant lady behind the desk. "Thanks again for your help," he offered as they walked through the metal detectors.

The librarian simply smiled as she wound the cable back to its original circle shape. "You're very welcome."

As the three made their way back out the large doors and down the steps of the brick building, Sean spoke up. "Allyson, you never said why Axis was so interested in all of this."

"That's right," her face was stoic. "I didn't."

She didn't offer anything else as she climbed into the front seat of the truck.

All he could do was shake his head with a smirk while he walked around to the back door.

42

SOUTHEASTERN TENNESSEE

I t had only taken the black Hummer fifty minutes to make the drive through the rolling hills and farms to Red Clay State Park. The ancient Native grounds were located in a very rural area near the Georgia-Tennessee border. Replicas of one-room log cabins, barns, and meeting halls dotted the meadows surrounded by the sacred woods.

Tommy had barely noticed the incredible display of fall colors during the journey. His mind had been busy considering when his luck would turn on him. So far, things had gone his way. He couldn't help but feel a sense of doom though. It was encouraging that Sean was on the trail, but how would Sean know how to decipher the code on the boulders?

Ulrich guided the giant SUV into an empty place right outside of the park's museum. Two other cars sat idly by to the right. The museum was designed to keep with the country-rustic aesthetic of the area. Wooden beams angled up from exterior trusses, and brown paint covered the natural paint siding of the entire building. It was capped with a cedar-shingled roof. A large deck was situated on the entire front of the building and wrapped around the right side. On the lengthy porch, old-fashioned rocking chairs silently rested, unoccupied.

Crows loudly bellowed from some high branches overhanging a picnic area while four college-aged kids were carelessly throwing a Frisbee in a field nearby. The crisp air was filled with the aroma from a tall stand of pine trees behind the museum.

"What now?" Ulrich inquired as the four men simultaneously set foot on the ground, exiting the vehicle.

Tommy nodded his head in the direction of the museum. "I guess we should check in there. They will have a bunch of information about the area. Maybe we'll find something."

The group casually walked up the front steps toward the building. Upon entering, they were greeted with what Tommy considered to be a pleasantly familiar smell. Museums of differing types always seemed to have a similar odor. It was only natural for Schultz to associate the scent he was now inhaling with the vision of ancient relics, pottery, weapons, or ordinary daily devices and utensils that people thousands of years ago would have taken for granted.

Behind the welcome desk, a man with reddish-tan skin and long black hair stood in a tan, short-sleeve, button-up shirt and green park ranger pants. He was busily typing on a computer that sat on top of the information counter. The nametag on his shirt read, *Cooper*. His job must have got boring.

Tommy figured the ranger could complete a round of solitaire in record time by now. The guy was probably not used to visitors during the week that were not part of a school group or some kind of educational tour.

"Can I help you?" the man asked as he stopped whatever he was doing and turned his attention to the four men, smiling with bright-white teeth.

Jens gave Tommy a nudge forward. Clearing his throat, Schultz tried not to act like a hostage. "Yes," he began, "I was just showing some of my friends around the area. They're not from around here," he continued, pointing at the other three who looked at each other, seeming confused. "I thought it would be cool to show them a little bit about some of the local history."

The dark-skinned ranger looked pleased. "Well, you've come to the right place. Feel free to take a look around our museum, just through those doors there. You can find all kinds of information about our rich past as well as many artifacts that have been discovered through the years right here on the property." Then he added, "If you would like, we have a twenty-minute video that will be showing in a few minutes."

Why would they have a movie at set times if there was no one there to watch it? Tommy didn't ask the question. The guy was obviously eager to share information with someone who didn't arrive on a yellow bus.

"Thanks. We'll just take a look around for a few minutes and maybe walk through the park."

"All right. Just let me know if you need anything or have any questions." Satisfied he'd done his job, the ranger went back to whatever he was previously doing on the computer.

Tommy nodded in appreciation and led the two flattops and Ulrich through the large double doors into a small museum area. Once inside, they were greeted by six-foot-high placards with pictures of Native Americans in full headdress. Smaller pictures with name plates and brief descriptions dotted the walls. Frames displaying Indians playing an ancient form of lacrosse were paired with some actual balls and sticks that had been used hundreds of years ago.

The *museum* was more like a large single room that had been divided by an artificial wall. Maybe the park thought it would seem bigger if it were split into two areas instead of just one. Display cases were propped around on the floor, showing a variety of old artifacts. Eating utensils, scissors, small bowls, sewing needles, and several other items of interest were presented in the first little spot.

As the group made their way around the room, they found containers displaying arrows and spearheads made from flint. Bows, arrows, rifles, pistols, and various other weapons were displayed on the walls behind these glass boxes. A few rusty knives hung precariously next to a picture of a sallow-eyed Native in what looked like a suit a lawyer may have worn in the 1800s. The name under the picture read, *James Vann*.

Tommy smiled and let out a snorting laugh when he saw this.

The men guarding him must not have noticed or even cared about their prisoner's private thought.

Ulrich interrupted the moment. "What are we looking for?" he said in a direct tone.

Tommy cast him a *buzz-off* glance. "We're just looking at this point. Red Clay was one of the most important spots in the Cherokee Nation. Logic would suggest that if the chambers exist, there is probably something that links to them here."

The answer to his comment was the feeling of a gun shoved into his left kidney. "I would suggest, Mr. Schultz, that you look faster. Time is of the essence."

Shivers went through his body, but Tommy remained calm. "Take it easy," he replied and took a few steps toward a large standup of John Ross. The story of Ross's life played out next to the image. It was a tale that Schultz knew well.

John Ross had been the primary leader of the Cherokee Nation before it was dissolved and moved to Oklahoma. He and many white members of the United States government had fought the removal of the Indians from their ancient lands for years before succumbing to a betrayal by a minority group acting on the Cherokee's behalf.

Along the walkway, the images of other great Cherokee leaders hung from the walls. More display cases contained what seemed to be random works of art: drawings, paintings, cups, and other pottery.

Both the guards had lost looks on their faces. Tommy was unsure whether apathy or incomprehension caused the blank look on his captors' faces, but he didn't really care either way. His eyes wandered the room, scanning all the frames, hoping that whatever it was he was looking for would pop out like one of those 3-D pictures that were so popular in the late '90s.

After a few minutes of searching, he finally saw it. In the shadows by the exit doors, a small glass case stood alone on a pedestal with a single floodlight shining onto it at an angle. In a few long strides, Tommy was standing in front of the exhibit. Wonder filled his eyes as he ran his fingers along the edge of the glass next to the *Do not touch* sign.

The men watching him were momentarily alarmed at how quickly Schultz had moved toward the exit, but when he stopped in the corner, they reholstered the pistols drawn a second before.

Mesmerized by the exhibit resting in front of them, the four men stared into the case. Within its confines, a piece of clay pottery about the size of a typical flower vase sat inconspicuously in the pale light.

Tommy squatted down to get a closer look at the jar. It looked more like it had come from an ancient Greek society than a Native American one. Fluid snakelike carvings decorated the front of the clay container in shapes that crisscrossed like an elaborate pretzel. As he scooted around to the back of the display stand, he beheld an image of two birds almost identical to the ones on the stone disc he had discovered.

"This is it," he whispered.

Jens appeared unimpressed. "What does it mean?"

Tommy had grown tired of these undereducated men. Nothing annoyed him more than ignorant treasure hunters who only searched because of the fame and money antiquities might bring.

He rose from his squatting position and sighed, "This is actually a very rare piece of history. As far as I know, only two of these have ever been discovered. One of them was found fifty or so years ago and is called Vessel Number One. Until now, I have never actually seen one that resembled anything close to that vase."

"And how is this clay jar going to help us?" Ulrich looked bewildered.

Tommy pointed to the front first. "You see, the first vessel that was found had almost identical snakelike drawings. But it did not have the bird designs on the back, like this one." He motioned at the carvings on the rear side of the pot.

Clearly, the three men still had no idea where he was going with this.

"The stone that I found in Chatsworth had the exact same birds carved into it. Don't you see?" His voice pleaded while his hands extended outward. "This means we are on the right track. The fact that this vase and the medallion have the same designs means the clues are related!" Tommy was ecstatic about the discovery.

"So, what do we do? Take the vase?" Ulrich took a step closer to the glass case, removing the gun from his jacket.

"No, no, no! Hold on a second," Tommy got in his way and put his hands up to hold the blond man back, a move his captor did not seem to appreciate as evidenced by the warning scowl on his face. Backing off a foot, he continued cautiously, "Look. We don't need to take it. Just give me a minute." Ulrich reholstered his weapon, seemingly willing to wait and see what the archaeologist was going to do next.

Tommy took a step back from the exhibit and looked around. Immediately, he noticed that there was no history placard or name plate identifying where the pottery had come from or why it was there. He retraced their steps through the corridor, looking to see if there was anything that contained information about the vessel, but he found nothing.

Finally, he said, "I need to get the guy from the information desk in here."

Ulrich looked at him suspiciously, deliberating over the request. Then he nodded his approval.

Tommy strode back over to the giant exit doors and gently pushed one of them open. The hinges obviously needed some kind of lubricant as the portal creaked loudly. He poked his head out and noticed the park ranger looking directly at him. The squeaking must have got the man's attention.

"Done already?" he inquired cheerfully.

"Actually, no. We had a question about something in here. Would you mind?" Tommy made a motion with his hand for the man to come over.

The ranger looked around. For whom, Tommy had no idea. Then he said, "Sure. What would you like to know?" He walked over to the doors and pulled them open to find the three men standing around the corner exhibit.

It seemed that the sight of the huddled group startled the ranger for a moment, but he recovered and continued into the museum. "So, how can I help you?"

The three captors remained silent. Again, it seemed Tommy would do all the talking. "We were wondering about this piece right here." He gestured to the vase. "How come there isn't any information about it? We thought that was strange. Sure is a spectacular piece though."

An odd look crossed onto the Indian's face. "What is it, exactly, that you want to know?'

The tone of the man's voice had changed from helpful to almost sinister. Maybe it was just Tommy's imagination, but the smile that had accompanied his jovial attitude had disappeared as well.

Stumbling through his words, Tommy said, "Well...where did it come from? How old is it? Who made it? You know, stuff like that?"

The smile returned to the weathered face, but there was something different about it. He eyed the other three men with a look that seemed like disdain. When his gaze returned to Tommy, it held a look of warning, though his voice had become pleasant again. "It is a ceremonial jar that was kept here in the Cherokee capital for a very long time. As to who made it, no one really knows. But it is an excellent example of early nineteenth-century Native artwork."

Tommy looked skeptical; something didn't seem right. "I'm sorry," he paused slightly. "Did you say that it was early nineteenth century?"

"Yes. That is correct. The Cherokee were a very artistic people. There was an entire caste of artisans, sculptors, painters. Creativity was encouraged by the Cherokee culture."

Tommy interrupted him, "Yeah, but I don't think that this is actually nineteenth century. That can't be right."

An annoyed look passed across the man's face. "I assure you, we have had the best experts in the region examine this, and they have all agreed to the same timeframe."

"Well, I don't know who these experts are, but I can tell you one thing: that vase predates the nineteenth century by at least, oh, I'd say a thousand years."

For a moment, the ranger's eyes squinted. Tommy's comments seemed insulting rather than inquisitive. "Really? And what makes you think such a thing, if I may ask," he responded, crossing thick, tanned arms.

"Well, first of all, as I was explaining to these gentlemen, this is an example of Weeden Island pottery. It's from the early Mississippian Age, at the youngest. But from the expression of the lines and the type of clay that appears to have been used, I'd say this thing is way older. In fact, it resembles some items that I have seen at a dig site in Lebanon. Phoenicians made some containers that look very similar to this one. And those were about three thousand years old." He tried not to appear too much like he was correcting the man, but this was an area in which Tommy considered himself to be a foremost expert.

Again, the look on the Indian's face changed. This time, though, it was an acknowledgement. "Impressive, sir."

Tommy was not sure how to react. Before he could, the ranger continued.

"It is, indeed, much older than the nineteenth century. Although, exactly how old, I do not know. Since you seem to know much more about our history than the average person, surely you know this vase has a twin."

The last comment urged an answer. Nodding, Tommy replied, "Vessel Number One. Yes, I've seen it."

Apparently pleased, the man continued while the two flattops and the blond looked at each other, bemused. "This particular piece of work has an interesting history. Originally, it was brought here by the oldest of the Cherokee. It was said that they kept the bones of a great tribal leader within it. As the legend goes, this man was more a king than a chief. He ruled vast lands and was a great warrior. When he died, those who took over for him believed that if they kept his remains, the kingdom would be blessed for all eternity and that he would watch over it from his place in the afterlife."

The ranger stopped talking for a moment and looked at the unassuming display, lost in thoughts that drifted through time. "This land we stand upon was considered holy by the Cherokee for thousands of years. Then, in 1838, the American government took it all away. Their lust for Native treasures and land pushed the tribe west to Oklahoma."

"But the vase remained here?" Tommy slipped the question in during a moment of reflection.

"No," the reply was vacant. "It was taken to a safe place near here."

"A safe place?"

"Yes. The nation's leader, John Ross," he said, motioning at the wooden representation of the old tribal chief. "Ross knew that the people had been betrayed by some of their own and that soon the United States government would force them to leave their land. So, he took their most sacred relic to the only place he thought it would be safe...a church."

Tommy's eyebrows furrowed at the revelation. "A church? I don't understand. Why didn't they just take it to Oklahoma?"

The dark-skinned man chuckled under his breath. To him, the answer was obvious. "This vase is as much a part of this land as the trees and the dirt beneath them. It was brought here by a great tribal leader, and here it must stay for all eternity. Even though many traditions were lost through the years and several Euro-American ones were adopted, there are still others that remain and will remain until the end of time."

"But if the white settlers could not be trusted with this, how did Ross know that he could trust a church full of white people?" It was a good question, assuming it *had been* a church full of white people.

"There were many people in the United States government as well as average, everyday citizens, who wanted the relocation to happen. No doubt, those people were in the majority. However, there were some who believed it to be a great evil and fought the forced removal with every resource they had. Davy Crockett was one of the most famous to fight against the government removal. It ended up costing him his political career. "But there were also local people who rallied for the Cherokee cause. One of those was the pastor of a nearby church. That place of worship still exists today. It's called the Beacon Tabernacle. Ross developed a friendship with this preacher over time and grew to trust the man as if they were brothers. In fact, there was a rumor that the reverend had even gone through the blood ceremony to become forever united with his new friend." The Indian stopped again and looked out through the double doors to make sure no one was waiting at the desk, a move that startled the two Russians momentarily.

Ignoring their jumpiness, he began again while Tommy listened eagerly. "A few days before the federal troops moved in, Ross went to the church. He walked in during a service and presented the jar to his friend. There it was kept for over a century until this park was established. Knowledge of this vase's importance to the Cherokee was passed down from pastor to pastor. When it was announced that Red Clay would become a protected state park, the then-leader of the church graciously returned the vessel to where he believed to be its proper resting place."

"So, what happened to the bones of this ruler?"

"The great king's remains were rumored to have been buried somewhere safe, but the location remains a mystery much like the story itself."

As fascinating as the whole tale had been, none of it really helped them with the bigger picture of finding the chambers. Tommy couldn't help but feel like this simple park ranger knew more than he was letting on. But how to get it out of him?

The Indian disrupted his thoughts with a whisper, just loud enough for Tommy's ear alone to hear, "You shall not find what it is you seek. Though you have come farther than any before, the chamber will remain a secret."

"What? Why?" He was confused by the sudden confirmation and denial all in one breath.

Ulrich leaned in to hear the exchange between the two men.

The ranger stepped back, resolution in his face. "You are not the one the prophecy foretold would lead us home." His finger extended toward the now-angry-looking blond man. "You will not find the chamber. Only death awaits you and your allies."

Pulling his gun from his jacket, Ulrich stood in front of the man and pressed the Glock to his forehead. He'd heard enough. "Tell me where the chamber is, fool, and perhaps I will spare your life."

A sick grin came upon the reddish-brown face. It was followed by a deep, slow laugh, becoming faster and louder until the entire hall was filled with the eerie sound. "Death is no threat to me. The location of the chamber will only be revealed to the pure of heart. Your heart is black as the night. I can see it in your eyes. It cannot be yours."

Tommy tried to intervene and stepped toward Ulrich. "Jens, don't do this! He's the only one that can help us. If you kill him, then we will never find the chamber. We need him."

The blond cocked his head slightly. "Hmm. Really?" Then, with a matter-of-fact look, he turned his attention back to the park ranger. "Well, if dying doesn't change your mind, perhaps pain will." A split second later, he had lowered the weapon to the ranger's leg. The loud recoil rang throughout the museum walls.

What had been a look of resolve on the man's face instantly contorted to agony and shock as he collapsed to the floor.

Ulrich's voice became louder, more commanding. "Tell me where the chamber is, and I will end your misery!"

The man said nothing, he just grasped his leg, trying to slow the bleeding from the bullet wound.

"Say it!" Ulrich yelled again. He aimed the weapon at the other knee and pulled the trigger again.

The kneecap erupted in a splash of blood and bone. Still, the man did not cry out, though his face betrayed a new surge of pain as he clenched his jaw tighter.

A small pool of red liquid was forming around where he was propped on the floor.

All Tommy could do was watch in horror, helpless to do anything, wrapped in the arms of the two guards. "Are you crazy? Stop it! We need him!" he screamed.

The blond's eyes turned for a moment to Tommy before another shot resonated through the building. This bullet went through the ranger's shoulder, directly into the joint. Blood trickled from the wound down the tan sleeve of the man's uniform.

Both of the guards looked visibly uneasy as they watched from a few feet away. They were busily looking around to make sure no one else was going to enter the room, paranoia on their faces.

Ulrich squatted down and put his nose close to the grimacing face of the Indian and pressed the gun against the man's temple. "Tell me where the chamber is, and I will end all of this for you right now. This is your last chance."

The agony on the ranger's face turned once again to a look of defiance. "I am already dead," he spat through gritted teeth. "My ancestors await me. And you shall never have the treasure you seek. My purpose is fulfilled."

"Have it your way then," the gun lowered to the ranger's abdomen. Another pop burst through the silence.

Bloody hands first grasped at the arms of the European jacket of the man that had certainly ended his life. Then, releasing the sleeves, he reached down with his hands and felt the warm, thick liquid seeping from the bullet hole in his stomach. His voice came in a gasp now, "The chamber will not be found."

A moment passed, and the Indian just lay there silently, looking at the ceiling with his hands on his belly, covered in the oozing crimson.

"Nooo!" Tommy yelled. Adrenaline took over as he broke the grasp of the guards and rushed toward the kneeling Ulrich.

The move seemed to catch the killer off guard for a moment as the crazed prisoner's shoulder plowed squarely into the man's right arm, jarring the gun from his hand. It clacked onto the hard carpet floor and tumbled a few feet away. Startled into action, the two guards pried the wildly swinging Tommy off of the blond before he could strike back.

One of the flattops bear hugged him into submission while the shorter one proceeded to punch him viciously in the midsection. Tommy lost his breath, and his body's natural reaction was to double over, but with the far stronger arms holding him up, his body couldn't reach the position it desired for relief. Another fist slammed into his jaw, causing the world to spin recklessly out of control. The guard released his grip, and unconsciousness teased him for a moment as he lay sprawled out on the floor.

Ulrich had recovered from the attack and was now standing over him. Through his captor's legs, he could see the huddled mass of the park ranger leaning against the wall. The man's chest still moved up and down, but a considerable pool of blood was collecting around his body. He held something in his right hand, unseen by the attackers. It looked like a cell phone.

"That was an unwise move, Thomas." Ulrich said, still standing over Tommy. "Why should I not do to you the same as I did to him?" His arm gestured carelessly toward the heaped Indian in the corner.

Tommy coughed, his breath returning. A thin line of blood streamed from his lip as he rose to his knees. He wiped the blood with the top of his hand. "You know why. I'm the only one that can help you find the chambers." Another cough racked his body and kept him on one knee.

During the punching session, Ulrich had recovered the gun from the floor and was now holding it level with Tommy's chest. "For now, Thomas, for now." He glanced over at the bloody mass by the doors. "Let's move."

Ulrich stopped by the body on the floor and turned around. "We will go to the church. Perhaps we will find a clue there."

"Maybe we should look some more here," Tommy tried to stall, hoping the Indian had got through to the police on the phone.

"And wait around for the authorities to find us? I don't think so. Move." He flicked the gun toward the door in a commanding motion.

Standing at the exit, Ulrich poked his head out to make sure the path was clear. No one stood in the lobby. The only movement in the open room was the slow revolution of a ceiling fan that hung from the exposed wooden ceiling. They slipped out of the doorway, careful to make sure there were no other visitors to the museum that might suddenly pop out of a restroom or some other area. The last thing they needed at this point was to be careless.

43

BLUE RIDGE MOUNTAINS

"I got nothin' over here," Will stood, looking at the caged rocks with a beleaguered look on his face.

Fifteen feet away, Morris, too, was deeply studying the soapstone paintings, unsure at what he was looking and even less certain what he was looking for. "Yeah, me either," he replied.

The two detectives had arrived shortly after leaving the site where the car had gone off the side of the mountain. Upon arriving, they had gone to the park ranger's office up the road and asked him a few questions.

The ranger had been less than helpful. After being asked if he had seen anyone in the area that morning, the ranger had said, "No. I ain't seen anybody up here today, but I didn't get to the office 'til an hour or so ago. Ain't like I gotta clock in." The old ranger's saggy skin shook as he let out a hearty laugh at his last comment. He then pinched a wad of snuff and carefully placed it in the pouch of his bottom lip. Both cops had looked at each other with a disgusted glance.

Now they were standing in the shadow of the highest summit in the state and didn't have a clue why. The ranger had begrudgingly told them the history and a few of the theories concerning the large boulders, but nothing had been much more informative than what the people in the diner had told them.

"Do you think that maybe this is just an ancient prank by a bunch of Indian teenagers from three hundred years ago? You know. They were sitting around getting high off some wacky tobacky one day and decided to do a little graffiti on some big rocks? Thought it would be a hoot and voila, here we have it." Will's theory was more humorous than insightful, which actually helped, considering they were finding more dead ends everywhere they turned.

Save for their cars, the parking lot across the field was empty. "Guess they don't get a lot of traffic up here on the weekdays." Trent's comment was as pointless as it was true.

Will didn't respond. He just continued looking at the rocks with an odd fascination.

Morris went on, "If they *were* here, they either didn't find what they were looking for, or they found it quick."

"What if they didn't come here?"

It was certainly a possibility. "Okay. Let's review," he started as he turned to head back to the vehicles. Will took the signal and joined him walking across the grass. "What reason would Sean Wyatt have for getting rid of Schultz?"

"Money," Will stated. "He would have complete control of the IAA and its finances. And they have a ton of money."

"Right. But doesn't the timing just seem really odd?"

"How so?"

Morris looked off into the trees, watching the wind push around the leaves. The dense forest was alive with critters of several types busily gathering their stores for the winter.

"I've been thinking about this since we left the McElroy place. Tommy was about to have a press conference. What was it for?"

"Nobody is really sure. But the rumor is that he'd been looking for something big. Speculation was he found it or something to do with it."

Trent stopped walking for a second. They were standing at the edge of the parking lot near a light pole. "Yeah. So, what, exactly, was it that he was looking for?"

His younger partner looked thoughtful for a minute. "I don't know," he finally answered with a shrug. "Did you hear something?"

Trent nodded slowly. "I didn't hear much. But I did hear something about Schultz looking for some huge treasure, had to do with some golden rooms or something. Now, I don't know anything about that kind of stuff, but that is what I heard."

"Golden Chambers?" Will appeared clueless.

"Yeah. Beats me. Sounds like another city of gold hunt to me. But from what I did hear, it sure seemed like it would be the discovery of a lifetime.

"The other thing I heard was that it is some kind of ancient Native American treasure."

"So you think that's what this is all about?"

"Schultz finds something and sets up a press conference. He goes missing. A professor who is a friend and contemporary gets killed. Now it seems like his best friend, our prime suspect, is visiting historic Native American sites with an expert in ancient Indian history. Then, Wyatt gets himself into a high-speed shootout with two unidentified gunmen. If I was a betting man, I would say Wyatt is looking for whatever it was that Schultz was onto, and someone doesn't want him to find it."

"All right, I'm listening," Will replied. "But what does that mean? Are you saying that Wyatt isn't behind all of this?

"No. He's still at the top of my list." Trent smirked, "Okay, he is the list. But something just doesn't seem right about this whole scenario." Bracing his shoulder against the light pole, he reached down to tie a shoelace that had become undone.

As he finished tying the knot, something on the ground caught his attention. Half-doubled over, Trent reached down and picked up the metal cylinder. He looked at the object and then started scanning the parking area, suddenly more alert.

"Is that a bullet casing?" Will asked as he stepped closer to see what Morris had found.

Trent nodded, flipping the small cylinder to his partner, who caught it with one hand. "Nine millimeter."

It only took them a second before they started noticing the shells lying around on the pavement. "They're everywhere."

"Another shootout?" the younger cop posed.

"Sure looks like it." Bending at his knees, Detective Morris stared closer at the light pole he'd just been leaning against only a few moments before. He removed a pen from his jacket and scraped a mark on the metal. Then he looked down and found another mark, this one on the concrete base of the metal post.

Will stepped over to see what his partner had found. "These shots came from over there," he pointed back across toward the other side of the parking lot.

Nodding, Trent stood and walked with him about thirty feet away, both sets of eyes closely examining the ground for more clues. "There are some more," he stated, as if the bullet casings were right where they belonged.

Both cops bent down to see the remnants from the firefight. "Forty cal," Will confirmed.

"Yeah," Morris agreed. "There was definitely an exchange of fire here."

"So, my question is this: Who was doing the shooting? There must have been a second group involved that wasn't part of the shootout on the road."

"No way to know that right now, but we do know they were here." He looked down the road that went up over the hill from the way they'd come just a few minutes earlier. There were two spots with heavy concentrations of empty bullet shells in separate locations. If Sean Wyatt was involved with this whole thing, then someone else didn't want him there. "We need to find out exactly what it was that Tommy Schultz was looking for and what he found."

"The guy was secretive, didn't really tell anybody what he was doing except for Wyatt and Borringer. And I don't think either one of them are going to be very helpful at the moment."

Trent nodded. "There has to be someone else who knows what he was up to. I find it hard to believe that he was traveling around all over the state on some treasure hunt, and no one knew what he was looking for."

Aggravation had reached its boiling point. He took a few deep breaths and ran his hands over his head from front to back and then to the top where he stopped and dropped them back down to his hips, exasperated. "Every time it seems we've found something that will help us, more questions pop up."

Will just stood quietly, letting his partner vent. They may have been a relatively new pair, but the young cop already knew enough not to say anything when Trent was frustrated.

Detective Morris was at his wit's end. With resignation on his face, he turned and said, "Let's get out of here."

"Where we goin', boss?" Will threw his arms up, not yet ready to give up the search.

"Back to Atlanta," his voice was resolute. "We'll search every scene again. Maybe something will turn up."

"Trent," Will pleaded, "maybe we should double check here. There's got to be some kind of clue that could show us where they went."

Morris shook his head. "I appreciate your enthusiasm, but this wild goose chase has gone on long enough. Wyatt has disappeared. We're not experts in archaeology or ancient mysteries. You heard the park ranger. People from all over the world have been coming here for decades trying to interpret those stones, and not a single one of them has been able to do it. You and I probably couldn't get any more out of those drawings than a three-year-old."

That last part was a good point, Will thought. "So we're just going to head back and retrace our steps?"

"Unless you got a better idea or someone that can tell us where the hell those guys went...yeah."

There was nothing Will could say. He just shook his head.

"Then we head back." Trent pulled his keys from inside of his pants pocket as he strode angrily toward the Charger. Will was on the other side of the cars, opening his own door when the cell phone in Morris's pocket began ringing.

"Jeez, what is it now?" He reached into the coat and pulled out the silver phone. After a quick glance at the caller ID, he slid the phone open and said, "This is Morris," his voice sounded irritated.

"Detective Morris?" the man on the other end of the line clarified.

Maybe they didn't hear the way he answered the phone.

"Yes. This is Trent Morris. Who is this?"

From the sounds coming through the receiver, the caller must have been in a vehicle driving down the road. Even with all the background noise, he was still able to hear the answer. "This is Sean Wyatt."

44

BLUE RIDGE MOUNTAINS

Detective Morris stood next to his car, dumbfounded. Wyatt had disappeared a little over twenty-four hours ago, which only made him seem more like the prime suspect. Yet here the man was, actually calling him.

"Sean," Trent started off with an overly friendly tone while inside, his mind raced. "You're a tough man to get ahold of. I had some more questions I needed to ask you."

The voice on the other end seemed unimpressed. "Well, sorry about that. Someone made it rather difficult to stay around."

"And who would that someone be?"

Will had closed his door when Trent motioned for him to come closer. He'd walked around the car quickly to see what was going on. Morris mouthed to him, "It's Wyatt."

Scribbling down the number of the cell phone that had appeared, he then handed it to the younger cop. Will knew exactly what to do and stepped away to a safe distance so Wyatt couldn't hear him speaking to the department on his own phone.

Sean replied coolly, "Check the bottom of the mountain near Brasstown. They should still be there."

"Oh?"

"Don't play coy with me, Morris. I'm sure you heard about that accident by now."

He decided to at least play along. "So, who were they?"

"How should I know? They didn't introduce themselves when they started shooting at us."

"Why don't you meet me, Sean? Then we can sort all this out. I'll come to you. Where are you right now?"

There was a pause on the other line. "Look, Detective. We just got shot at twice this morning. That makes three attacks since I talked to you the other day. No offense, but I am not sure exactly who I can trust at this point." His voice was emphatic.

"Yeah. I know. I don't blame you. But if you will meet up with me, maybe I can help you. We can figure it out..." Hesitation lingered in the phone's receiver. "What did they look like, the guys who were after you?"

There was something muffled on the other line, like Sean was giving directions to someone.

"What?" He clearly didn't hear the detective's question.

"I asked what the men who attacked you looked like."

"I gotta be honest, Trent. I didn't really stop to take a good look at the guys in the ravine. Probably woulda taken me a few hours and a lot of rope to do that." Obviously, killing the two passengers in the other car was something Sean felt was justified. "But the other guys later on...yeah, I got a real good look at them. Two of them looked like they were twins, except that one was taller than the other. Both of 'em had flattop haircuts and wore matching suits like they were some pop star's bodyguards."

On a pad of paper he'd removed from his car, Trent was busily taking down a few notes about the men who had supposedly attacked his main suspect. "Anyone else?"

"The guy who was holding Tommy was tall, probably several inches over six feet. He had blond hair. Dressed like he was going to a trendy nightclub or something. Very European."

This last bit of information came as a bit of a shock. "Did you say a tall, blond European guy?"

"I don't know if he was European. Just said he dressed like it. You know, like a German or something. I couldn't get close enough to ask him where he was from or how he came to America."

Again with the sarcasm, Morris thought. "We had reports of a guy named Jurgenson that was posing as one of our own running around town."

"Yeah, Mrs. Borringer said that he came by."

Another shock. "You went to Borringer's house?"

"Yep." Sean decided not to share the drama that had unfolded the night before when they had been hidden in the bathroom while the detective was downstairs.

"When was that?"

Ignoring the question, Sean began again, "Look, Detective, all I know is this guy is bad news. I'm not sure if he is the one who is pulling all the strings, but it sure seems probable. If I had to put my money on it, I'd say he was the one that killed Frank."

"What happened during the firefight with those men?" Morris continued to string the conversation out.

"I put a couple of rounds directly into the flattop twins, right in their chests."

"They dead?"

"No," Sean sounded irritated. "Pretty sure they had vests on. Makes me wonder how available those things are to the general public."

It was a well-known rumor that some less-than-ethical police were selling some of their equipment on the black market to drug dealers and gangsters, something that seemed to happen in nearly every major city. Trent ignored the implication. "I'll look into it. But there are a lot of places to get those things now days. What about the blond, Jurgenson?"

"Don't know. Didn't hit him. He was using Tommy as a human shield."

"How did they get away?" Morris felt like he was asking a lot of questions, but the longer he kept Wyatt on the line, the easier it would be to triangulate his cell phone signal. He hoped that whoever Will was talking with was working quickly.

"They drove."

"Of course." Trent set himself up on that one. "But you don't know where they were going?"

"Hard to say. We're trying to figure that out at the moment." It was a half lie.

Trent paused a moment, trying to think of what to say next. He looked over at Will, who was mouthing that they had not got a location on the signal yet.

"Listen, Sean. Why don't you meet up with me, and we can try to figure this out together. I'll meet you wherever," his voice sounded uncertain, and he was starting to repeat himself.

There was no reaction from the other end of the phone line for a few contemplative seconds. Then, "No can do, Detective. We're too far away from the city at this point, and we can't afford to lose any more time. For all we know, they may have killed Tommy and left him in a ditch. I don't think those people will kill him until they have what it is they are looking for. But I can't risk it."

"And what is it that they are looking for?"

"Sorry, Detective. My phone is...what did you..." The connection started cutting out.

"Sean. Can you hear me? Sean?"

"We...mountains..." Then the line went dead.

Trent pounded the phone in his fist. "Did you get the signal?" he looked pleadingly at his partner.

Will shook his head. "No."

"Why not? It shouldn't have taken that long." Morris was boiling at this point.

"I dunno, man. Maybe he has some kind of signal isolator on his phone. But HQ said they were having problems locking onto it." He stood next to his car with arms open, as if begging for forgiveness.

"It's not your fault," Morris sighed.

Sunlight poured down on the two of them as they stood next to their cars, wondering what the next move should be. Suddenly, his phone rang again. "Sean?" he answered the phone without looking at the caller ID.

"Is this Detective Morris?" It was a woman's voice.

"Yes," he said dejectedly as his shook his head at his partner to indicate it wasn't who they'd hoped.

"My name is Marla Tinsley. I work at the public library in Dahlonega."

Trent looked over at Will with an eyebrow raised, wondering what this call was about.

"Yes, ma'am," he responded politely. "What can I do for you?"

"Well," she began, "About an hour ago, an odd little group of people came into the library here wantin' to use the computer. We are a public library, ya know. So, I pointed them to the computers that we have available so they could get what they needed. I figured they wanted to use the Internet. Hardly ever get people in here doin' research with books anymore."

Her nostalgic demeanor was wasting his time.

Morris tried to be patient with her, not quite sure where this was going. "Ma'am, you said there was a group that came into your library? What did they look like?"

The woman sounded irritated at his disinterest in the walk down memory lane. "Well, there was a girl and two men. She was kinda tall with brown, curly hair. One of the guys was probably in his late twenties or early thirties. The other man seemed to probably be in his forties. Hard to say about him."

Trent's interest was piqued. There was no way his luck could be this good. "What did these people want?"

"Said all they needed was to use one of the computers. I told them to go ahead. Seemed harmless enough. But something seemed mighty suspicious about 'em."

"What did they need a computer for?"

"Didn't tell me. But they did have a digital camera that they hooked up to it. Overheard them talking about stones and ancient Indian symbols."

He'd been staring at the ground, concentrating on listening to what the woman was saying, but when he heard this last little fragment, his eyes shot up to his partner. "We got something," he mouthed silently.

"Can you tell me what they found?" He went back to the lady on the phone.

A moment of quiet came over the line before she answered. "Yeah, the older guy started looking at this Indian painting that we have hanging up. He was gazin' at it for a couple of minutes before something musta struck him about it. They talked for a few minutes about what it meant. The picture must be real old, been here as long as I have. Anyway, something about that painting made them real excited. They went back over to the computer for another minute or two and then started talking about the old Cherokee capital."

"Cherokee capital?"

"Yeah. They said something about going to a place called Red Clay. Sounded like that anyway. Never heard of it myself. As soon as they walked out the door, though, I called Sheriff Jenkins's office. For all I know, they coulda just been travelers passin' through, but like I said, something struck me funny about 'em. A few minutes later, the sheriff put me through to Atlanta, and that's how I came to talking with you."

Morris had been busily writing down notations of what the old lady had been saying. He had to really focus on what she was saying in her thick Southern drawl to make sure that he got all the details right. "Was the man in his thirties tall, dirty-blond hair, blue or gray eyes?"

"Yep. That was him." There was no hesitation from the other end. "They in some sort of trouble?"

"We just want to ask them some questions, ma'am," he said politely without giving away what was going on. The last thing he wanted was a rumor going around Dahlonega that there were fugitives on the loose. If that news spread too quickly, they might never find Wyatt.

"Did you happen to catch any names of the people in this group?" He was merely looking for absolute confirmation at this point.

"Yeah. They were calling the older one Mac. I think the younger guy's name was Sean." She thought for a moment. "Didn't catch the girl's name."

"Thank you, ma'am, for the information. You've been a big help."

He hung up the phone in the middle of her saying, "You're welcome."

Sliding the phone back into his pocket, he said, "We're going to a place called Red Clay."

"What's that?" Will was lost as to what had just transpired.

"We got a witness up in Dahlonega that says Wyatt and McElroy are headed there. I don't know where it is, but apparently it used to be the site of the old capital of the Cherokee Nation."

"How far is it?" Will asked, again opening his door.

"Don't know. But we're about to find out."

Trent hopped into the Charger and searched for Red Clay on the car's navigational system. A minute later, he said, "We can be there in an hour."

The car tore out of the parking lot, spinning bullet casings in its wake.

45

BLUE RIDGE MOUNTAINS

"Very good. You may hang up the phone now."

Marla Tinsley stood behind her desk, staring at the two strangers, a man and a woman. The librarian hung up the receiver carefully. "What is this all about?" she asked, terrified. "We don't have any money in here. What is it you want?"

"Nothing." The brunette's cold reply was punctuated by a puff of smoke from the barrel of a silencer.

Fear turned to shock on Tinsley's face as two more quiet clicks sent bullets ripping into her chest. Her legs buckled beneath her, and she collapsed to the ground.

The woman with the gun stepped quickly around behind the counter and stood over the victim. Tinsley's shirt had quickly become soaked in red as flowers of blood bloomed from the black holes. A thin matching line streaked from her lips.

With troubling ease, the woman in black raised her weapon once more and fired a final shot into the librarian's head. Then she turned to the man who'd accompanied her. "Call the Prophet. Give him the update."

"Yes, Ma'am." He had started to retrieve his cell phone from his jacket when he stopped and turned back to her. "Should I tell him about this one?" A gloved finger pointed toward the body.

She gave him a look that he understood meant "No." "Just tell him we are still observing. Nothing else."

He nodded and pressed the talk button.

Stepping across the body, she made her way toward the front window of the library. Outside the glass, the little town only presented a few wayward pedestrians, none of them seeming aware of what was transpiring within.

She heard her assistant finishing up a short conversation with their boss. He would certainly not be pleased to know that they had killed the librarian, which was why he didn't need to know about it. She was an innocent stranger, but she was also a loose end. And loose ends were never a good thing.

Her assistant walked up and stood next to her, putting the phone back in his jacket pocket.

She continued looking out the large window. "What did he say?" she asked even though she knew the answer.

"Just to continue on observing." He glanced over at her, not sure what she was thinking.

"We know where they are going from here. Let's just try to make sure there are fewer contacts with random people between here and the goal. I'd prefer not to leave a blood trail wherever we go." She gave a quick glance over her shoulder toward the area where the body lay.

He nodded in agreement.

"Okay," she said after another moment. "Let's go. We don't want them to get too far ahead of us.

The two stepped across the threshold and onto the sidewalk outside. A bright sun beat down on their black outfits, warming their bodies against the chilly autumn air.

No one around even noticed as they slipped into their black sedan and drove off.

46

SOUTHEASTERN TENNESSEE

Sean and Allyson stood waiting at the information desk in the welcome center of Red Clay State Park. Since they'd arrived, no park worker had been seen. Joe had lingered in the entryway, checking text messages, more than likely, from an angry Mrs. McElroy.

Time was of the utmost value, and the absence of someone who could provide useful information would certainly be a hindrance.

Allyson breached the silence. "Should we just take a look around? We've been standing here for five minutes." Her patience was obviously running thin.

"Sounds like a plan," Sean concurred. "Hey, Joe, let's see what we can find."

McElroy nodded and flipped his phone closed, sliding it into a front pants pocket.

Sean pointed to a pair of large double doors close to them at an opposing wall. A blue sign marked *Exhibit* hung above the museum entrance. "Let's try in there first."

Upon entering the display room, they noticed an acrid odor that filled the room. It was distinctly different than what a museum normally smelled like.

"Something isn't right here." Instinctively, Sean reached for his weapon. He was thankful that Joe kept a secret stash of ammunition in the tool box of the pickup truck.

Cautiously, he held the weapon at his side as he crept past the display boxes and pictures. At the corner of the false wall that divided the two rooms of the exhibit, he stopped and signaled the others to do the same.

Joe and Allyson had detected the smell, too, but they weren't sure what was going on, so they obeyed, halting short of where Sean stood.

Sean warily peered around the edge of the wall down the other corridor of the small museum. That's when he saw it.

The body of the park's keeper lay motionless on its side in the corner of the room near the exit. Thick puddles of blood spread out underneath his form, the liquid seeping slowly into the thin carpet.

After seeing the man on the floor, Sean rushed over to the scene with Allyson and Joe confusedly following behind. As they rounded the wall, the two beheld what had caused Wyatt's change of demeanor.

"Looks like they're still a step ahead of us," Joe commented grimly as he arrived at the exit.

"Yeah," Sean nodded with a sigh. He reached down and checked for the man's pulse on the darkly tanned neck, but felt nothing. "He's gone."

Allyson had seen bodies before. It was something you had to be able to cope with if you were going to work for the agency. Still, she had never truly grown comfortable with it. "Why would they do this?" she wondered aloud.

Both men shook their heads. "Either this Jurgenson felt like the ranger knew too much, or the guy tried something." Sean squatted down to one knee, examining the multiple gunshot wounds. "Or maybe he could ID them, and that made him another loose end that had to be tied. At any rate, the police haven't been here yet."

"Which means we better get the heck out of Dodge," Joe finished.

"Right." Sean began to stand when he noticed one of the ranger's hands clutching something. A cell phone. Cautiously, he reached down and pried the device from the dead man's fingers, afraid that the police or perhaps a park visitor would burst through the door at any moment.

Then something else caught his attention. In the corner of the room was a small display pedestal with a glass case surrounding a vase. Taking a quick step over to the pottery, he examined it with a look of distant recognition.

Joe, too, became curious with the artifact. "You know what that looks like?"

"It seems like I have seen it somewhere before, but I can't place it."

"Looks like Vessel Number One to me."

"Weeden Island stuff?"

"Yeah. But I didn't realize they had anything like that in this museum." Joe frowned while examining the piece.

"There's no information about where it came from or who found it either."

"Guys," Allyson cut in, "I don't mean to interrupt, but there is a dead boy in the room, so if you don't mind hurrying up your discussion a little..."

Ignoring her for a second, Sean went on, "I wonder if this vase is the next clue."

"Would make sense," Joe agreed. "It's the only thing in the room that doesn't fit with any of the other artifacts. Sure is curious. I'll say that."

Even after a few closer looks, though, Sean was unsure what clue the vase could hold. Unfortunately, they didn't have a lot of time to analyze the artifact. "I wish there was some kind of information about this thing."

Sean looked at Joe and shook his head, turning his attention back to the phone. They wondered if the dead man had called for help before his demise. Surely not. If such a call had been placed, the authorities would already be on the scene.

He pressed a button that illuminated the small screen. Instead of pulling up a menu, though, what appeared to be an unsent text message flashed onto the display. An odd message, Sean thought. The message read, *Beacon.*

Joe came closer to see what had grabbed his friend's attention. "Beacon?" he wondered out loud. "What's that supposed to mean?"

Allyson was baffled. "Why would the ranger leave a message like that on his phone if he was dying? Seems like he would have called 911."

"Not sure, but we can't stick around here to figure it out," he answered with growing concern then motioned toward the door and placed the phone back in the curled hand of the park ranger.

The three made their way out of the exhibit room and into the main lobby, heading to the front entrance. Sean reached the inner door to the building first and started to open it when he froze in his tracks. Outside, in the parking lot, two county police cars had pulled into a few empty spaces thirty or so feet away from their own vehicle.

"What?" Allyson asked.

"Police are here," he responded pseudo-calmly.

"But how did they...?" Joe started to ask, but Sean cut him off by motioning for the group to move back into the building. Fortunately, the glass doors to the Information Center were tinted, so seeing people inside from the parking lot was nearly impossible. Sean looked from right to left, trying to find an alternate exit. There was a set of stairs to the right of the information desk, an option he didn't like because it immediately cornered them in whatever was on the second floor.

To the left was a door underneath the word *Theater.* Thinking that most theaters had exits, Sean quickly said, "In there."

The door to the movie room closed behind them a split second before the two police reached the top of the porch outside.

It hardly seemed like much of a theater. There were four rows of auditorium style seats with a medium-sized screen on the wall in front. Sean stood near the doors for a moment, listening closely. When he heard the inner of the two front doors to the building open, he quietly ushered the other two toward the front row. As he'd suspected, there was an exit near the front of the room.

Moving quickly, the three companions made their way beyond the seats over to the single door with the red *Exit* letters hanging over top of it. Upon reaching the door, Sean hesitated a moment. Some doors had automatic alarms on them so that in case of an emergency, a warning would sound throughout the rest of the building. As his hand pressed down on the handle, he hoped that this wasn't one of those.

The device clicked and opened easily into the early afternoon daylight. No alarm sounded as they slipped out of the building undetected and back around the front of the building to the truck.

47

SOUTHEASTERN TENNESSEE

F inding the Beacon Tabernacle proved to be easy enough thanks to the Hummer's navigational system. Fifteen minutes after leaving the state park, Big Guard whipped the SUV into the parking lot of the church. There must have been a thousand words to describe what the men in the car were thinking as they stared at the monstrous building. But silent awe was all that was projected.

The Beacon Tabernacle was situated in a valley of rolling hills right on the crest of a slight rise. From the parking area, the view of the surrounding mountains and hillsides was serenely beautiful. Patches of orange, red, and yellow forest dotted the landscape, the trees' leaves on fire for the season. In between the dense cropping of woods, a few small farms dotted the land.

Tommy looked around at the scenery. "They sure picked a nice spot," he whispered to himself. No words had been spoken since they had left the museum. He was still in disbelief at the brutal manner in which Ulrich had killed the innocent park worker.

Still, something about the Indian seemed as if he had been prepared, almost looking forward to the whole thing, like it was part of a bigger plan.

Ulrich and the two guards exited the SUV and also took a brief glance around. Their reason for looking was more to make sure no one had followed rather than to appreciate the stunning visuals.

A solitary gray pickup truck sat quietly outside the entrance. He assumed the vehicle belonged to the church's sexton. Most churches didn't require a person to work during the week, due mostly to the small number of people using it. This building, though, boasted more than three thousand patrons. Despite its large seating capacity, the church was forced to offer three services during the mornings just to accommodate everyone.

The four men cautiously approached the building. Unlike many churches in the South and Northeast that were essentially boxes that angled up to a point in the roof with a steeple at the front, the Beacon Tabernacle was most certainly a unique piece of architecture. Not cathedral-like either, its roof gradually rose to one side of the building and then dropped off dramatically. And there was no steeple, only three steel beams of varying heights precariously placed off to the side of the entrance on a separate patch of landscaping.

Another interesting point of note was the lack of crosses. Most Christian churches he'd seen had several crucifixes decorating windows, doorways, pretty much everything. It seemed odd that there were none at this location. In fact, the building seemed to be missing many stereotypical decorative items of Christianity. Two rows of slender stained glass windows decorated the pale brick walls of the exterior. But even though the sheer size of the place was impressive, the design itself seemed somewhat simple, almost made to look plain.

The shorter guard reached the large wooden doors of the church first and grabbed the brass handle. Apparently, the door weighed more than he expected, and the jerking motion pulled him off balance for a second. Slightly embarrassed, he held the door for the other three to walk in first.

Upon entering, the four men found themselves in something that completely offset the outside of the building. Just past the second set of large doors, the ceiling dramatically vaulted up into a five-story-high angled glass roof that extended the length of the room. On the other end of the vast atrium, a tiled staircase extended upward in front of elevator doors.

Even the usually stoic guards seemed impressed. The dumbfounded looks on their faces spoke to the fact that they had never seen anything quite like it. The church's lobby wasn't more amazing than the Sistine Chapel or any of the other great cathedrals of the world, but the striking beauty of the inside, when compared to the ordinary exterior of the building, truly was an amazing contrast.

As they stepped farther into the giant room, they saw an older man with a white head of hair at the other end of the mezzanine behind a welcome desk. He must have heard them enter because he was in the process of folding up his newspaper.

Ulrich's patience with allowing Tommy to ask the questions had seemed to wear thin, and he spoke directly to the church worker. "We are from out of town and heard of your church from our friend here. Would it be possible for us to look around?"

It was unbelievable. Was this the same man who had just gunned down an innocent park ranger not half an hour ago? Now his demeanor had done a complete 180. He spoke smoothly and politely to the old man and did not appear to have any desire to hurt him at all, like a snake waiting quietly in the grass.

"Certainly," the sexton replied. "Feel free to take a look around. The rooms and offices across the way there are closed for the day." His skin-and-bone hand extended toward the place about which he was speaking. "But you can go up the elevator to see the balcony, and you may take a look around in the main floor of the sanctuary as well." Thin lips pursed into a welcoming smile.

"Thank you," was all that Ulrich offered.

Five sets of stairs led into the main sanctuary. Above, a small chapel was situated on the second floor, the outside wall of which was covered by a spectacular painting of multiple scenes from Jesus's ministry. The pictorial history climaxed emotionally at the top with a depiction of the second coming. The canvas alone was at least fifteen feet in length and another eight feet wide.

Hurriedly, the four men moved toward the first set of stairs going into the inner lobby of the church. Once inside, several sets of windows allowed the faithful to see into the colossal main worship hall, probably to help the church members decide on a place to sit before actually walking through one of the four sets of wooden doors.

At the very front of the great auditorium, behind the pulpit, was one of the most impressive sights that Tommy had ever seen. The group slightly slowed their pace and passed through one of the doors on the left. Almost reverently, the group eased down the aisle toward a gigantic pipe organ that reached from the floor of the elevated stage to nearly three stories up to the wooden plank ceiling.

Its enormity wasn't the only thing that made the instrument so impressive though. Intricate wooden carvings decorated the beast from top to bottom. Trees, vines, flowers, birds, and other animals looked almost as if they could come to life from the wood into which they'd been carved.

Above them, the sanctuary opened up like a huge airplane hangar. The angled roof soared to its apex near the left wall then dropped off to a much lower point on the right. In the very back, the church balcony loomed with an additional several hundred seats and the control center for the sound and video systems.

Tommy's attention went back to the side walls of the church and the stained glass windows. From outside the tabernacle, the windows looked very dark, not quite black, and the colors were much duller. This made it difficult to see the details of the panes. But from the inside, the colors showed much more brilliantly. There were especially a lot of blues and reds used in the mosaic of jagged glasswork. And in each individual window, there were what seemed to be random white dots interspersed through the darker colors.

He let his eyes gaze at several of them before making his way, almost unconsciously, toward the stage and up its front steps. Closer up, the organ was even larger than he'd thought, with ladders and small platforms built up inside so maintenance workers could have easy access to the necessary spots.

Tommy turned to Ulrich, his mind leaving the instrument for a moment. "What do you expect to find here?"

Ulrich cocked his head, "That's why you are here, Mr. Schultz."

"I don't even know what to look for." He'd become exasperated. The events of the last few days had taken their toll, and his brain hurt from the emotional and mental roller coaster.

"Try."

Minutes went by. Tommy scanned the entire chamber, searching for something that could possibly be a clue. He could find nothing. No pictures, no words, not even any symbols that could be translated were to be found anywhere. And there was certainly nothing of any Indian influence to be seen.

Out of nowhere, the sexton appeared in a doorway near the base of the large stage. "Do you gentlemen have any questions or need help with anything?"

"Actually, sir," Tommy answered, "I do have a couple of questions."

"Yes?" The man looked happy to be able to help.

"I was curious about the size of this church. It seems fairly large for an area with such a small population. How did that happen?"

The old man smiled. "Originally, this church only had a dozen members or so. That was back in the mid-1800s. Shortly after the church was organized, the founding pastor came into a great deal of money. No one really knows where it came from. He claimed that the money had come from a generous donor who believed in the ministry of the church but who wanted to stay anonymous. Down through the years, the church has been remodeled and expanded many times to accommodate the growing numbers of members. Where you stand now is the result of the final renovation in the 1950s. Down in the basement areas, the original flooring and foundation still exist to this day."

"Would it be possible to get down there and see some of the original structure?"

A slight chuckle ensued. "Oh my, no. There is only one door that leads down into that area, and it is completely sealed off. Quite impossible to get down there."

"Why is it sealed off?"

"I have no idea. It seems to me that it would be an interesting part of the church's history to include that as part of the tour, but for some reason, it was closed up long ago, before this final version of the building was ever completed. If I had to guess, I would say there must be some kind of safety or insurance concern with having people in that area."

The answer seemed an honest one. Still, the mysterious origin of where the church got its money was never made clear.

"That organ," the sexton went on, "is the largest bellows-driven pipe organ in the eastern half of the United States and one of the biggest in the entire world." He must have noticed Ulrich and the two guards pretending to admire the massive instrument. They all gave the man a blank stare of disinterest.

"If I may," Tommy went back to the issue in his mind, "you said that nobody knew where the money originally came from?"

"That is correct, sir. Of course, now the church has a rather large number of members on its books, so money comes in regularly from tithes and offerings."

There was something suspicious about the story they were being told. Tommy believed the church worker was mostly telling the truth, but it seemed like the connection between the dead park ranger's story earlier and the way that this church seemed to thrive so quickly was more than just a mere coincidence. His eyes once again searched the room, trying to find something that would tip him as to how.

His gaze stopped on one of the colored windows. There was something different inside it.

The sexton seemed content to simply stand by and help answer any questions the strangers had. Clearly, he was bored with his job.

Tommy obliged him. "I do have another question to ask you. These rows of stained glass windows on the walls, where did they come from?"

"Ahh. I believe they were made somewhere in Spain. A very

specialized glassworks company created them, and they were shipped over here. It must have been a difficult thing to communicate back and forth with a company so far away about the specifications of the windows needed for the church."

As interesting as Tommy found the history of the windows, he was more concerned with the oddity in their appearance. "What I was really curious about was the white pieces of glass that seem to dot each window. Are they just there to throw in contrast with the dark colors, or is there another reason for them?"

The old man smiled. "I'm so glad you asked. You see," he explained, "those white pieces of glass are actually a tribute to one of the most revolutionary forms of communication ever developed."

Tommy and the other three stood waiting for clarification.

"The white dots of round glass inserted in the windows are actually Morse code."

"So the clue is in the windows." Tommy spoke a little louder than he'd intended.

The statement took the church worker off guard. "I'm sorry. Clue? What clue?"

He was given no answer. Instead, Ulrich began examining the windows as well, in an attempt to figure out what it all meant. The effort was short lived and futile though.

"What does it mean? How do you know where to begin?" Tommy asked.

A curious look came on the wrinkled face. "I'm not sure what you're so frantic about. It's just a Bible verse. It begins on that window, over there," he pointed to a window in the top of the front right corner of the sanctuary, "and reads all the way around, down to the next level, then finishes over there in the back."

Ulrich looked as if he'd just won the lottery. "The Bible verse, what does it say?" he demanded.

"It's just a text from Genesis. Many people around here know about it. Not like it's a secret."

More impatient now, Ulrich insisted, "Yes, but what does it say?"

The man appeared thrown off by the sudden change in temperament, but he replied anyway. "It's from Genesis 8, all taken from verses 7, 8, and 20."

"Show me."

The sexton raised his arm and pointed at a large Bible sitting on a stand directly below a raised baptismal pool. "Here, take a look." He shuffled over to the gargantuan book and flipped a few chunks of pages then, one by one until he found the right spot.

"See, have a look."

Ulrich and Tommy stepped up to the podium that held the huge book.

Verse 7: And he sent forth a raven, which went forth to and fro, until the waters were dried up from off the earth. Verse 8: Also, he sent forth a dove from him, to see if the waters were abated from off the face of the ground. Verse 20: Then Noah built an altar to the Lord.

"What is this? The raven and dove? What is that supposed to mean?"

Confused, the elderly man replied matter-of-factly, "Well, um, it is a kind of motto for this church, sir."

Ulrich was incredulous. "What do you mean a motto? What kind of motto is this for anything?"

"Well," he was stuttering at this point, unsure about why it mattered so much to this foreign visitor. "Our church is called the Beacon Tabernacle. A beacon is a type of guide, in a manner of speaking. So, the designers of the building thought it appropriate to use this verse because the raven and the dove were used to guide Noah to dry land."

"That's it?" Ulrich stepped over to the old sexton and grabbed him by the shirt and tie and lifted him with both arms, pressing him against the wall beneath the baptism. "Answer me, old man. Is that all you know?"

A look of innocent fear swept across the sexton's face, replacing the confusion that had been there. His voice scratched as a result of the fists cutting off his breath just below the neck. "I...don't...know what you...want me to tell...you. The church represents the altar that Noah built. What else do you want to know?"

Strong hands clenched tighter around the man's thin neck, and the pale, wrinkled skin began turning a slight reddish-purple color.

"What are you doing? You're hurting him!" Tommy yelled but was restrained by the strong grips of the guards.

Ulrich turned as if to say, "I don't care," when suddenly, another familiar voice filled the sanctuary.

"Put him down!"

Both of the guards looked instinctively over to an open doorway where a man with hair that almost matched his dark-khaki pants stood holding a pistol in the direction of their boss.

Turning his head toward where the voice had come from, Ulrich glared at the new threat that dared interrupt his interrogation. At first, his eyes went immediately to the drawn weapon in the man's hands, aimed squarely at him. After a moment, though, he focused on the person holding the gun.

Sean Wyatt had caught up to them. Again.

48

SOUTHEASTERN TENNESSEE

For a long moment, everyone stood frozen in a stalemate. Ulrich and Wyatt glared at each other as if waiting to see who would make the first move. Even though it must have only been half a minute, it felt like an eternity.

Sean wasn't willing to risk a shot, afraid the old man might get hurt.

The two guards stood at the ready, each holding Tommy tightly, also making them difficult targets.

"So, Mr. Wyatt," Ulrich broke the silence. "You just won't seem to go away." Then in one quick, fluid motion, he grabbed the sexton and jerked him around like a rag doll, clenching the old man around the neck with his arm.

"Most people think of it as an endearing trait." Sean kept the gun trained on the blond assailant.

Ulrich snickered, "Hardly the time for joking." With another swift movement, he pulled his own pistol out and pressed it hard against the side of the old man's head.

Though Sean had surprised the group, he was at a major disadvantage. He could see Joe and Allyson crawling behind the cover of one of the church pews on the other side of the sanctuary. That evened the numbers a little, but now the bad guys had two hostages, and the risk of hitting one of them was too high at the moment.

"So tell me, Sean. How did you find us here?" Ulrich was talking again.

"It was dumb luck really." Sean edged slowly behind the nearest church pew. He didn't want to be a completely exposed target. "That park ranger you killed left a message on his cell phone that said, Beacon. After leaving the museum, I did a quick search on the navigation system in the car. The only thing within twenty miles with the word beacon in it was this church. I figured it was worth a shot."

"How fortuitous."

Ulrich leveled the pistol with a quick snap of his wrist and fired off two quick volleys that erupted into splinters in the pew right in front of Wyatt. The quick action by the blond man had sent Sean sprawling to the floor below the bench seat. Another shot sounded from somewhere else as a bullet thudded into the wood above his head. One of the guards must have started firing.

On his elbows and knees, Sean scurried across the carpet to the end of the row. Leading with his gun, he peeked around the corner of the bench and saw that the larger guard was holding Tommy while the shorter held his weapon at the ready, looking to the end of the pew where he'd just fired.

Across the aisle, Joe and Allyson were crouched in a similar position. Sean gave a quick motion of the hand for his companions to give some cover fire.

Allyson acknowledged the request and surprised the two suits with a volley of her own, careful not to hit the hostages. Her rounds narrowly missed the stocky attacker.

Joe was a good shot with long-range weapons as evidenced by his success as a big game hunter. But smaller weapons were a whole different animal, and bullets wildly splashed around the feet of the three men on the stage, a few pinging off the metal of the pipes behind them.

Allyson gave him a stern look as she pulled him back below the pew. "Why don't you let me handle this?"

"Probably a good idea."

Ulrich and the guard both turned their attention to where the new shots had originated.

"I see you brought some friends, Mr. Wyatt." Ulrich launched another bullet toward their position.

As poor as Joe's aim was, the distraction was exactly what Sean had needed. Both enemies appeared confused as to where to concentrate their aim.

Sean rounded the corner of the pew again, kneeling as he squeezed off three quick bursts of his own. One bullet harmlessly lodged into his target's Kevlar vest, another completely missed, but the third found its way into the thick upper thigh.

Suddenly in pain and bleeding, the henchman dropped to the ground, momentarily letting his gun drop at his side.

From his position, Ulrich couldn't see anyone, so he sent four shots in both directions, pinning Allyson and Sean under the cover of the church benches. The pungent smell of gunpowder lingered with the smoke that was beginning to fill the air.

The shorter guard was still on one knee and trying to stand as blood oozed from the wound in his leg. He lifted his weapon slowly, hoping to return fire if Wyatt popped out again.

Instead of poking around the edge of the seat, Sean slid underneath it and took a quick aim, only pulling the trigger once.

The guard noticed Wyatt's new position too late. For a second, the stump of a man had a surprised look on his face. His eyes stared forward, blankly. Then the black hole in his forehead began trickling red liquid down his nose seconds before he fell forward and down the steps.

Ulrich's head turned toward the dead body of his associate as it rolled to a stop at the base of the stage. He pointed the barrel at where the mortal shot had come from and unleashed another quick succession of rounds.

The larger guard who had previously been occupied with Tommy was forced to join the fray. With an almost superhuman strength, the bulky man seized Tommy with one hand and fired his weapon with the other. His .45-caliber resonated louder than everyone else's, thundering explosions off the walls as he fired.

With one bad guy down, the fight was a little more even, but the hostages still made things dicey. "Just let the men go, Jurgenson or whoever you are!" Sean yelled from behind the church pew. "It's over! The police are on their way here right now! And you don't have many more bullets left in that gun."

"I don't believe you would call the police, Sean. Besides, *you* are the one they are looking for." As he answered, his eyes checked out two closed doors with an exit sign over them about twenty feet away. The guard looked over and noticed Ulrich had motioned with his head to follow out the exit.

The big man nodded his silent acknowledgement and popped off two quick shots at both Allyson's and Sean's hiding places. Then immediately, he dragged Tommy by the neck across the stage and down the steps, right behind the tall blond.

"What do we do?" Joe mouthed across the aisle.

"I don't know," Sean replied. "I can't get a clean shot."

Allyson shook her head. She had no angle either.

Suddenly, a muffled shot came from somewhere else in the building. It sounded like the front corner of the sanctuary.

Sean risked a look over top of the pew he'd been hiding behind and saw the empty stage. His stomach turned at the realization.

Rising up from his cover, he scanned the corners and crevices of the church, keeping his gun leveled. They were gone.

Allyson stood too, mimicking Sean's position. "Where did they go?"

Through the ghostlike smoke, Sean noticed the doors at the front of the sanctuary.

They sprinted toward the exit, stopping short to risk a peek in a small square window at the top of the thick wood. Through the opening, Wyatt could see a small antechamber on the other side. There was a short bench, a water fountain, a flowery-upholstered couch, and two legs with black shoes sticking out from around a corner.

Sean pushed open the door, leading the way with his gun. He

rounded the corner of the small room and found the sexton lying on the floor. The chest of the man's white button-up shirt was beginning to soak with blood. Just beyond where he lay, the short hall ended abruptly with two more doors leading outside into the parking lot.

Joe took a knee next to Sean, who was crouching over the old man. Allyson ran over to the outer doors, holding her weapon next to her face while she peeked out the window.

"You...must not...let them find the chamber," the sexton gasped.

"Just hang on there, old timer," Joe replied. "You're gonna be just fine."

Allyson was grabbing her cell phone to call 911.

The old man kept talking, "We have kept the secret long enough." His body racked with a cough, and a small trickle of blood seeped from the corner of this mouth. "They are too close now. You must...go to where the raven and the dove meet. Do not...let them succeed."

Allyson was talking on her cell. "Yeah, we have a man with a gunshot wound at the Beacon Tabernacle. Send an ambulance right away. He's in the front of the building in a room off near the stage entrance. Address? I don't know the address. Just hurry." She ended her call and rejoined the group.

"Where the raven and the dove meet," the old man continued. "That is where you will find it. The first chamber...it..." his eyes grew wide with fear, and he gripped Sean's arms tightly. "You must not allow them to find the next stone."

"But where is it? Where is the stone?"

"The raven...and the dove face each other. Let their stones guide you...they meet in the middle. The altar...you must find the...key. Climb the stairs...of Heaven."

With that, the man's head went limp, and his eyes closed. Joe laid the gray head down gently on the floor. "Poor old guy."

"He's not dead." Sean pointed at the bony chest slowly rising and falling. "Just unconscious. There's nothing we can do for him now. Cops should be here soon. If we don't get out of here now, we may never catch those guys."

"We can't just leave him here, Sean."

"Allyson called an ambulance. They will arrive any minute. If the police get here before we're gone, we will get arrested and have no chance of saving Tommy."

Joe seemed to consider it for a second.

"Look, Mac. You heard what the man said. He wants us to find the chamber. We have to go."

Nodding, Sean's friend stood up, a look of resolve on his face. "Let's go get 'em then."

"Right."

The two men darted to the door with Allyson right behind. Sean eased open the heavy portal carefully. The asphalt was empty except for the beat-up Silverado and what they assumed to be the sexton's car.

Once again, the men who'd abducted Tommy had slipped through their fingers.

"Got any idea where they went?" Allyson asked as she put away her gun.

"Yeah, I do now."

49

NEVADA

A handful of afternoon guests sat busily on the veranda of the palatial mansion. They chatted about investments, the economy, and the various properties they had acquired or sold in recent weeks.

Hardly a hot-dog-and-beer crowd, most sipped on rare scotch, top-shelf vodka, and well-aged whiskey. Smoke from a few cigars wisped around, spiraling up and into the open air of dusk.

The host of the party stood near the outdoor bar sipping on a glass of twelve-year-old Jameson Irish whiskey. It wasn't the most expensive of drinks, but it was by far his favorite. Smooth and warm, it was his regular drink of choice.

He had been chatting with his colleagues, but something was keeping him on edge. In fact, he'd probably had a few drinks too many, and the one in his hand wasn't going down slowly either.

It had been a few hours since he had heard anything from his contacts, and the anticipation was driving him mad.

For ten years, he had searched for something that would help him find the trail to the Golden Chambers. A decade of frustration and disappointment had almost caused him to give up hope.

Then, from the ashes rose the most random of opportunities. An archaeologist in Georgia discovered the first stone, the beginning of the trail...

He'd met with the man several weeks before and discussed a financial proposal so he could purchase the piece. Thomas Schultz had hardly been accommodating. Whether it was foolish pride or haughty defiance, he had been unwilling to part with the object.

The man had made a second offer, an astounding amount of money even for someone with the means of wealth that Schultz possessed, and still, the proposal was denied.

So he left Schultz's office empty handed and angry. He had worked too hard and spent too much time and capital to be denied by some insolent archaeologist.

Indeed, Schultz probably did not even realize the entire story behind the Golden Chambers. There were only a few on the planet that knew the beginning part of the legend. But the end, that was what the old man was truly interested in. The gold itself was but a small portion of the true reward that waited at the end.

Most of his guests didn't even notice him slip away when the cell phone in his smoking jacket began to ring.

"Hello?"

"Ulrich is out of control, sir. He is leaving a blood trail in his wake, and I fear his recklessness is drawing too much attention. I recommend you let us intervene." The voice of the woman on the other end was concise and direct.

The old man twisted his head around in both directions to make certain no one was listening. "Where is he now?"

"On the interstate, headed south. I'm not sure where they are going though."

He pondered the situation. Ulrich had become sloppy. Then again, he knew this would happen. He would never invest so much without doing his research first. The blond contractor had served his purpose thus far. "Continue following them. Watch the situation closely. If it gets out of hand, you know what to do."

"Sir, I highly advise..."

"I know what you advise," he cut her off, "but they are up to something. Follow them, and see what it is."

He paused for a moment before adding, "Are the other players still in the game?"

"Yes, sir."

"Good. Let them continue on as well. They may still be useful after all if Ulrich becomes more of a nuisance."

"Anything else, sir?"

"No. Keep me updated."

"Of course."

He ended the call and slid the phone back into his pocket. For a few seconds, he stood by a stone pedestal that supported a bronze urn. Things were going well, almost exactly as planned.

A new guest arrived through the side door of the adjacent room, and he decided it was time to go back to being sociable. With a big swig, he finished off his whiskey and headed back into the gathering.

For the moment, the pawns had to play the game by themselves.

50

SOUTHEASTERN TENNESSEE

"Why did you shoot that old man? Are you crazy?" Tommy yelled at Ulrich, who swerved the giant SUV through the country roads toward the interstate.

The large guard sat in the back with the angry prisoner.

Tommy continued the tirade, "He didn't do anything! And you killed him!" He started to reach an arm forward toward the blond driver when he felt a sudden thud across the side of his face. The world spun for a moment from the shock of the punch and his jaw throbbed as he curled up in the corner of the seat.

"Your sentiment is touching, Thomas. Do not think you are by any means safe at this point. Remember what I will do if you do not cooperate."

Through the ringing in his ears, Tommy got the message. Sean's parents could still be in danger, an element to this whole scenario he, unfortunately, continued to forget.

The guard reached over, about to smack Schultz back to a more alert state, when Ulrich waved him off. "That's enough."

He nodded his head slowly.

"Good. Now, what I need to know is, where should we go next? Hmm?"

Tommy's voice was low as he sat up straight, eyeing the guard. "How should I know? You killed the guy that could have had the information."

"Now, now, Thomas. You don't know that he died. And you need to dwell on the things that can help. Tell me, what do those Bible verses have to do with any of this?"

For a long minute, Tommy stared out the window of the truck as they sped along the rolling countryside. He looked at the other cars that passed by, knowing the passengers had no idea what was going on inside the black SUV. His mind came back to the present. Right now, he needed to focus.

"I can only think of one place that has any sort of correlation with the clues at the church."

"And that is?"

"It will take us a while to get there."

"How far?"

"Probably four hours at best."

Ulrich seemed to contemplate how long it would be. "You are certain?"

"As certain as I can be. I didn't really get a lot of time to investigate back there, what with all the shooting and using me as a human shield and all."

"What is this place?" He ignored Tommy's sarcasm.

"It's called Rock Eagle, down in East Georgia. That seems like the only place that would match up with the clues of the raven and the dove." He laughed, "Actually, I'm a little annoyed that I didn't think of it before. It seems kind of obvious now."

"Why is that?"

"Because Rock Eagle and its sister site, Rock Hawk, are the only stone effigies of their kind in the United States. They are essentially two giant birds made out of piled rocks." He paused for a moment and released an exhausted sigh. "You'll see when we get there."

Then Tommy laid his head back against the headrest of the seat in an effort to relax the pain pounding from his jaw. Ulrich watched Tommy out of the corner of the rearview mirror, wary of his every movement.

51

SOUTHEASTERN TENNESSEE

The phone only rang twice on the other end before Sean heard, "Wyatt, you better have a good explanation for all this!"

Sean smirked, "I take it you're at the church, then, Detective?"

"Yeah, we're at the church. It's a bloody mess over here. Got an unidentified corpse at the base of the stage in the sanctuary and a church worker in the hospital. You wouldn't happen to know anything about that, would you?"

"The corpse shot at me first," Sean replied plainly. "How is the old man?"

"Critical but stable. Docs think he will be okay. Lost a lot of blood, but the bullet missed his vitals. He's hurt, but he'll live."

"That's good to hear. I guess they shot him to slow us down. They were gone once we got to the parking lot."

Trent's voice took on a quieter tone, "Look, Sean, there's a lot of people that still want to ask you some questions. FBI's here now. I'm way out of my backyard at this point. I got no jurisdiction at all."

"So, do you still think I am the one going around killing people?"

"No. I know you're innocent. We saw the security tapes from the museum. But you still need to turn yourself in. There's a dead man here that you did kill, and with your help we might be able to find the others and bring this to an end."

"Sorry, Detective. No can do. We don't have much time. Jurgenson and his other thug are on their way south. I think they are headed to a place called Rock Eagle down in Southeastern Georgia."

"What makes you think that?"

"Kinda difficult to explain at this point. I really don't think you would understand."

"Sean. Listen to me. These guys are obviously dangerous. Let me help you..."

"If you want to help, find out who is behind this," he responded with clenched teeth.

"I'm working on it. The guy in the video footage from the museum doesn't come up on any of our known databases. This Jurgenson's a ghost."

Sean considered this last bit of information. He'd run into men like this before, assassins, hit men, contract killers. They come by many names. Sometimes, they were sloppy. Usually, they were very good. He was unsure which category this Jurgenson fell into. So far, the guy's only mistake had been ignoring the presence of the security cameras in the museum. Maybe he'd not even thought that such a small place would have measures like that in place. Either way, the man was lethal. But something was making him impatient, a fact Wyatt might be able to use to his advantage. Or so he hoped.

And then there was the other component of this mysterious man's existence. If he was a hired gun, as Sean suspected, that meant that someone else was pulling the strings. This was somewhat more disconcerting. Usually, even if the contractor was taken out, the guy behind it all simply disappeared, leaving the trail cold. Just like with the assassination of John F. Kennedy. No one will ever know who really ordered the hit. One thing is certain, though, Lee Harvey Oswald was no mastermind.

Joe changed lanes, glancing back in the rearview mirror to make sure no one was following. A white luxury sedan passed in the far right lane and continued farther and farther ahead.

"Sean, you there?" Morris's voice snapped him back to the moment.

"I don't think Jurgenson is the one calling the shots."

"No?" Trent sounded surprised.

"Nah. The way that this whole thing has been going down, it makes me think he's just the manager of the team."

"But not the owner?"

"Right."

"So who is?"

Sean could tell the cop's voice was being kept a little low. He imagined an entire crime scene investigation going on in the background. Trent must have surely been huddled in a corner of the church somewhere so no one else could hear the conversation.

"I'm not sure. There are only a few people in the world who even know about the legend of the lost chambers. Until this whole thing started, I didn't really know much. And most of what I knew about it came from Tommy."

"You said a few people. Who else would fit into that category?"

"I don't know. I've been racking my brain trying to figure that out, but no one comes to mind. Tommy never did any presentations about the chambers story. It was something that he and I talked about in private. He was always really secretive about his research on it, too. I can tell you this though: Tommy put his life into that search. He wants to find the lost chambers more than anything else. It's completely absorbed him."

"Not one person comes to mind that he may have been in contact with?"

For a moment, Sean looked out the window of the truck, watching the fiery colors of the forest blur by. "There was one guy that I saw leaving Tommy's office once, about six months ago. I had never seen him before. Now that I think of it, I don't think I ever saw him after that either. He was an older gentleman, walked with a fancy-looking cane and dressed in a pinstriped Armani three piece. Not sure why it was, but he had a scowl on his face, like someone had just stolen his last piece of candy."

"Didn't get his name?"

"I went in and found Tommy sitting at his desk with his hands crossed. Guess he was thinking pretty hard about whatever he and the old guy had discussed. But he never told me what they talked about or who the man was."

The detective silently contemplated the scenario and the few details they had.

Sean decided to go on. "All I know is that I have a chance to stop these guys, and that is exactly what I intend to do."

Resignation came from the other end. "I guess there's no changing your mind, Sean. You know that I could call the police down where you're headed."

"I realize that. But you know as well as I do if you get other authorities involved, we may never get Tommy back."

Morris contemplated the problem. "Ok, Sean. I will give you a little more time, twenty-four hours. But that's it. After that, I want your full cooperation with this. You hear me?"

"Yeah. I hear ya."

"Good. Just don't get yourself killed."

"We'll see."

The line went dead.

52

SOUTHEASTERN TENNESSEE

"You sure that was a smart thing to do, tellin' that cop where we're headed?" Joe cast his friend a skeptical look in the mirror. "I mean, why wouldn't he just set up a road block and bring us in?"

"I don't think he'll do that."

"Well, why *did* you tell him where we were going then?"

Sean smiled, "Because, Mac, we might need some help when this thing goes down."

"Well, I don't like it." Joe cast a glance at Allyson, who had remained somewhat silent the last few minutes. "Isn't there someone you can call on this? I mean, you work for Axis, right? Can't they do something?"

"I'm not sure what they would do at this point. The FBI is already involved. As Sean knows, our agency tries to keep a very low profile. I'm afraid we might be on our own in this one."

Sean nodded in agreement.

"On our own again, huh?" Joe echoed. "Great. So, tell me something, Sean, how did you figure Rock Eagle was the next place we need to go?"

"The thought had crossed my mind before. It seemed like the

only logical spot on the continent. But what really gave it away was when the sexton started talking about an altar."

"An altar?"

"Yeah. The history of Rock Eagle and Rock Hawk is a pretty big mystery, as I'm sure you know."

This time Joe nodded. "Yep, those are a couple of odd spots for sure."

Allyson was confused. "What is this place you guys are talking about?"

"Rock Eagle and Rock Hawk are located down in East Georgia, fairly close to Augusta," Sean explained. "The names eagle and hawk refer to two giant stone effigies that are in the shape of birds. Rock Hawk was built out of a darker stone, so it appears almost black. A few miles away from there, Rock Eagle was constructed out of white stones. They are actually quite amazing designs."

"So what does this have to do with the Golden Chambers?"

"Well, the riddle mentions a raven and a dove. Maybe whoever gave the name Rock Eagle and Rock Hawk was just trying to help keep the mystery hidden."

"Makes sense," Joe added. "I'd never actually considered that before. And the altar?"

Sean smiled. "Glad you remembered. When the first excavations were done at the sites, researchers believed that the stone mounds were some sort of mass graves. They expected to find dozens, if not hundreds, of human remains underneath."

"Did they?" Allyson asked.

"No. In fact, they only found two skeletons, one at each site. Turns out, the bones found at the Rock Hawk site were of a female, and those discovered at Rock Eagle were that of a man. What tipped me off, though, was an odd little detail of the story."

He paused for a moment, reflecting. "It is said that Indians from many parts of the region would make a pilgrimage to both sites to place stones there. Over the years, there must have been hundreds and hundreds of rocks brought from all over the southern part of the continent to be placed on the giant stone birds. Generations of

Indians traveled to the altar where "the sacred bones lay." The two people buried there must have been extremely important. Perhaps even the first Natives to settle the area."

"According to the new theory, the first Egyptians to settle here," she realized.

"Exactly. They were the father and mother to a new nation."

The moment was heavy in the truck as the last little detail sank in.

"So, you think these two birds will lead us to the chamber?"

"More than that, Allyson. I think the birds watch over it."

Joe and Allyson cast a questioning look at him.

"Think about it. The medallion Tommy found has two birds on it divided by some kind of line or pole. I think that line marks the location of the first chamber."

"You know," Joe added, "I think you might be right. But how do we find that line?"

"Well, I wasn't sure about that until I remembered another oddity in the area. You see, the two birds face each other even though they are miles apart. Almost exactly at the midpoint between them, a set of totem poles was erected."

"That is interesting."

"Even more fascinating, these totems were built out of stone, not wood. Now why would the Natives go to so much trouble?"

"They wanted them to last forever," Allyson jumped in.

"Exactly. But there is one more piece to the puzzle. And if I know Tommy, he has already figured it out. If he's smart, he will take those guys to the totems without the key."

"Key? What key?"

"Remember the riddle," Sean continued. "It said there was a key."

"Do you know where this key is?"

"I think so. When the bones of the man were discovered at Rock Eagle, there was only one other artifact recovered with his body: a quartz arrowhead."

"Quartz?" Allyson inquired.

"Yes. It was an odd material for Natives to use, considering they made most of their weapons from flint in the early days. Spearheads and arrowheads were almost exclusively made from the soft, gray stone. So, when the archaeologists found one that was made from quartz, that naturally seemed strange."

"And you think this arrowhead is the key to the chamber?" Joe looked hopeful.

"I do. It's the only thing that could make sense."

"Where is this key then?"

"It should be at the museum at Rock Eagle. My guess is it should be on display there."

"How do we know that Jurgenson won't get it before us?"

"We don't," Sean said with determination. "But if Tommy's smart, he will take them to the totem poles first, which should give us enough time to get the key."

"And just how do you plan to do that?" Allyson asked skeptically.

He answered with a sly grin. "I'm sure the museum can make an arrangement for one of its principal contributors."

53

EASTERN GEORGIA

Between the majestic peaks of the Blue Ridge Mountains and the plains of Southern Georgia lies a happy medium. Putnam County's rolling hills. A little farther south, the golf course famous for dogwoods, azaleas, and green jackets rested quietly awaiting that fabled weekend in early April.

One of the perks of being wealthy was the ability to attain the unattainable. And no sporting event in the world was less attainable than a ticket to the Masters at Augusta National.

Being an avid golfer, Tommy had paid an outrageous amount of money to make the pilgrimage to the annual tournament among the pines and flowering bushes. Sean had tagged along more for the story than anything else but was dazzled by the immaculate beauty of the course. He had gawked at the explosion of colors and had wondered at how the groundskeepers could shape nature into such perfection.

Tommy's mind snapped back from the brief daydream as he and his two captors approached the welcome center of the Rock Eagle Effigy Mound. The lengthy drive seemed to take forever, and his legs ached from inactivity.

Brown signs pointed the way to a picnic area nearby. Ulrich had not said much for the last few hours. The SUV came to a stop in front of the building, and the three men got out amid a flurry of schoolchildren. Apparently, their field trip had run a little late. Tommy wasn't sure if he would rather be in his current situation over having to drive one of the buses back with the screaming kids on it.

"Where to, Thomas?" Ulrich interrupted his thoughts.

Tommy glanced around for a second then pointed to an enormous pile of rocks about sixty feet away.

Perhaps the most amazing thing about Rock Eagle was that it looked as if someone had been standing on a thirty-foot-high scaffold, directing the placement of the stones. Why they had done it was a whole other matter.

Tommy led the way over to a historical information plate that stood a few feet from the base of the stone bird's tail. An elderly couple had just finished reading the placard; they were slowly making their way back toward the parking lot.

His eyes scanned the raised metal words. He'd probably read hundreds of those things over the years. According to what the sign said, a sort of earthen wall had originally surrounded the bird effigy. It went on to say that the entire stone representation was raised about four feet higher than the rest of the ground around it. Historians could not offer a logical explanation as to why it was there, but a few details were mentioned that Tommy thought interesting.

Of course, he already knew the story. Archaeologists had assumed the sites to be mass graves, but the remains of only one human had been found at both Rock Eagle as well as the sister site of Rock Hawk —only a few miles away. He was also aware of the quartz arrowhead that had been recovered from the bones of the male skeleton in the pile of stones before him, a little detail that needn't be mentioned to his captors at the moment.

Ulrich seemed unimpressed by the information. "What does this mean?"

"Nothing. I just thought there might be some helpful info here.

It's just the story about how this place was discovered. Maybe we should check out the welcome center and see if there is anything helpful in there."

Ulrich only thought for a second before he nodded and fell in behind Tommy, who was headed toward the old wooden building.

Having been there a few times, Tommy remembered that inside the information center, artifacts on display were few in number. The three men entered through the single glass door and casually made their way over to a map in the corner of the room. A small group of schoolchildren was filing out, complaining that they had to go back to school. If they had been able to understand the concept of time, they would have realized that by the time the bus got back, school would be out for the day.

Ulrich seemed uncomfortable around the children, and the guard, in particular, looked a bit out of sorts.

Tommy smiled to himself as he stepped closer to a poster-sized aerial photo of the location. "Okay. This is us," he said as he pointed at the building in which they were standing, marked by the usual *You are here* dot. His finger then traced the outline of the giant stone bird effigy from where they'd just come a few minutes prior.

"This is Rock Eagle," he stated. He then moved his hand to another, similar formation opposite of the one he'd just mentioned. "And here is Rock Hawk." He tapped the map and took a step back. Staring at the map, Tommy was puzzled by the entire scene.

"So where is the chamber hidden?" Ulrich asked plainly.

Tommy gave him a *drop dead* look. "Beats me. There's a lot of land between the two formations. Rock Hawk is about seven kilometers from here. It could be anywhere."

The clock on the wall read, 4:25. Right on cue, a nondescript woman wearing the light-brown button-up shirt of a park worker announced that the building would be closing in five minutes.

Tommy ignored the woman, still gazing at the map in an effort to find a hint, anything that might show them the way. The screaming voices of the elementary students just outside the windows made thinking difficult.

His mind wandered to the ancient people who'd built these places. The reason behind Fort Mountain was clear to him. A three-dimensional stone replica of the Nile was a clue to the early settlers' mysterious past, but the giant rock bird effigies stumped him. Though animals were revered in ancient Egypt, it was still unclear why they would be here, unless that's all it was: a clue to the past.

Perplexed, he pulled the sketch of the amulet he'd found out of his pocket. His eyes pored over its contents. The clue on the back was clearer, but not complete. They'd found the birds the riddle spoke of, but something was still unsolved. Tommy examined the picture of the birds again in hopes that there was something that would spark the answer.

His two captors remained calm, standing a breath away, but Tommy could sense the urgency in Ulrich's eyes. The man had become extremely impatient, jittery even. It was a characteristic he'd seen in many treasure hunters throughout his life. The closer they came to their goal, the more inexperienced treasure hunters hoping for unimaginable wealth could almost taste their dreams of a life of ease and luxury. Even this trained killer seemed to have caught the fever. Or was it something else that bothered him?

The woman in the brown shirt had started closing up her counter and was about to announce that the park was closing when Tommy had a thought. His eyes locked onto something in the picture. "Excuse me...Miss?"

"Yes, sir, can I help you?" The response from the frumpy woman was forced. She must have been tortured by the high-pitched voices of the youth all day. Her eyes had bags under them, and her hair was tangled like she'd been running her hands through it in frustration.

"I know you're about to close, but I just have a quick question for you." Tommy's understanding seemed to ease her frustration momentarily. "This picture here, with the totem poles...where was it taken?"

He knew well that the ancient Mississippian Natives of the area had constructed many such monuments, but the ones he was looking at in the picture seemed different than most.

"Actually, it was taken just a few miles from here. If you look right here in this area," she pointed to the map at a spot between the two bird formations. "There are eight totems here in a place the Indians used to call, "Khan Ug." They are remarkably preserved, and scientists have dated them to before the time of Christ. The most interesting thing about them is that they are some of the only stone-made totems on the continent."

"Did you say there are eight in this location, and they are made out of stone?"

"Yes. And another interesting point of fact is that the location is exactly three and a half kilometers from Rock Hawk and Rock Eagle. This demonstrates that ancient Indians who lived here might have actually been using the metric system long ago." She looked at her watch, obviously done being courteous.

"I'm sorry to bother you," Tommy could hardly contain his excitement. "But how would we get there?"

She gave them an annoyed sigh and then a few quick directions before excusing herself to finish closing up.

Tommy nodded his head in the direction of the door, and the two men followed him back outside. The sidewalk area in front of the building was finally void of the noisy children.

"So we are going to the place on the map?" Ulrich asked as they neared the vehicle.

"Looks that way. I'd say the place is at least worth taking a look at. It'll be getting dark in a little while, and that's pretty much the only guess I've got at this point."

Ulrich looked awkwardly at the prisoner. So far, Tommy had been right on with every guess. And, surely, they were getting close. It just seemed too easy. Still, he had no other choice.

The woman's directions had been accurate, and it only took about five minutes to get to location she'd shown them on the map. As seen in the picture, eight tall stone carvings ominously stood in a small patch of grass. The setting was surrounded by an amphitheater of looming oaks and narrow pines.

Tommy slammed the door of the truck carelessly, unable to take his eyes off of the magnificent structures as he stumbled toward them.

Seven of the poles were similar in height, around fifteen feet from what he could tell. But the one in the middle was different in every way. First off, it was several feet higher than the others.

The differences didn't stop with mere height. More intriguing was that each of the other seven totems displayed carvings of animal groups. One had birds, another showed cattle and other agricultural animals, and so it was with each monument. Though each one contained different animals, the animals were part of a similar species group. On the largest piece of stone was a representative animal from all of the other seven, like some kind of montage.

Moving slowly with both guards in tow, Tommy walked from one pike to the next, examining the intricate handiwork. He stopped at the largest one in the middle and ran his hand over the face of a fierce-looking cat, a cougar as far as he could tell. Then he stepped over to the other three, his face alight with admiration.

"Amazing," he finally broke the silence. "It must have been an extremely painstaking effort to create them."

The silent guard seemed to be slightly interested. Ulrich was less intrigued. He stood, arms crossed, with a stern demeanor.

Tommy stopped at the last sculpture and examined it closely. The animals on it were foxes, wolves, dogs, coyotes, and what looked to be something like a hyena. He traced the stonework with his finger, still amazed by what the ancients could do.

"What are you looking for, Mr. Schultz?" Ulrich's annoyed voice interrupted his thoughts.

He'd been crouching over slightly and at the question, had stood back up straight. "I don't know for sure."

Ulrich motioned for the guard to start looking down at the other end.

Tommy finished inspecting the first pole and moved to the next, Ulrich staying close with him. They spent several minutes meticulously checking the surfaces of the stone without coming across anything out of the ordinary. He walked around the granite center-piece, still hoping there was something there to be found. This had to be the place. Everything they had found thus far had pointed to it.

As he came back around to the front of the chiseled stone, he noticed it. Small, almost invisible at first glance, Tommy had not seen it before, even though he'd thought he was looking carefully. An owl stared at him, its eyes lifeless and eerie. The animal's face contained amazing detail. Its mouth, in particular, caught his attention because unlike the other animal carvings, the beak was open.

He moved his finger up to the opening. "This is it."

"Are you certain?"

"Yeah," Tommy replied. "I'm sure. It makes so much sense now. In ancient Indian lore, owls were guardians to the other world. They protected the spirits of ancestors who were already on the other side. It was also believed that sometimes the bird itself was a long-gone relative who had returned as a guide for a person or people. Seems logical that whoever built these would have put an owl here to protect their greatest secret."

Ulrich stood up straight again. "So, what do we do now?"

Tommy sighed, thinking for a moment. "There must be some kind of key we have to use here. If my guess is right, whatever the key is probably fits into this owl's mouth."

"Why do we not simply pick lock?" The guard suggested in broken English.

"We can't do that."

"Why not?"

"Do you honestly think that the ancient people who put this here would have hidden everything so well and simply closed it up with a padlock? My guess is it is probably rigged with some kind of antima-nipulation device. If we try to mess with it without the correct key, we may lock ourselves out of the chamber forever or something worse."

"So how do we find this...key you speak of?" Ulrich asked, as if Tommy could make it appear out of thin air.

"You mean this key?" The male voice interrupted the conversation from behind.

All three men turned around quickly, surprised by the sudden intrusion. Sean, Joe, and Allyson stood about fifteen feet away, guns trained on the two villains.

In his left hand, Sean held something small and white, precariously gripped in his fingers, was a quartz arrowhead.

54

EASTERN GEORGIA

The astonished looks on the faces of Ulrich and the guard were priceless. Tommy's head went back and forth, not sure if he was hallucinating. "Boy, am I glad to see you guys."

"It's good to see you too, Schultzie."

Joe echoed the sentiment. "We weren't sure if we were gonna see you again."

"Likewise," Tommy replied, reflecting on the past forty-eight hours.

The guard and the blond man stood frozen, a deer-in-the-headlights look on each of their faces.

Sean cautiously stepped toward the group. "Wasn't that difficult to find you, actually."

He glared at Ulrich. "Shooting the old man was a mistake, but leaving him alive was a bigger one. He gave us the final clue." Sean laughed. "Although I have to admit convincing the park that the IAA center needed to borrow this arrowhead for analysis was a bit more difficult than it should have been."

Tommy stepped away from his kidnappers. "Thanks, gentlemen. It's been real." He smiled, "So, Sean, how did you know that the arrowhead was the key?"

Wyatt handed the little rock to his friend. "I remembered seeing a presentation about this place a few years ago. The speaker had mentioned the oddity of the quartz arrowhead that had been buried with the body in the bird effigy. That's when it clicked with me, "The key with sacred bones does lay.""

Realization washed over Tommy's face. "Of course. I should have thought of that." He raised the arrowhead to examine it more closely, admiring the precise detail. Every edge of it appeared as though it had been shaped by a laser.

The pinkish-white stone was small, only about three inches long and half as wide. "It must go into the mouth horizontally." He walked back to the pole while his captors eyed him warily.

Then he motioned toward Allyson. "Who's the girl?"

"Allyson Webster," she answered.

"She's with Axis," Sean added.

"An agent? Really? Did you make a phone call or something?"

"Actually, no. Pretty sure she was already on your trail."

Allyson just smiled back, obviously not interested in giving away any more details.

Wyatt turned his attention to Ulrich and the bewildered guard. "Now if you two boys don't mind, please move out of the way." He waved his gun in a motion indicating they should step to the left. "First, though, you are going to need to go ahead and drop those weapons that you're carrying in your jackets. And do it real slow. I have more than enough excuses to waste you two right now."

They complied, carefully reaching into their jackets then dropping the guns to the ground.

"Good. Now step away."

The two shuffled sideways, moving away from the pistols. Ulrich never took his cold gray eyes off of Wyatt. Even unarmed, the man's gaze was menacing.

With his free hand, Sean reached into his pocket and pulled out a cell phone. Keeping the gun leveled at the two men, he held up the device up to his face.

"Detective, we got 'em."

"What do you mean you got 'em?"

"We got Tommy and the guys that kidnapped him. Joe and I are holding them at gunpoint as we speak."

"What's your location?" Morris's voice sounded urgent.

"A couple of miles from Rock Eagle, standing in front of eight big totem poles."

"Okay, I'll get the local authorities over there as quickly as I can. Will and I are on our way; we're about fifteen minutes from there."

"You drove down here?" Sean was a little surprised at the cop's persistence.

"Like I said, I got a lot of questions for you. You won't be able to answer them if you're dead. And I thought you could use some backup."

"Don't worry about us, Trent. The situation is under control. See you in a few."

Tommy had been busy taking a closer examination of the quartz and the mouth of the owl. "I hope we don't need to get it back out."

With that, he cautiously slipped the arrowhead into the mouth of the chiseled bird. It was a perfect fit. With his index finger, Tommy pushed the quartz all the way into the open hole. As the projectile went deeper, there was a click then a few more until it was completely inside.

Suddenly, the large totem pole and the earth underneath their feet began trembling. For a brief second, Sean took his eyes off the two men, bracing himself by bending his knees slightly. His gun, though, stayed pointed at them. The entire group took a few steps back, not sure what was happening.

The seven smaller poles began to move slowly. To the left, all the rods were sinking into the ground. On the right, they were rising but the post in the center never moved. The bizarre event lasted for only a minute, but when the pillars had stopped moving, their heights had changed to a more staggered look, like a staircase.

All five witnesses stood in silent awe for a minute, gazing at the oddity.

"So, what now, Schultzie?" Sean broke the silence.

Tommy looked perplexed. "That should have been it. Something's wrong."

"Maybe you didn't do it right," Joe chimed in.

"No. Pretty sure that was it and that had to be the key." He looked around as if expecting some kind of sign from Heaven to point the way to their goal. None came. "I don't understand."

The two captives stood silently while the others attempted to solve the problem; Ulrich's eyes locked on Joe like a rattlesnake eyeing its prey.

Sean looked curiously at the scene. "Mac, keep an eye on those two."

"What is it?" Tommy asked.

Tossing the gun to Tommy, Sean ignored his friend's question for a moment and walked over to the totem that had lowered to where the top was only about four feet high. "They're steps," he finally answered. "The ancient Natives had a ritual for new warriors. It was the final test they had to pass. They had to stand on top of a pole like one of these for an entire night. If they could accomplish this without falling off, they would be initiated."

"Realization came to Tommy. Of course. How did I forget that?"

"Beats me," Sean said, hopping up onto the short log. "You're the expert on Indians." He grinned cynically down at his friend.

"Hope you know what you're doing."

"It's only about five or six feet in between them. The problem isn't the jumping, though. It's the landing. The gradual escalation isn't going to help either."

He steadied himself on the two-foot-wide platform and leaped to the next one, making it look easy enough. Below, Tommy rejoined Joe and their new prisoners, still watching as Sean jumped to the third pole.

He made it to the center pole with relative ease. Again, he repeated the maneuver up to the fifth. The platform was up about fifteen feet at this point, and the jumping was becoming riskier each time. Thinking ahead, the final leap would be to a height around twenty-five feet, a point at which the danger would be broken bones or worse. He tried to shake the fear from his mind, but it was still in front of him as he made the next two leaps. The lack of concentration nearly cost him on the seventh as he shorted the distance by about a foot. His fingers caught the front lip of the stone, gripping tight, and his feet dangled below. Tommy made a quick movement to get below him in case he fell.

Struggling to keep his hold on the top, Sean hung over the ground, kicking his legs in an effort to worm his way up. With his right foot, he found the nose of a wolf's face sticking out of the front of the tall facade and used it to brace himself while he hugged his way onto the platform.

His allies below exhaled a breath of relief as Sean hoisted himself up and readied for the last jump. "I'm okay," he assured them. "Just lost my concentration for a second there."

He let his eyes search the surroundings for a brief second, hoping that the location would be revealed from his current vantage point. It wasn't. So, with trepidation, he moved to the very edge of the pole. He was surprised at how much his legs were burning at this point. Sean took pride in the fact that he exercised regularly and had very high endurance for physical activities. This routine must have been working out muscles that he was unaccustomed to using.

With every last ounce of leg power he could muster, Sean launched himself across the void. This time, adrenaline must have taken over because he almost overshot the thing, landing on the very back edge and waving his arms like a gymnast on a balance beam to keep from toppling over.

Steadying his weight back on the center of the beam, he gazed out across the landscape. Rolling forests lay out before his eyes. He couldn't help being a little surprised at how such a small elevation could improve one's view of things.

Sean's eyes passed across the horizon as he turned around a full 360 degrees.

"You see anything?" Tommy shouted from below.

"Just a bunch of woods, the road..." Then his gaze locked onto something. "Wait a minute. There *is* something." He pointed over toward what, to the group on the bottom, appeared to only be a thick growth of trees.

"What is it?"

"I don't think you can see it from down there. But I see another totem, sticking up from the trees on that small hill, over in that direction."

Tommy stood on his tiptoes in an attempt to locate what his friend had found.

Allyson, too, took a few steps closer to the row of stone faces to see if she could glimpse what Sean was pointing at.

For one second, Joe took his eyes off of the blond and Flattop to take a glance toward the forest. A second was all Ulrich needed to pull the hidden gun from his back and fire off three quick shots.

Joe stumbled and dropped his gun as one of the bullets found its mark, sending the man reeling backward, shock on his face as he collapsed to the ground.

In another instant motion, Ulrich had spun forward and grabbed Allyson around the neck, immediately putting the gun to her head.

Tommy looked on helplessly. He stood frozen, completely stunned by what had just transpired.

"Drop the weapon, Mr. Schultz. I may still have need of you, so don't do anything stupid."

Sean was crouching down on his perch, now looking at the scene below. Joe was still down, wet crimson soaking his shirt.

"Mr. Wyatt, if you would be so kind as to join us now." Ulrich motioned for him to return the way he'd just gone.

Going down was much easier than the jumping up had been, and in less than a minute, Sean was back on the ground. The guard had retrieved his gun and now had it trained on Wyatt.

To say that Sean was frustrated would be an understatement. He'd forgotten the cardinal rule of his training. Always check a detainee for other weapons. Now they were all back to square one. Worse than that, now Allyson was in danger. "Leave her out of this," he demanded.

She squirmed against Ulrich's grip, and a look of terror filled her eyes.

"Now, now," Ulrich whispered. "Don't struggle. I would hate to have to kill you, my dear." He didn't respond to Sean's request.

Her mouth couldn't form the angry words she wanted to say. The man's vice-like grip around her throat barely let in enough air.

"Let her go!" Sean shouted this time. "She has nothing to do with this! The cops are on their way. What are you going to do? It's over!"

The blond man answered with a twisted smile. "Then I suppose we should hurry." He motioned with his gun at the area Sean had pointed out a few minutes before. "Now! Or I kill her right here!"

"We can't just leave him here." Wyatt motioned to his friend lying on the ground, motionless.

"You will do as I say, or she dies!"

Tommy and Sean had no choice. For a moment, their eyes locked, desperate and bewildered. Then they started trudging into the forest, Sean leading the way. The guard was right behind them, holding his gun at waist level, followed by Ulrich, who'd taken his arm from around Allyson's neck and forced her to walk in front of him, holding the pistol at the small of her back.

"What are we gonna do, Sean?" Tommy asked. His voice sounded like a child's.

"I don't know, Schultzie." He looked around as they waded through the tall grass, hoping the police were on their way. "But we're running out of time."

55

EASTERN GEORGIA

Ulrich forced the group to move quickly through the forest. He had overheard Sean's conversation with the police so time, he knew, was running out. With a feverish urgency bordering on madness, the blond man trudged through the undergrowth. He snapped his head left and right every time a twig broke under someone's foot.

The guard, too, looked uneasy, making sure he covered a 360-degree area with his gun as he swung it around wildly.

Sean's thoughts wandered to Joe. He hoped that the police would find him fast enough to get him medical treatment. The wound hadn't looked good, and Mac must have lost a great deal of blood in a short amount of time.

After a few more minutes of marching through the trees, the group arrived at the spot Wyatt had seen earlier.

Tommy stared at one of the most impressive monuments he had ever seen. Loose dirt surrounded it, indicating that the massive thing was mostly buried, if not totally underground.

The woods had been somewhat flat up until they got to that point. There, the forest floor gave rise to a small hill with the enormous totem pole at its base. Just beyond it, at the foot of the hillside, gaped an opening to a cave.

Ulrich motioned toward the entrance, "Quickly, inside!"

The three captives obeyed and swiftly scurried over to the opening. It was a hole about seven feet high and four feet wide. A pile of grass and dirt lay next to it, alluding to the fact that the entrance had been covered for centuries. Ulrich removed a pen-sized aluminum flashlight from a cargo pocket. The guard did the same.

Sean turned around at the edge of the dark corridor. "Are we supposed to just go on through the dark?"

The blond replied with a fake pitying grin and tossed him the small light. "Lucky for you, I brought an extra. Now move!" He flicked the gun, herding Sean and the others into the darkness.

Sean led the way in with Tommy just behind, followed by the stumpy guard, then Allyson and Ulrich. There were cobwebs everywhere, and it was a struggle just to maintain sanity while brushing them away every five or six feet. Apparently, the spiders that had spun them had long since died or given up trying to catch anything in the ancient place.

The walls of the walkway were smoothly carved stone cut with laser precision. Overhead, the ceiling was also a perfectly scored surface.

Tommy broke the awed silence as they moved farther underground. "Do you realize what we are seeing? No one has been inside of this hall for maybe thousands of years. We are the first humans to set foot here in millennia."

"Yeah," Sean responded only half interested. The current situation overwhelmed his admiration of the surroundings.

The passageway came to a corner and turned ninety degrees to the left, sloping down somewhat steeply. Another twenty or so feet, the same turn was repeated, continuing downward almost like a spiral staircase without the stairs.

After turning left several times, descending deeper into the earth, the group came to a point where they could go no farther. In front of them stood a wall made from the same stone as the rest of the corridor. The difference was that the other walls had no identifying markings. This one did.

Hieroglyphics of amazing detail jumped out from the solid rock canvas before them. There was no mistaking the inscriptions' origin. Various Egyptian deities, animals, symbols, and other characters were easily recognizable even to the novice historian.

"Amazing," Tommy whispered.

Sean reached out slowly so the two men with guns wouldn't freak out. He traced the outline of a glyph that he'd never seen before. It was a picture of some kind of boat with figures of people and animals surrounding it.

"That must be one of the boats that brought the Egyptians over to the Americas. Looks like they brought a bunch of animals with them. Probably as a food source."

"Would make sense," Sean agreed. Then he turned his attention to a couple of oddities on either side of the path.

Carved into the stone were two hollow spaces. Within each vacancy sat a stone bird. The two animals faced each other from across the corridor, and each had a small inscription below it.

Ulrich was obviously irritated by their halt in progress. "Where is the chamber?"

"He always like this?" Sean jerked his thumb toward the blond man.

"You have no idea," Tommy chuckled in spite of himself.

"I'm glad you two are comfortable with the fact that you are about to die," Ulrich threatened.

Sean's smile disappeared for a moment as he turned to face the murderer's blue-gray eyes. Then he turned back to his friend. "Still, I think those guys down in Peru were way worse."

Tommy couldn't help but outright laugh. "Yeah. Probably."

"I knew it!" Allyson exclaimed as she gave Sean a chiding glare. "I knew you guys were up to something in Peru!"

Obviously tired of the little trip down memory lane, Ulrich forced the gun barrel to the back of her head.

Both friends' faces turned somber.

Tommy spoke up. "All right. All right. Obviously, we can't just move this wall. It's got to be, like, two or three tons, easy." His eyes scanned the smooth surface.

"What do these markings say? Can you translate it?" Ulrich urged.

"Basically, it's a story of how the people came here. Apparently, there was one man who they believed to be some kind of a savior for their people, someone who would take them to a new land."

"Sounds like the Moses story from the Bible." Allyson final spoke up.

Glad to see she was no longer in shock, Sean turned to her. "Sort of like that. But this story predates that one. These hieroglyphs are from a much earlier Egyptian kingdom." He paused for a moment, thinking. "I wonder what they wanted to get away from?"

"Yeah," Tommy continued. "You can tell from the construction of the characters, the lines, the way they have been carved, these are some of the more ancient forms of Egyptian writing.

"You see," he went on, "eventually, the Egyptians went to a more abbreviated form of writing called hieratic. It was much simpler and faster for their scribes to use than what you are looking at right now. This must come from the time around the Old Kingdom."

While Tommy kept reading the wall, the guard's attention had been distracted by the bird in the left wall. His right hand held the gun, but the man's curiosity led his left hand to the smooth stone of the carving's head.

He was just about to feel it when Tommy yelled, "Stop!"

The guard yanked his hand back, startled.

"Don't touch anything," Tommy ordered. "There is a riddle here. I think this whole place might be booby trapped."

Ulrich cast the guard a warning glance.

"It says, 'To find the way, the birds will guide you. The one that returns shall doom bring forth. The other shall lead you home.'"

"Ok," Sean said. His face contorted into a sarcastic smirk. "That seems simple enough. To move the wall, we have to do something with one of these birds." He looked at one and then the other.

"Yeah, but if we choose the wrong one, we may not get out of here alive," Tommy added.

"How do you know which bird? They look the same to me," Allyson asked.

"I'm not sure," Tommy replied, scratching his head. "The one that returns...I wonder what that means."

"It must have something to do with the writing beneath the birds. But the language is different than on the wall. Looks a lot like the writing on the back of the stone I found at the Vann house." Tommy pondered the problem.

"Can you read it?" Ulrich butted in.

"Not really. That was why I sent the stone to Frank to begin with."

Sean reached into his pocket. "You mean this stone?"

He opened his palm, producing the medallion.

"Where did you get that?"

"Joe had it. I guess Frank mailed it to him before Blondie here could get his hands on it."

Tommy took the stone and examined it closely then looked at one of the stone birds. He stepped over to the sculpture and pointed to the word underneath it. "These birds must be the raven and the dove."

"Which is which though?"

Ulrich watched silently off to the side, keeping his gun on the hostages.

"We have to assume that this one here is the raven. It is the first one in the riddle and the word on the stone matches the writing below. But that is only half of the solution."

"Which one returned?"

"I'm not sure." Tommy stepped across the small space to the other bird. "Both of the birds look the same."

Then he leaned down to look at something that appeared to be clutched in the bird's claws. "Looks like some kind of branch."

"That's it!" Sean exclaimed.

"What's it?"

"It's an olive branch. In the flood story from the Bible, Noah released a raven and a dove from the ark. The raven came back. At first, the dove did as well, and when it did, it carried an olive branch. A week or so later, Noah sent the dove out again; the second time, it did not return."

Sean knelt down at the base of the stone dove, examining it closely. With both hands, he reached around the bird's head and pulled. The sculpture gave way to the force of Wyatt's hands and bent forward. A deep grinding sound reverberated through the ancient passageway, and the dusty floor beneath them shook violently as the huge stone wall began to rise slowly. All five of the visitors could not help but stare at the sight of the heavy door being lifted. Even Ulrich looked a little shocked by the power that must have surely been required to move such an enormous weight.

Not surprisingly, a tremendous amount of dust hung in the air after the huge stone's journey had finished at the top of the portal. Ulrich motioned for the prisoners to go on through to the other side. Beyond the cloud of debris in front of them, more darkness awaited.

Sean stepped cautiously across the threshold, hoping there weren't any crazy booby traps like he'd seen in so many movies. In his experience, he'd only come across a few things like that. For the most part, though, measures that were set up thousands of years ago to prevent intruders had long since rotted away or lost their effectiveness. Still, better to be safe than sorry.

"Move," Ulrich insisted with a nod.

"It's imperative that we be careful here. You don't want to end up with a dart in your eye or something." Sean said sardonically.

Ulrich wasn't fazed by the comment, but the guard looked around, his eyes filled instantly with paranoia.

They were all safely on the other side of the wall when Allyson spoke up. "Do you guys smell that?"

"Yeah," Tommy agreed. "It smells like some kind of gas."

Flattop's head darted left to right, up and back, panic all over his face. It was easy to tell the man was not comfortable being in a place so far under the ground. It probably didn't help that they had no idea what was waiting for them down there.

"Anyone got a match?" Sean requested.

"You're not going to light a match down here, are you? You guys just said you smelled gas. Are we going to just blow ourselves up?"

Sean smiled at her. "No one's going to get blown up." His light pointed to a torch hanging on the wall in a sconce that appeared to be carved from the same rock as the wall. "Why would someone put a torch there if something was going to explode?"

She supposed he had a point. Ulrich flicked a small book of matches at him, hitting Wyatt in the chest. Sean snatched it out of the air before it could fall to the ground.

A few moments later, the tightly wrapped rags on the piece of wood were burning brightly. Sean pocketed the matches, figuring the German wouldn't care, and gave the flashlight to Tommy. He purposefully took a few more steps forward and stopped. The hallway where they'd been for the last ten minutes opened up into an enormous, square chamber. In the center, rising up from an inset lower floor, a pedestal stood as the only furniture in the room.

The most striking thing about the room, though, wasn't what stood in the center of it. It was the fact that the chamber was empty.

56

EASTERN GEORGIA

"Where is it?" Ulrich demanded loudly. "Where is the gold?!" He grabbed Tommy by the shirt and pressed the gun deep into the skin underneath his jaw.

"I don't know," Tommy stammered. "This should be it." Something in his eyes said that he was telling the truth.

Ulrich released the gun from his hostage's neck and carelessly pushed him away. "Is this it, Thomas? Is this your golden chamber?"

"I don't know where the gold is. Maybe someone beat us to it. It should be right here. Let's just look around. If we're lucky, we might find a clue as to where it went."

Sean stepped down into the center of the room, lowering his light to get a better look at the pedestal. It was a simple design: a perfect, rectangular stone cube. Unlike the blank walls surrounding it, the plinth was covered in hieroglyphs, not unlike what they had just seen on the colossal door a few moments ago. As Sean drew closer, he noticed an object resting on the top of the platform. His eyes widened in realization.

"Schultzie," his voice was firm, trying to contain the excitement. "You might want to come take a look at this."

"Is that what I think it is?" he blurted out, nearly missing the step down into the lower part of the chamber.

"Yeah."

They both stare at a stone disc of nearly identical size to the one Sean had in his pocket. The medallion was lying on one side, a picture of an odd-looking spider carved into it. Both friends looked at each other quizzically, unsure what to make of the piece.

Ulrich and the guard ushered Allyson over to where Tommy and Sean were standing.

"What is it?"

"I think it's the clue to the next chamber," Tommy replied.

"But where is the gold?" Ulrich had had enough of the games and riddles. "This was supposed to be a GOLDEN chamber. Not an empty one!" His voice echoed off of the solid walls.

Tommy shrugged. "All I know is that this amulet is probably the next piece to the puzzle and..." While he spoke, his right hand reached over and grasped the stone disc, lifting it off of the podium.

As soon as Tommy had lifted the weight, the ground beneath them started vibrating. Ulrich and his cohort braced themselves by bending their knees and putting their arms out to their sides. Sean grabbed Tommy's wrist and looked quickly at where the stone had just been resting a moment before. A small button protruded from the center of the pedestal.

"Not good," Sean said quickly.

As he did, the grinding sound of stone on stone filled the room as the floor began slowly rising toward the ceiling

"Put it back, Schultzie!" Sean shouted over the noise.

Tommy's obeyed immediately, realizing what was happening. He hurriedly put the disc back on the top of the stand. As expected, the floor stopped moving. It had risen about three feet closer to the ceiling.

"Don't do that again," Allyson requested.

Ulrich and the guard frantically looked around, concerned the floor might begin moving up again, and if it did, they were jumping back to the main floor where it was safe.

Puzzled, Tommy and Sean looked at the stone cube before them, trying to interpret the hieroglyphs.

"Always good to read the instructions before you activate a three-thousand-year-old death trap," Tommy commented with a sideways glance at his friend. "Must be some kind of weight and counterweight system."

Sean snorted a quick laugh. "Yeah. This looks like a story of some kind." He ran his finger across the stone.

"Two men of truth, bring a gift to the great god," Tommy translated. "By giving up what they had, it looks like the glory of the gods was revealed to them."

Sean moved around to the other side of the pedestal. The epiphany hit him. "The other disc. We must have to put it on this thing with the other stone."

Tommy stepped around to look at what his friend had found. A two-inch-deep circle had been cut into the stone. "It makes sense now. According to the story, whoever finds their way here must bring the first disc and leave it before they can find what they seek."

Ulrich was now leaning in close to monitor the discussion while Flattop stood back, still uncertain about what was going on.

Feeling in his coat pocket, Sean produced the original stone disc.

"Boy, am I glad you brought that," Tommy sighed, eyeing the artifact with relief.

"Yeah." Sean crouched down to one knee. The circular indention in the stone podium mirrored the carving of the two birds, except that the two birds were raised, not indented like on the medallion. Quickly, he removed the spider disc from the top and slid the stone into place and pressed it down firmly. Somewhere in the cavern, there were a few clicks and then silence.

Nothing happened.

"What is the problem now?" Ulrich demanded.

Ignoring the question, Sean then took the medallion with the spider on it and placed it on top of the one Tommy had found.

The ground began shaking again, and the grinding sound of the ancient stones resumed at full decibel. This time, though, instead of rising, the floor began to sink.

"It's an ancient elevator!" Tommy shouted over the noise as the enormous device continued to move downward.

Sean looked a little more suspicious but was anxious to see where the lift would take them.

The floor above was gone as they descended into a shaft cut perfectly into the sandstone. Then, around the edge of the moving floor, a gap opened up, growing larger and larger until with a thud, the old machine came to a thunderous halt. The eyes of its passengers searched the dark corners of the room cautiously. Resting on either side of the stone lift were two enormous golden obelisks pointing majestically toward the ceiling of the room. Their torches and flashlights flickered off of the walls.

Sean stepped off the platform toward something that looked like a bronze birdbath. With a quick nod, Ulrich motioned for the guard to follow Wyatt.

Arriving at the large dish, Sean looked inside it briefly then touched his torch to the material it contained. Immediately, the fuel roared to life, lighting up the entire quarter of the room.

What their eyes beheld was more stunning than anything they had ever imagined. Sean stepped backward a moment, nearly bumping into the guard, who stumbled briefly then caught his balance.

Before them was an entire wall made from square golden panels.

Tommy barely spoke above a whisper. "We're here."

57

EASTERN GEORGIA

T
ommy hopped down from the stone platform and rushed over to the wall. He ran his finger over the incredible pieces of yellow metal. It was more amazing that anything he had ever seen.

Ulrich, too, seemed in awe of the scene. He moved almost unconsciously from the platform of the elevator to the main floor of the chamber, his mouth slightly agape at the sight as he moved closer to the shimmering partition.

The wall made of pure gold stretched forty feet from corner to corner, reaching around twelve feet in height. Its shiny surface was covered with hieroglyphic pictures and strange text, similar in appearance to the words on the original medallion Tommy had found. Four other dishes accented the corners of the room. In between the dishes were four stone boxes resting on the floor. They looked like sarcophagi, but Tommy wasn't sure. The large containers had the same odd-looking words chiseled into them.

"This...it's incredible. I had no idea it would be so...spectacular." His voice choked.

Sean smiled, half-excited, half-desperate to find a way for them to survive. He knew they only had a few minutes to make their move. Stepping over to the wall on his left with Flattop in tow, he made his way to another large fire plate. This one was made from silver. Again, he dipped the torch into the ancient fuel, and the wall before him came to life in the fiery glow.

He repeated the illumination process at a third dish, this one made from what looked like onyx.

Allyson watched Sean's progression from the safety of the elevator, amazed by the radiance of the room. As he made his way to the final saucer, Sean gave her a quick flash with his eyes. What did he want?

Again, he gave a quick look over to her left with his eyes toward the pedestal on the elevator.

The disc. Sean wanted her to remove the disc so the elevator would start going back up again. She shook her head.

He mouthed to her, "It's okay. Do it."

She looked over at Ulrich who was now standing directly behind Tommy, raising his gun to the back of Tommy's skull. Sean was nearly to the last dish. Her eyes shot back toward Tommy and again to Sean. As soon as Tommy was executed, the guard would take that as his cue to kill Sean. Then she would be next.

"I really must thank you for your help in finding all of this, Thomas. It has been quite an adventure," Ulrich finally said.

Tommy turned around to find a gun barrel between his eyes.

"Unfortunately, your services are no longer required."

Sean gave her a quick nod as he ignited the final plate's fuel. The guard stood directly behind him, raising his weapon as well. His thick face was completely vacant of any emotion.

Biting her lip, Allyson reached down and pried the medallions from the podium with her fingers. Immediately, the ancient elevator rumbled to life again, rising slowly from the floor.

Neither Ulrich nor Flattop saw Allyson's sudden move. So when the giant mechanism started moving again, they both spun around instinctively.

Ulrich's reaction was less shocked as he realized quickly what was happening. He twisted his arm away from Tommy and fired off two quick shots that narrowly missed Allyson, who crouched behind the stand of the rising platform. As he started to lunge toward her, something grabbed him by the ankle.

Tommy's grip was firm, and Ulrich felt himself lose his balance, toppling over with a thud. Both elbows smashed unexpectedly onto the solid stone floor. Pain immediately shot through his arms, and the crash caused the gun in his hand to rattle free.

Across the room, the guard's reaction to Allyson had been less coordinated. The big man seemed momentarily confused by what was happening. However, he quickly followed Ulrich's lead, and he took aim at the woman.

A shot was never fired from the stocky man's weapon though. Before he could pull the trigger, a sharp and burning pain shot across his head and face with bits of dripping flame flying past his eyes.

Sean had taken the moment of surprise and moved quickly, swinging his arm as hard as he could. The torch bashed against the man's temple, sending sparks and fire swarming around the man's head.

For a second, the large body staggered, dizzied from the strike. Instinctively, he dropped his gun and reached up to his face with both hands, screaming in pain. Sean followed the blow with another swing.

This time, the stocky man was ready. He recovered from the initial blow and raised his other arm just in time to block the flaming staff from hitting him again.

It was Sean's turn to be surprised. He had not anticipated the strong man's ability to stabilize so fast. After blocking his attack, the man grabbed the torch with one hand and Wyatt's throat with the other.

Sean tried to pry the fingers loose that were cutting off his supply of air, but the grip was too strong. He swung wildly at the guard's face, only getting in a few glancing blows that seemed less than ineffective.

The room began to spin as the lack of oxygen started taking its toll. His lungs screamed to breathe, but he could not force open his throat. With a last-ditch effort, Sean jumped and lifted both of his legs in a running motion, essentially stepping on Flattop's chest then his face with both feet. The odd movement worked as Sean's legs forced free the man's grasp and sent him reeling backward toward one of the flaming urns.

Wyatt landed on his side and gasped for air, his lungs filling gratefully in relief. He only had a moment, though, as the guard had caught himself and was charging toward him like a bull. Tommy staggered to one knee with a hand still on the ground. Only a few feet behind him, another of the dishes burned brightly. The idea came just quickly enough.

Running at full speed, Flattop squared his shoulders into a tackling position, ready to drive Wyatt to the floor. But just as he was about to hit him, Sean rolled out of the way and caught the guard with his boot.

The man stumbled forward out of control, and before he could stop, he crashed into the fiery platter, sending it toppling to the ground. He reached out his hands to the floor as he fell, but they landed in the fire that now spread along the floor. The man let out a yelp and withdrew his hands, but when he did, his body collapsed into the flames. His black suit roared to life in a burst of yellow-and-orange heat.

He screamed and struggled to roll out of the flames as his entire body became engulfed. Finally, after a moment, the man was able to worm his way onto a part of the stone surface where the fire hadn't reached, and he continued to turn over in the dust. A few seconds later, the flames had been smothered. The skin on his face and hands peeled and blistered from the burns and his flattop haircut had been singed down to the scalp.

Then he opened his eyes to see Sean Wyatt standing over him with his gun. Without hesitation, Sean raised the weapon and clicked off a shot. The bullet smashed into a knee, shattering the joint into a bloody mass of tissue and bone.

Wailing, the man collapsed onto his side, both hands gripped the bloody mess where his kneecap used to be.

"Don't move," Sean remarked casually as he turned to leave the man twisting in agony on the floor.

Wyatt's attention went to the other side of the room as the elevator continued its ascent.

Tommy was hanging onto Ulrich's foot for dear life, but the strong blond man was dragging him along, struggling to get to the gun that was only a few feet away. Across the room, both combatants saw an orange-yellow flash followed by a howling scream and then a gunshot. Neither one could see beyond the giant column that was pushing the platform of the elevator up.

Ulrich was only a few inches from the gun, his fingers scratched against the hard floor in an attempt to pull closer to it. He kicked a couple of times, once catching Tommy in the face. Still, the man would not let go.

Tommy realized his attempt to impede Ulrich was futile. His jaw ached from the black shoe striking it. There was only one thing he could do. In one sudden movement, he released the blond man, who tumbled forward just beyond the gun. All Tommy could do was dive behind one of the stone boxes for cover before Ulrich could get off a shot.

The unexpected momentum had thrown Ulrich off only for a few seconds. He recovered quickly and snatched up the weapon, squeezing off three quick rounds at the sprawling Tommy. The bullets ricocheted off the sarcophagus and bounced, momentarily, around the room.

"Very clever, Thomas!" The voice was sinister as Ulrich stood up, firing another shot just over Tommy's back. It pinged off the golden wall beside him.

"But now your little game is at an end," Ulrich continued. He took a step forward, moving in for the kill, when another gun popped from somewhere else in the room.

Ulrich froze in his tracks. Looking down at his chest, he noticed blood slowly seeping into his shirt. He spun around quickly to return fire, but his reaction was too late.

Four more shots came from the other weapon, all of them finding the blond man's torso. His legs wobbled for a moment then gave way, sending his now-heavy body to the ground.

Sean lowered the weapon and walked over to the man lying on the cold stone floor. Blood trickled down Ulrich's face from the corner of his lips. His icy-blue eyes were wide with shock. His lungs gurgled beneath the crimson-stained shirt, struggling against the damage the bullets had inflicted.

With a final act of defiance, Ulrich tried to raise his pistol.

Another loud bang from Sean's gun punched a dark hole through the man's forehead, and the hand holding the gun dropped lifelessly to the floor.

Tommy peeked out from behind one end of the stone box. He saw his friend standing over the body of the dead Ulrich. Sean dropped the pistol onto the ground next to the body.

"Cuttin' it a little close there, weren't ya?" Tommy joked, staring down at his kidnapper.

"Sorry. I was a little preoccupied," he jerked his thumb backward in the direction of the moaning henchman.

"What'd you do to him?" Tommy asked, not sure he wanted to know.

"Let's just say, he won't be winning any dance contests...ever." Sean forced a smile.

"Should we call Allyson back down?" The elevator had gone all the way back up to the top.

"Give it a second, Schultzie." He slapped his friend on the back. "This is what you have spent your life looking for."

They both gazed in awe at the unimaginable scene before them. Their heads turned a full circle, taking in the scene.

"It's amazing. I can't believe we actually found it. Do you realize we are probably the first people to see this in thousands of years?"

"You've earned it, buddy."

Then Tommy turned to Wyatt with a big smile. "Thanks, Sean, for everything. You've always been there for me. I knew you would come."

"Someone's got to take care of your dumb ass," he said with a wide grin.

58

EASTERN GEORGIA

Detective Trent Morris stared in utter disbelief at the scene before him. Around two hundred feet of pure- gold walls wrapped around the entire chamber. The ceiling panels too, were made out of gold. It was unlike anything he'd ever seen in his entire life.

The place was crawling with federal investigators, and a CSI unit had arrived shortly after the other squads. A coroner was there, as well, to tag and bag the body of the mysterious Jens Ulrich.

"He's an international mercenary," Will said, pointing a finger at the black bag. "Interpol has been looking for this guy for a few years. He's been implicated in several assassinations and other murders all over the globe. But no one has ever been able to catch up with him."

"A fistful of aliases and the right amount of money can get you a great deal of anonymity," Morris added.

Sean nodded, glancing over at the burned guard being wheeled out on a stretcher, still moaning in excruciating pain. His first stop would be the hospital. After that, it would be on to a cell, probably for the rest of his life.

"Docs said your buddy McElroy is going to be okay. He'd lost a lot of blood when the paramedics found him, but it looks like the bullet didn't hit anything vital."

"Not that it matters now. I'm sure his wife is going to kill him when he gets home."

"Well, we'll keep homicide on alert." Morris returned the grin.

Sean let his eyes wander through the room. Tommy was busy analyzing the golden tiles of the walls while talking on the phone with the IAA. At least a dozen researchers and archaeologists were already on their way to the site.

Schultz was in his element, and whatever fatigue he may have had was replaced by the excitement of discovery. *Tommy deserved it,* Sean thought.

His eyes switched to another spot. Allyson sat nearby on one of the stone boxes, sipping a bottle of water. She noticed him staring at her and offered a practiced shy smile. It was the kind of grin that could pull a man across a bed of hot coals without him ever noticing.

For a moment, his attention went back to the officers who were still going on about all the things that had happened. "So if you could come by sometime next week, it would really help me with filling out my report," Morris was finishing his spiel.

"What? Oh, sure. No problem. I will give you a call next week." Then Sean's attention went to a man and woman dressed in black in a corner by themselves. The woman was on a cell phone, but whatever she was saying could not be heard. "Who are they?"

Will looked back over his shoulder at the couple. "Those are agents Sewell and Yates. They're with the feds. Apparently, they have been after Ulrich for a while too. I don't trust them. They're not very sociable. Haven't said a whole lot to us since they got here."

"Interesting."

Trent gave his young partner a quick nod. "Let's get out of here, Will." Then he turned back to Sean as they started to walk away. "Next week, okay?"

"You got it."

The detectives got on the giant platform of the lift along with the medics. Will removed the disc from the pedestal, and the ancient elevator started its slow ascent.

Sean's eyes played back over to where Allyson was sitting. She was listening to Tommy, who had apparently finished his phone conversations. He was going on about the different languages that were represented, four in all, one on each wall. She was clearly only half-interested.

Making his way over to them, he stood over his friend and the young journalist/agent. "Sorry to interrupt your history lesson, Schultzie, but Ms. Webster scheduled an interview with me, and I really have to keep that appointment." He lifted his right eyebrow at his friend.

Tommy looked at Sean and then at her and started laughing. "My bad. I don't want to keep the good readers of the *Sentinel* waiting."

With that, he stood up and headed back over to a couple of people who were tagging some of the panels with Post-it notes and started directing the cataloging effort.

"Well, Ms. Webster, how about that interview?" His eyes smiled more than his mouth.

"You do remember I'm not really a journalist, right?"

"We can pretend."

59

NEVADA

The old man hobbled over to his desk hurriedly to answer the phone. It was ringing furiously, interrupting his nightly dose of brandy by the fireplace in the study.

He leaned his cane against the bulky desk and reached over to pick up the device. No answer to the caller was given. The white-haired man just waited.

"It is done," the young voice came through the receiver.

"Both of them are dead?"

"Ulrich is. The Russian he hired was still alive when I got there, though he was badly burned. Wyatt shot him in the knee, as well.

"You said *was* alive."

"Correct. He will not be a problem anymore."

"Excellent work. I knew I could count on you. Ulrich had become so sloppy."

"He served our purpose in the end."

"Indeed." The old man stood, contemplating his next question. "Did you find the next clue?"

"Yes, sir. The girl had it, but I instructed her that it would be needed as evidence for the crime scene."

"I'm sure those pesky agents from the IAA will be clamoring to get their hands on it for their museum." He coughed as he finished the sentence.

"It will be of no concern. I have already contacted the best stone worker in the country and requested a duplicate be made. By the time those fools have their artifact, we will be well on our way to the next chamber."

"Good. I knew I could count on you. God be with you, my son."

"Thank you, Prophet."

The old man hung up the phone and retreated to his enveloping leather chair by the fireplace. He raised his glass of brandy in satisfaction, filling his nostrils with its rich, warming aroma. *Curious,* he thought while eyeing the half-filled tumbler, *that alcohol was forbidden by the church's teachings.* Soon enough, though, they would be following his doctrines, as would the world. He finished the drink in one gulp and set the glass back on a stand near the chair.

~

"Who were you talking to?" Morris asked as he met up with Will at their car.

"Oh, that was just my girlfriend. Had to tell her I would be home late tonight."

"All right, buddy, let's get back to Atlanta. Good job, Will."

"Thank you, sir." The young detective stood for a moment as his partner entered the car. "Thank you," he repeated, almost inaudibly, peering back at the totem poles nearby.

Everything is going to according to plan, Will thought. Soon, the wicked would perish and the world could start new again.

AUTHOR'S NOTES

With any good piece of fiction I have ever read, there are always notes from the author at the end. So in keeping with what my favorites have done, I thought I would provide some of the details behind *The Secret of the Stones*.

Gold really was one of the biggest reasons the United States government wanted to relocate the Native American tribes. In North Georgia, there have been several documented finds of Indian Gold in different places. Talks about the *Indian Problem* began as early as the Jefferson administration and ended with the Trail of Tears moving the last great tribes to the west. The government never did find the enormous treasures they had hoped for.

The IAA and the Georgia Historical Center are both fictional. However, at Dalton State College, about an hour north of Atlanta, a new North Georgia Historical Center has been opened and contains a tremendous wealth of history and artifacts.

Chief Vann's House and the story as relayed in the book are real. His home is situated in the small town of Chatsworth, GA. The two-hundred-year-old plantation house is still one of the best preserved historic sites in the United States

Etowah Indian Mounds State Park, Fort Mountain, Track Rock, Red Clay State Park, and Rock Hawk and Rock Eagle are all very real. The mysteries that these locations present are truly amazing, and I highly suggest visiting them in person. The original location of the Cherokee capital was actually near Cartersville, Georgia.

The riddles and theories concerning the arrival of the first Native American settlers were entirely my concoction. It was extremely interesting, though, to find so many similarities between the ancient cultures of Egypt and the Native American tribes during my research. Also, the likeness of the wall at Fort Mountain when compared to the Nile River is quite fascinating, though that monument's purpose continues to remain a mystery to historians.

One historical note that I did have to alter was the relationship between the Mormon settlers and the Native American migration. All of the details are true except for one. The Mormon church was not actually founded for almost another decade after the Trail of Tears. That fact does not mean that the Mormons could not have helped the tribes later on though. And their paths certainly crossed many times in the Midwest and beyond.

During the course of the story, the characters find themselves in a church called the Beacon Tabernacle. This church does exist in the small town of Collegedale, Tennessee. I changed the name of it to better suit the flow of the story, but all of the details are as close to the truth as I could make them. The Bible verse that appears in Morse code on the stained-glass windows also exists, but I did take the liberty of changing which verse is displayed.

As to the Golden Chambers themselves, I must admit that they are only a theory of mine. However, much of the research I have done seems to point toward the number four in conjunction with the existence of a Native treasure. And the more research I do, the more I start to realize that the chambers could be a very real possibility.

Thanks for reading my book. I hope you enjoyed the story and will check out the other Sean Wyatt books I've written. If you liked this book, share it with a friend.

There are a lot of books out there, and I appreciate that you took the time to read mine.

If you don't mind, take a minute, and swing by the place where you got this book and leave a review. Reviews are so helpful for both readers and authors. So thanks for helping everyone out.

OTHER BOOKS BY ERNEST DEMPSEY

War of Thieves Box Set
When Shadows Call
Shadows Rising
Shadow Hour

COPYRIGHT

Made in the USA
Las Vegas, NV
21 August 2022

53738399R00184